SEASON OF THE BLOOD

STEPHANIE M. FREEMAN

SHADOW LILLY PUBLICATIONS
YORK, PENNSYLVANIA

Cover Designed by: J.L Woodson www.woodsoncreative studio.com
Interior Designed by: Unique Hiram www.authorumhiram.com
Editors: Naleighna Kai and Kelsie Maxwell
Betas: Debra Mitchell, Christine Pauls, Anita L. Roseboro
ISBN (eBook) 978-1-7367985-8-4
ISBN (Trade Paperback) 978-1-7367985-9-1

Freeman Stephanie M.. Season of the Blood (Diamonds, Blood and Shadows Book 4) (p. 6). Shadowlilly Publications, LLC

UNFINISHED BUSINESS

DEDICATION

For Dolores Ann Wilkes Freeman

"I kept my word."

ACKNOWLEDGEMENTS

We are only as good as the company we keep. I had excellent company (and midwives). Thank you Naleighna Kai for all that you do today and every day. Special thanks to J.L Woodson for the awesome book cover! And to my Editors and Beta Readers D.J. Mitchell, Christine Pauls, Anita L. Roseboro, Kelsie Maxwell. Thank you all for your sharp eyes, attention to detail and your voracious appetites for reading!

"Monsters are real, and ghosts are real too. They live inside us, and sometimes, they win." - Stephen King

CHAPTER ONE

"Everything is for sale. Even the screams," he said swallowing hard at the gorge burning the back of his throat.

"Indeed, Detective Garrett. Rigor and body temp puts the time of death at two possibly three hours ago tops. Corneas are missing. Wouldn't be surprised if other organs are missing too." The stained white hazmat glove on the coroner's hand dwarfed the ink pen he used to sign off on a document on the clipboard.

Homicide Detective Gabriel Garrett lowered the heavy plastic and grabbed the zipper to close the body bag. After the gurney was wheeled away, he studied the coroner Max Caldwell as he scribbled a signature on another clipboard. Mud and a dark substance bathed the coroner's biohazard suit the color of death. The goggles that hid his usual craggy bearded face did nothing to conceal the tears in his ancient blue eyes.

"How many, Max?" Gabe asked then winced at the crackle and whine from the feedback in his helmet.

Max shrugged and looked back toward the pit. With a flick of a soiled, gloved hand, a small caravan resumed its descent to the makeshift walkway pushing gurneys carrying body bags and grey body recovery containers.

The tents erected around the walkway concealed the grisly work from the crime scene lice— those people that seemed to materialize no matter how remote the location of a murder. Reporters joined the onlookers in jockeying for position beyond the crime scene tape. The one winding road that led to the mountainous vacation spot to the city of Serenity disappeared into the waning crime scene lights behind them.

More skeletal remains were excavated from the putrid soil near The Pine Barrens, the local densely wooded hiking trail just outside of New Serenity. The longer he stood there, images of his mother sitting on the back porch filled his mind. Gabe prayed the stench didn't blend with the winter jasmine in her garden.

"When I was a boy, I read somewhere that tribal nations gauged wealth by how many they could stand to lose in a war," Max said.

The old man's voice always reminded Gabe of whiskey poured over jagged ice. Even in scrubs, Max looked very much like a grandfather waiting for retirement or a coronary to end his watch as Medical Examiner for the state of Maryland. More times than not, Gabe and the coroner stood on scene just like they were now: worrying some bit of philosophy between them, searching for some polished way to process the horrors they witnessed on a regular basis.

"Mom told me something like that once," Gabe said as he scanned the area once more. "She said if thousands died then a tribe was rich indeed."

Max took a step back and waved a gloved hand dismissively over the pit. "How rich... I mean my God, Gabe. When and if we do, establish idents, who's going to tell the families that a piece of their soul was thrown into that darkness like so much garbage?"

"People like me. Come on. Last thing I need is for you to fall in there," Gabe said steering the old man away from the pit and back toward his triple black pick up with magnetic bubble lights on the roof.

He remembered the squelching sound each of his steps made through the stew of mud the first time. If his grip failed, Gabe knew he'd go in after the old man and the sounds would haunt the quiet places of his mind forever.

Gabe stripped out of his hood and gloves. A female forensics technician ran up and handed him a bottle of hand sanitizer and some paper towels.

"Trade you Detective," she said before holding out a biohazard bag for the men to put their helmets and gloves in.

"Sherrie, make sure you put some of that menthol under your nose before you open that bag again," Max, followed suit as another attendant came over with more paper towels and to take away the helmets.

"My people will remain on scene as long as needed. Botany and Entomology will be here when the sun comes up. Called in a favor and got some bone specialists coming from out of town to help classify and hopefully identify the remains. Local Labs and Coroner's offices got an invite too," Max said as he scrubbed his face with a wad of paper towels doused in the alcohol-tinged gelatinous mixture.

"You sounded like your father just now. Same height and build but one look at your eyes and all I see is…"

"I know; my mother," Gabe finished. He winced at the icy slimy texture of the sanitizer coating his hands.

"How is Alana, these days?" Max asked as another technician walked by with a biohazard container.

Gabe drew in a deep breath and frowned. "Aunt Myra and Uncle Mark spend time with her, but you know Mom."

"Yes. I suppose I do. Ethereal, regal and something darker all rolled into one," Max accepted his glasses from another attendant and slipped them on. "Sounds an awful lot like you too."

"Hardly. I'm more like my dad. He's the one—" the words died in his throat as a shard of his heart choked off the memories. "*Was* the one," he corrected before clearing his throat and focusing on the crowd behind the crime scene tape. Max tapped the back of his hand.

Gabe tried on a smile that ached around the edges. "Sorry Max, what were we talking about."

"Your parents cast a long shadow in this town, but yours eclipsed theirs a long time ago," Max said with a nod. "You and the group you run made quite the name for yourselves over the years. With you at the helm, there's bound to be more highlights for the reel."

Gabe moved to answer him when a group of attendants rushed past them. Max gripped the arm of one of his attendants. "Talk to me. What's wrong?"

"They found a survivor, sir." One of the technicians said over his shoulder.

CHAPTER TWO

Her silence rivaled the odor of decay that crawled from the room.

From where Gabe stood, the plaid curtains drawn around the bed concealed her body but not the small group of young doctors congregating in the corner of the room. Anxious snatches of conversation from the medical personnel entering and exiting the room made it clear. The girl's condition was deteriorating by the second. No ID on the body made calling next of kin impossible. When one of the doctors rushed out and threw up in a nearby trashcan, Gabe bowed his head and said a prayer.

"She won't survive the night. She can't," he said stumbling over to a garbage can.

Gabe lifted his head to see a nurse with purple hair staring at him. She nodded once then dragged the young male doctor behind the nurse's station. "Pull yourself together, Dr. Marsden."

"She's in there throwing up maggots! She needs a doctor," The young man blubbered as he stuck his head further into the trashcan.

"You *are* the doctor, Tommy," The nurse said rolling her eyes while wrinkling her nose in disgust.

"I know that, Tiana. You don't have to remind me of that," Marsden snapped before staggering to his feet. He swiped at his mouth with a lab jacket sleeve. "It was a shock that's all," He explained to two of the doctors standing around the nurse's station.

Gabe straightened to his full height and inched closer to the doorway. Dr. Marsden cleared his throat and straightened a navy-blue silk tie. Gabe winced at the faint sour cloud that followed the young doctor back into the room.

"What is your name sweetheart? Do you know what happened to you? What is your name?" The young doctor yelled.

"Mi cosecha es blanca," a small, cracked female voice responded.

"Your name honey. What's your— Christ did she say anything to the EMTs on the way in?" Marsden asked, over his shoulder to a group of doctors standing in the corner. "What about that guy outside. Does he know her?" He inquired.

"Noches doctor. Mi cosecha es blanca," She repeated.

Dr. Marsden continued asking the same round of questions as if the rise in volume would somehow make her understand. Gabe finally pushed through the curtain. Brenda, the same older heavy-set nurse that ushered him to the emergency department waiting area hours earlier rounded the hospital bed and reached for his arm. Gabe tilted his head as if to dare her.

"Detective, we understand that you need to interview the patient, but as you can plainly see, she's in no condition to talk to anybody. So, if you would please just wait outside," Brenda said gesturing with her head.

The girl picked and pulled at another nurse's hands trying to pin her shoulders to the bed. Dr. Marsden, still reeking of vomit, continued with his same line of questioning. Gabe moved closer and the woman in the bed went still. The wildness in the patient's eyes made him ease Brenda aside and approach the bed.

"Well, I don't know what you think you can get from her," Marsden said as he gave Gabe a once over. "I'm calling in Behavioral Health."

The crisp white lab coat, smart blue tie and shiny stethoscope made

Gabe wonder if the good doctor ever rolled up his sleeves to touch a patient let alone sit and talk with them. One of the nurses thumped Marsden on the arm then pushed a roll of mints into his hand.

Gabe smoothed an imaginary wrinkle out of the blanket then put a hand on the patient's forehead. He tried not to react to the waxy and cold texture of her skin. Her gaze shifted in a pool of oily tears. "What she's asking for doesn't require a name," Gabe said before tucking the blankets tighter around her.

"She's talking out of her head. Behavioral health needs to have a look at her," the doctor insisted as he tossed a couple of the disk-shaped mints in his mouth.

Great Now he smells like spearmint flavored vomit.

Even under the light with bandages all over the place, the faint scent of decay permeated the air. The whites of her eyes were stained a putrid yellowish green which made the twin crystal-clear blue pools of misery staring back at Gabe more brilliant and painful.

Brenda shouldered her way past Dr. Marsden forcing the shorter light skinned man to step back and almost trip over some unseen piece of equipment. He straightened the pocket protector of pens and stroked his stethoscope. "Well, as her provider, I think she would benefit from-"

"We can't move her until she's stable, Tommy. So, Behavioral Health is not an option. Look all of y'all are underfoot. Either help me or leave. And before you fix your face to say another word Tommy Marsden, you're a Resident. That doesn't make you my boss," Brenda snapped.

Marsden's mouth fell open as he scanned his colleague's expressions. His face flushed red before he cornered one of the other doctors, a shorter brunette woman, into a private conference.

"We are in mixed company, and I will not discuss this patient's mental state—" he said in a theatrical whisper that made the female resident he conversed with wilt under his hot garbage breath.

Gabe turned his attention back to the patient. "She's not crazy, doctor. She told you something in Spanish only you were too busy talking *at* her to get it," Gabe snapped as he glanced at the two doctors in the corner," Didn't you?" Gabe asked as he straightened the pillow under her head.

Both doctors inched toward the bed while two others vacated the room. Even the nurses stopped working as the patient tried to sit up.

"No, no honey, you need to rest," Brenda said reaching over to coax the girl to lay back down. Gabe backed off far enough to give her room to work.

"Noches doctor. Mi cosecha es blanca. It's what you said right?" Gabe returned to the bedside and smoothed the greasy brown hair back from her face.

"Yo llamo Abra." She closed her eyes and tears spilled back over her temples. "Mi Cosecha es blanca."

Gabe removed his hand from the woman's forehead and scanned the group. "I'll have two officers posted outside her door."

"Okay, enlighten us. What did she say?" Tommy asked, cramming more mints into his mouth.

Gabriel let his green gaze drift to the window beyond the bed. He nodded at Max's reflection standing in the doorway dressed in fresh scrubs.

"I have no right to ask, Gabe," the old man offered as he walked into the room. "Would she even accept a call from me?"

"This can't happen over the phone, Max," Gabe explained without bothering to turn around. "If I ask her to help it's face to face."

"Alana knows how to walk into nightmares and bring people out on the other side," Max said as he walked into the room. "Seen her do it hundreds of times."

The medical personnel made a wide berth around them while Brenda and another nurse continued to work. She punched in a password and documented her notes in the computer on a wheeled terminal stationed at the head of the patient's bed.

"You really think she'll do it?" Max asked, as he reached for Gabe's arm.

Gabriel chuckled softly and backed away holding his hands up in mock surrender. He sidestepped around Max before walking to the door. "What would be the point? According to Tommy the vomiting resident out in the hall, she won't survive the night."

"Alana is the foremost authority—" Max started.

"On what? Surviving didn't make my mother some expert. This town that she and my dad cast a long shadow in nearly destroyed both of them." Gabe bit down on the last of the words and struggled not to curse. "Most of the people here still treat her like a leper no matter what she does to help."

Dr Marsden fixed his tie and summoned the courage to walk over to them. Max followed Gabe's line of vision turning so abruptly that Marsden flinched.

"Excuse me Dr. Caldwell, but as part of Jane Doe's treatment team we need to know anything that could help in her treatment," he said directing his comments to Gabe.

Gabriel glanced back in the direction of the bed. Brenda had drawn the curtain once more. He tipped Max a casual salute before turning to make his way down the corridor to the elevators; his boots sounded as hollow as his response.

"Her name is Abra. She said Good night doctor, my harvest is white."

CHAPTER THREE

Gabe put the last of the breakfast dishes in the dishwasher and thumbed the lock in place. The soft pale yellow and brown accents in the kitchen always reminded him of coffee and sunflowers. The large window over the sink offered a spectacular view of the screened in deck his father built and the back yard he played in as a boy. Winter jasmine, Christmas roses, and a healthy spray of purple crocuses bloomed next to the neatly manicured shrubs lining the white picket fence that surrounded the yard. The wooden owl perched on one of the fence posts housed a motion detector and surveillance camera that scanned the area.

And there, just like the wooden owl sat his mother like an old sentry waiting for night to surrender to morning. Alana Symone always curled up in the chair on the right. The left chair still had his father, Cassiel's intricately carved black wooden cane resting patiently beside it for a man who would never return. The faded blue oval carpet near her chair where Gabe read comic books and completed his homework assignments looked smaller somehow. She tilted her head as if to listen to music as a strange sad smile whispered across her face.

Think long and hard before you ask her son.

The warning his father had given him years ago sent chills down his spine. Gabe dried his hands on the dishtowel and pushed his way out onto the porch.

"Mom, I really think you should move to Shadow Bay with me. Uncle Mark and Aunt Myra are always begging you to come stay. This house is too big. Too many rooms. Too many ghosts." Gabe hunkered down next to her chair. "Sorry Mom. I didn't mean…" He said eyeing the grey and black lettering on his father's FBI Mug. Her pale, tissue paper soft fingers hooked under his chin.

"My memories, son. *My* ghosts," she said tracing his cheek with her thumb.

"I won't ask if you miss him." He kissed the palm of her hand and rested his face against it. Tears gathered at the corners of her eyes and Gabe looked out at the yard.

"Good. Then I won't have to lie," she said softly.

Out of the corner of his eye, he watched as she settled back in her chair.

"So much like your father. So handsome... so haunted," she said tracing his sideburn with her thumb.

"There had to be more. Nicholas Levine pulled Dad into it. I mean, why Dad? He wasn't short-staffed. Bastard didn't even attend the funeral."

Alana put the mug aside and sat forward. "What was there to say, son?" she asked.

"You were retired, Mom. You both were. Levine made a career on the work you all did. The sacrifices," he said swallowing hard at the lump growing in his throat.

This old argument sprouted from any conversation he had with her. For every answer, his mother gave more questions seemed to grow.

"I asked Levine not to come; to spare you and Monet." Alana slid her thumb over the left corner of his mouth.

"Doesn't matter. I still blame Levine. Look— just move in with me. You're all alone out here."

"Monet is married with children. Women in your bed but none by your side. It's you that shouldn't be alone," she said releasing him.

Fine strands of silver streaked her fiery red hair. Her hellfire gaze drifted over his features bringing him comfort while stripping him of any shred of pretense.

"I can't come out here and find that you died alone Mom," he said retreating to the safety of scanning the yard once more. He hazarded a glance in her direction to find her watching him with keen interest.

"You won't. I'd leave before I let you or your sister see me like that," she said in a matter-of-fact tone.

"You wouldn't leave me and Monet like that." He swallowed hard before hazarding a glance at her.

She leaned forward pressing her face to the side of his head. "I did it before son or don't you remember? Come inside. I'll top off your travel mug." Alana pressed a kiss to his temple as she rose from her rocking chair and Gabe followed. She settled down at the kitchen table and ran her slender fingers over the edge of the detective's shield and his shoulder holster.

"Your father wept when he gave you your first shield and your service weapon. Do you remember?" she said the nostalgia in her voice still had that slow intoxicating cadence that lulled him to sleep when she read bedtime stories.

Gabe sat down and took her hand and marveled at the smooth blank surface and the scar that sliced across her palm like a lifeline. "And there you were in the audience eyes glittering with tears just like now," he said trying hard not to notice the telltale moisture threatening like a summer squall that swam up out of nowhere.

"Your father calls to me from the corners of every room." Alana closed her eyes and took in a shaky breath. "It's hard to breathe without him."

"Mom, I didn't mean to—"

She blinked away the tears and focused on him.

"The youngest Police Lieutenant in the history of the Shadow Bay PD. Highest arrest and conviction record in the state. Mark tells me you still haven't moved into your office. Said you stopped taking calls from the FBI," she said as her green gaze grew a shade darker.

"Never asked for the stripes on my dress uniform or for the scrambled eggs ribbon on my hat," he admitted. "Never wanted or expected any of the commendations or promotions from the police or the military. I hunt monsters like you and Dad taught me. Can't hunt sitting behind a desk sequestered in an office away from my squad now, can I?" he quipped.

Alana took in a breath and pushed herself to her feet. "We taught you many things including the utter uselessness of small talk. I noticed it last night just after dinner. Tell me what you and Max Caldwell found in the dark." She walked over to his mug and peeled off the lid. The sun was just reaching the edge of the garden.

He swallowed hard before meeting her gaze. The tears were gone and the thing that moved behind her eyes hunkered down as if to prepare for war.

"A lot of bodies Mom—" he managed before pocketing his badge and reaching for his shoulder holster. "And a girl that shouldn't be alive."

***

Gabe switched off the ignition and stared straight ahead. The words were on the tip of his tongue and every time he turned to say them, more dread stitched another row around his heart.

"I always went in to talk to Dad first. He wasn't one for small talk either. If I called from a crime scene, he'd tell me to clean myself up before I came to the house," Gabe said as he hazarded a glance at her.

With hands folded neatly in her lap, his mother looked like she could have walked out of a book or across a charred rocky terrain on some distant alien shore. The older he grew, the younger she looked. Other than a few strands of grey, she still looked like the same woman that taught him basic rock-climbing techniques. The first time he fell, she folded herself around him breaking his fall, but cracking two ribs in the process.

"Think long and hard about what you're about to ask her, son. If you even think it's going to hurt, then don't ask," she warned, turning to face him.

"You heard us talking," Gabe gripped the steering wheel and put his head down.

She rested the back of her hand against his cheek, and he looked at her. "Why this morning."

Gabe started to shrug, but he felt her fingers dig in as she grabbed his shoulder.

"You know better than to shrug at me. Talk," she snapped, her tone left no room for debate.

"Dad was right. Let me take you home," he said reaching for the keys. Before he could turn the key in the ignition, Alana was out of the truck closing the door behind her.

***

The second the elevator doors opened; his heart sank. Medical personnel rushed in and out of the girl's room which was little more than a glass cubicle situated behind the nurse's station. One of the officers Gabe posted at the door jogged over.

"Morning Sir. She started convulsing and throwing up this black stuff all over the place."

Before he could respond to the young officer, Alana was off the elevator moving toward the chaos.

"Mom, wait," he called after her.

By the time he pushed his way into the room, Alana was ducking under a doctor's arms. The thrashing on the bed ceased and the coding team looked around at Alana. She reached over to smooth the matted hair from the girl's face. She took one look at Alana and screamed.

"Get her out of here," Brenda commanded, as she pushed Alana toward the door and into Gabe's arms.

Alana calmly walked over to the nurse's station. She kept her back to Gabe as the alarms grew louder. She flinched each time they yelled 'clear.' Gabe focused on the fine pale scar that started somewhere deeper in her hairline but flowed down her neck and beneath her collar. He pressed his forehead against the back of her neck and breathed in the warm coconut fragrance of her shampoo.

"Come on, Mom." Gabe moved her in front of him as he tried to steer her to the elevator. "I'm sorry I brought you here."

Alana raised her hand and he stepped back from her as the rest of the code played out.

"Mom, please. I was wrong. Let me take you home. Let me—" The room behind them fell silent. Alana gripped his hand and shook her head softly.

"Time of death," Someone called, and another voice answered.

Alana rotated in the small space he allowed her. She cupped his face in both hands like a precious gourd and made him look at her. The anguish in her eyes made him look away.

She caught his cheek in her hand and made him face her. "Her name is Abra St. Clair, son, and you were right. She wanted to die."

CHAPTER FOUR

"Letting them all die would have been better. The shipment—"

"Stop calling them that, Tiana," Olivia Calderone warned as she tugged a green scrub top over her head and looked in the mirror. Even without her glasses, the purple patches of exhaustion under her dark brown eyes announced to the world that jet lag was a real and hateful thing.

"Why? It won't bring her back," Tiana snapped, muttering a curse under her breath. "I didn't mean it like that."

Olivia let the silence expand between them before grabbing an ink pen from the top shelf of her locker. "You're right. It won't," she said finally. "I won't think any less of you if —." Olivia swept her thick mane of rich, dark brown hair into a messy bun and shoved the pen in place to secure it.

"Don't do that," Tiana snapped. "I made a promise same as you."

"Have you heard from Maji?" Olivia asked as she slipped on a white sneaker.

"You already know I did. Sat in the back of that SUV smoking a blunt the whole time. You trust somebody like that? Not even sure if it's a man or a woman," Tiana said exhaling hard enough to whistle through her teeth.

Before Olivia could answer the locker room door opened. "Hey Doc, glad you're back. How was the conference?"

Olivia glanced over her shoulder as her scrub nurse Christine Meadows pushed the door open.

"Take your pick. They aren't particular. Besides, I trust Maji with my life and so should you. I'll call you later," Olivia said while pressing the disconnect button on her earpiece.

Olivia focused her attention to Christine as she placed her tablet and lab coat on the bench. "Boring. Way too many windbags sucking the air out of the room with their egos." Olivia said running her finger over the electronic grease board operating room schedule.

Christine giggled as she leaned over to retie her candy pink sneaker. "How is that even possible, Olivia? You were in Miami in the land of hot sweaty men and umbrella drinks. Did you at least go to the beach?" she asked

"No time. We were in breakout sessions most of each day. Besides, it was a business trip remember? Professional Development and CEUs," Olivia tapped the screen to minimize the schedule and put on her other shoe.

Christine stood and peered in the mirror beside the lockers. "Please, you could have stayed here, finished the homework, and took those open book quizzes for an easy five grand. How come they don't offer those kinds of perks to the nurses? Christine asked while running a pinky over her lip gloss-stained bottom lip.

Olivia smiled softly and shook her head. "Believe me I wish they did Chrissy; as hard as you guys' work," she murmured. "I see Stewart scrubbed in this week." Olivia planted her elbows on her thighs and rubbed her eyes, suddenly tired.

"Yeah, Doc Stewart took care of a hot gall bladder and that emergency that got wheeled in here last night," Christine said "Some girl was found in the Pine Barrens covered in blood and maggots. I hear Tommy

Marsden came unglued and begged for a doctor," Christine said as she peered over her shoulder, "The cops were here too; the place was deserted by the time I clocked in. You know Doc Stewart is on a roll after maternity leave. He's already talking about having another one."

Olivia chuckled and pulled on her lab coat. "Has he asked his wife about that?"

Christine grabbed Olivia's stethoscope and glasses from the top shelf of the grey locker and handed them over. "Figured you'd get a book. You and your poetry." Christine sucked her teeth and smiled pulling a book from the shelf.

"Friend of mine turned me on to poetry when we were kids. The written word in my opinion is still the best drug known to man." Olivia held out her hand and Christine handed the book to her.

Olivia smoothed her thumb over the gold lettering on the spine of the Langston Hughes Poems book before she stood and put it back. Her mind flooded with the feel of Gabriel Garrett's arm around her as he flipped the pages of a book they were reading. A wicked chill snaked down her spine as she slammed the locker door. She looked back at the scrub nurse hoping the woman hadn't read too much into what she said. Christine twirled her braids into a knot and secured it with a scrunchie before turning around.

"So, you mean to tell me you didn't go on a date or play some night games while you were there? Six packs, tight asses and you didn't get bent over a balcony? Not even once?"

"No, and I wasn't dressing for the occasion either," Olivia said smacking Christine on the arm before grabbing her tablet and heading to the door.

"Hmph, you need a hit off somebody's peace pipe. Those books you sleep with put your brain out when you know you need that Vitamin D men swear, they have in abundance." Christine did a little shimmy before she sashayed through the door.

"Will you stop?" Olivia giggled as she shoved her friend into a short jog.

Olivia had to smile, it had been a long time since she sat across a table having an adult conversation that didn't include best practices in suturing and palliative care. Staying busy was easier than admitting that her bed was empty and no prospects waiting in the wings.

If they weren't talking about their careers, then they were priming the pump for office gossip or some way into the country club set. Only one was stable enough to be serious, but between his attorneys, ex-wife and a teenage daughter that hated her on sight, the single life suited Olivia just fine. She looked back in the direction of the locker room and frowned as the familiar ache that gnawed at her left side seemed to burrow deeper.

The way he arranged her against his side still hurt. His arm wasn't just thrown over her shoulder, he held her against his side as if she were some exotic extension of his body. Some days Olivia could almost convince herself that it was nostalgia and nothing more. Other days, the pain was so acute that she found her hand clamped to her side applying pressure to a wound that didn't exist.

Olivia continued down the hallway taking in a breath that hurt far too much as reality washed in and the fathoms of memory threatened to drag her under. Olivia tugged on the stethoscope to even out the weight. Her fingers fell to the name embroidered in black over the pocket of the freshly starched lab coat she knew Tiana her other scrub nurse left behind.

"So, tell me some more about that case last night, Chrissy, the girl from the Barrens."

"Not much to tell. Cops are bound to be back though. You know how cops like to worry shit worse than a dog with a bone."

She followed Christine around the corner to a group of residents congregating around the nurse's station. Christine winked at her before she straightened her back and marched forward.

"All right kiddos, summertime is over. Back to school. Now that you've all finished your rotations down in the Pathology and the Emergency Departments, it's time to step it up a notch. Your Chief of Staff, Dr. Olivia Calderone will do grand rounds with you, then give you your assignments for the day. Don't get underfoot or ask a bunch of long-winded, know- it- all questions. Dr. C is *not* impressed."

Some of the residents snickered as they looked over at Tommy Marsden straightening his pocket protector lined with red and black ink pens. He finally looked up and nodded.

"Now Dr. Calderone has surgeries back-to-back and there's a scheduled downtime from eleven this morning until three. I want cleaner paperwork than last time," Christine said as she took a clipboard from the Unit Clerk behind the station and handed it to Olivia.

Olivia scanned the document quickly then signed and handed it back to Christine.

Then she fished in her pocket for a pair of glasses before looking up at the group. "Good morning, everyone. Some of you were here last night when that patient came into the ER. Let's start there."

CHAPTER FIVE

The yellow crime scene tape twisted and writhed in the bitter late morning wind as murder scene technicians moved about in the necropolis below.

"Jesus, you walked around down there?" Calvin Ford asked as he inched over to the edge of the pit. He pinched the bridge of his nose to hold the light blue face mask in place.

Calvin shuddered and stepped back from the edge. Sunlight bounced off Gabe's shades making his eyes water as he slipped them on. He surveyed the area once more before focusing on his partner being helped down from the scaffolding. Calvin tugged a black Shadow Bay Saints watch cap beanie down over his ears. The bear of a man patted the attendant who helped him down on the arm before picking his way across the hardpack to where Gabe stood.

"Dispatch gets a call from someone claiming to see a dead body in the road. I get here and there's a male vic in the street with a burner phone. I pan my flashlight down at the ground to see the bloody footprints in the snow. Followed them over to a uniform. Couldn't get a word out of him.

He's just pointing his flashlight in that direction," Gabe gestured with his head to an area now covered with makeshift tents and walkways.

"I walk over and there's a severed hand in a medical waste bag sticking out of the snow. Uniform dropped it and parked himself on that rock over there and turned himself into a barf bag. I found more ruptured medical waste bags with more gore further down. The girl, Abra St. Claire was buried back over there." Gabriel waved his hand dismissively in the direction of the pit.

"It's cold as fuck out here and it still smells like spoilage and shit," Calvin mumbled as he cinched the collar on his green and black parka shut.

"What is that? French fries? Is it true the kid opened the bag with the hand in it? No gloves, just raw. Goddamned 'Boot'," Calvin said. This is basic stuff, G. DTS. Don't Touch Shit." Calvin rolled his eyes.

"Took a while to coax him off that rock. From the looks of him, he doesn't want to be a cop anymore," Gabe said remembering the tears in the young man's eyes as he stared down at the remains of his dinner freezing in chunks on his coat.

"What was he expecting a color TV? The Pine Barrens are the perfect place for your friendly neighborhood murderers to dump bodies, but you went down there?" Calvin looked off in the direction that had Gabe's attention and shuddered.

"Other units arrived, and I went in wearing wading boots. I could have walked around for hours and still missed her. Hell, I did miss her." Gabe shrugged as he glanced over at his friend and partner.

 Gabe pointed off to their left. "Found more body parts and skeletal remains. I was up and out of the mud by the time they found the girl."

"That isn't just mud in there. The sun is up, and they still have to use lamps," Calvin frowned in disgust.

"Yeah, Calvin. Putrefaction seasons the air with a distinctive bite. There's blood in the mud and the house knows why."

"There you go being all poetical and shit. Probably have that written on one of those tattoos you got. No ass or tit ink just poetry. I'd ask who does that shit but there you stand, living the dream," Calvin stifled a laugh.

Gabe grinned as he spun on his heel and made his way down to his truck with Calvin right behind him. Max walked over rubbing his gray woolen gloved hands together for warmth.

"Hey Max, anything new?" Gabe asked when he came to a stop.

"Lot of bodies. Some intact others; not so much. Ages are all over the place. Time of Death are all over the place too. The girl and the dead kid in the street were the freshest." Max reached over and fastened the helmet on one of the attendants. He pounded gently on the man's shoulder before turning back to Gabe and Calvin. "Mayor carved out some space at the airport and we may need all of it. I heard about the girl an hour after it happened. She was too far-gone, Gabe. If the sepsis didn't kill her, the organ failure would," Max said as one of his assistants dressed in another full body suit handed him a clipboard.

Max flipped through the paperwork then signed off on the last sheet before handing it back. Gabe stuck his hands in his pockets as another body bag was loaded in what amounted to a tractor trailer with plastic sheets hanging over the back doors.

"I thought they had incinerators or medical waste collection places for this kind of stuff," Calvin said with a grimace.

"We do, Calvin. Somebody got sloppy or just didn't care," Max said while pushing his glasses back in place with a knuckle then he leaned closer to Gabe. "Is Alana, okay? I'm sorry. I was the one that suggested it."

"Don't. According to her, she *chose* to go to the hospital," Gabe said as he scanned the area once more. The shame blossoming in Gabe's gut had risen to his scalp making it itch with regret.

"Now why doesn't that make me feel any better?" Max asked giving a curt nod to another attendant.

Gabe bit down on a curse. "I know right? What time is Abra St. Clair's autopsy?"

"We're backed up with that arson from earlier this week, but I'll make the time. Abra huh? Means light. Suits her. Suits this place. In her last minutes on earth, she shed light through a crack in Hell's ceiling,"

***

Tomato soup, grilled cheese, and frying oil permeated the air around Gabe as he chose a table in the corner where he could put his back against the wall and see the entire cafeteria. Hospital staff scurried back and forth carrying trays over to the collection area or to their tables. Quiet conversations and the soft clatter of dishes all but drowned out the classic music being piped into the area. A man sat a few feet away feeding an older woman some soup from a bowl. He dabbed at the woman's chin with a napkin before offering another spoon filled with egg noodles and bits of chicken.

Gabe poured over the notes he had taken earlier as they canvassed the community and few businesses surrounding the Barrens. Other detectives were at work slowly widening the radius, grid sweeping and following the usual investigative protocols. Gabe and Calvin focused on the hospitals and clinics in New Serenity before finally reaching the emergency room department at Shadow Bay General. He was in the middle of transferring his notes from the yellow sheets of paper from that morning when his mother's words filled his mind.

Surgical incisions from a procedure.

Gabe shrugged out of his brown leather bomber jacket and dropped it on the chair beside him. The young man seated across the aisle steadied the straw near the older woman's mouth and she took a sip and gave Gabe an impish smile and nod. When the woman's son looked over and smiled Gabe nodded and put his head down.

He had barely put the truck in park before she was out of the truck taking the stairs by twos. As they reached the Homicide Division, Calvin Ford, Gabe's partner rose from his desk.

"Good morning. Calvin Is the Commissioner in? Alana asked. The sheer size of Gabe's partner made his mother seem smaller.

Calvin stared at Gabe standing behind her as his eyebrows went up in his usual silent way of questioning. Alana touched his arm and Calvin flinched and looked down at her. "He was just leaving. Is everything okay? I mean uh. Mmm Morning, Mrs. Garrett." His gaze drifted to Gabe's once more.

Alana nodded once then and went down the hallway with Gabe fast on her heels. He reached the door first and turned the knob.

"Okay G, you want to tell me what the fuck happened down at Shadow Bay General? Mark asked while scanning a form in his hand.

Gabe leaned in the doorway as his mother came in. Mark dropped the papers, rounded the desk, and reached for her.

"Alana, what are you doing out so early, huh?" Mark brushed a kiss over her cheek then led her over to a chair. His uncle and Supervisor stared at Gabe before he closed the door behind them.

"I asked Mom if she would come and talk to a victim. The doctors couldn't get anything out of her that made sense," Gabe said hating the way the words felt in his mouth. The weight of his mistake landed in his gut and spread with a sickening speed.

Mark glanced over his shoulder. "You brought a civilian into your investigation, G? You know better than that."

Alana patted Mark's arm and he put his focus on her direction. "I'm hardly a civilian, Mark. The girl is dead. She died screaming after she saw me."

Mark's mouth fell open.

"What she means to say is...," Gabe offered and both of them turned around.

"Never known your mamma to not say what she means, G," Mark said turning back to her. Mark scooted to the edge of his seat and released her hand. He scraped his thumbnail over the space between his eyes and sighed, "Okay, start over Alana."

Gabe sat down on the sofa across from them. The dread and guilt he felt earlier multiplied. What color she had was fading. He scrubbed the bottom half of his face then leaned forward to listen.

"Your victim's name was Abra St. Clair. Quite a few students from the University do Work Study at my center." Alana slipped an errant lock of hair behind her ear. "She was in her junior year as a Foreign Languages Major at Shadow Bay U."

Mark reached on his desk and grabbed a legal pad and pen then tossed both to Gabe.

"I knew she was stealing from the center, Mark," she said. "They all do from time to time. Food from the pantry, clothing from the donations closet. The bandages were new. I followed her to a crack house one night. Inside was a young man nursing a wound. Well, not really a wound but a fresh surgical incision with sutures neatly done,"

"Alana, I know you know this town like the back of your hand, but you shouldn't be out there like that," Mark warned, gripping her hand.

She waved her hand to silence him before she continued. "There were others Mark. Most people would have assumed that they were sleeping off a high, but I saw the blood." She squeezed Mark's hand to make him pay attention. "I also overheard some of the kids talking about selling blood products and their organs for profit. Kept calling it a payday party."

Gabe looked up from taking notes to see Mark staring at him. Alana patted Mark's hand to get his attention. "Went to one of the ones I saw not far from my center and offered a cup of soup and my business card. He pocketed the card. He kept saying 'My harvest is white.'

Mark ran a shaky hand over his salt pepper grey beard. "Alana, do you have any idea how dangerous— course you do. Why do I even bother to ask?" Mark sat back and studied them both.

"Same thing Abra said to me over the phone about a week ago. Sounded familiar," she said squinting at some memory.

"Alana, can you give us locations… anything like a description? What about names? Did you know anyone else's names," Mark asked before releasing her hand.

Alana sat back and gripped the armrests. "No names; just faces. I saw one at Robey Medical Center and another across town at Bayview. They all made the same comment.; 'My harvest is white."

"Uh yes ma'am you have a blessed day too," Calvin said snapping Gabe back to reality as his partner and best friend Calvin Ford's rich booming voice filled the small area at the back of the cafeteria. He held the tray out of the way as the man and older woman inched by him.

Calvin reminded Gabe of his uncle Mark. Both men dressed in off the rack suits with blue or white button-down shirts as if they were kids wearing their Sunday Best and hating every minute of it. Even in jeans, his best friend had that former linebacker size and height that scared most people before he even opened his mouth. Calvin's laid-back nature was reminiscent of everybody's favorite uncle flipping burgers at the family BBQ with a dishtowel draped over one shoulder, sweating harder than the bottle of beer on the counter.

Nothing about the man shouted cop, until it came down to details.

Calvin could sit for hours picking through unrelated bits of materials or conversations with a mug of coffee and an endless supply of hot pork rinds close at hand. He was the only man that could find pinpoint discrepancies that when further investigated grew into gaping holes in alibis but brought confessions and convictions in equal measure.

"So, what's next, G?" Calvin asked as he pushed a cup of coffee in front of Gabe and took a sip from his own.

"Check out some more of the buildings in and around my mom's community center. Sooner or later, we have to get back and set up the murder boards," Gabe replied, as he closed his notepad and moved his cup in a small circle on the table.

"What, you think this has something to do with your mom's place?" Calvin asked before sitting the tray on the table behind him.

"Mom knew the victim." Gabe stared at the empty table across from them.

"She doesn't like me." Calvin frowned as he peeled the plastic wrap from around his blueberry muffin.

"Who, my mom?" Gabe asked before taking a sip from his cup and putting the lid back on.

"She can look at you and even if you didn't do anything, you feel like you better confess to something."

"She always knew when I was up to something," Gabe chuckled as he slumped down in his chair.

Calvin scanned the room before he leaned closer. "Can she read minds? "He asked.

"Sure, as hell seems to. Which is why me and my sister never cut school,"   Gabe sat back in his chair and laughed.

The one and only time he did, was a trip to the movies. When she calmly asked him to pass her the popcorn, his friends scattered like rats. Leaving the two of them to finish the movie before she dropped him back off at the school without saying a word.

"Think she'll let me bring Marcy over to meet her?"

The hopeful look on his partner's face made Gabe chuckle. Calvin always tiptoed around Gabe's mother as if she were an ancient mythical creature that would burst into a thousand points of light around him.

Gabe peeled the lid from his cup and threw it on the table. "Don't you want your Mom to make dinner and size her up?"

Calvin pulled the top off his blueberry muffin and crammed some of it in his mouth. "You kidding? My Moms has that grandbaby lust," he said with a shudder. "When are you getting married? When you planning to have kids?'" Calvin whined as he imitated his mother.

"Monet gave her three grands, but she's hinting around about me settling down," Gabe said with a shrug.

Calvin swallowed hard and chased a bit of the pastry with his coffee. "You're about the most settled down guy I know and that's without a lady in the picture. You could walk away from the Force tomorrow and make a cool million off the guitars you make."

"Hardly." Gabe took a deep sip of his coffee then pulled out a granola bar. He opened the foil package and took a bite. He chewed thoughtfully then swallowed. "Mom thinks I'm lonely."

"You? Bruh, all you gotta do is turn sideways in a chair and women be in a line trying to polish your crotch with their drawers." Calvin scanned the room again before popping another piece of muffin in his mouth.

"Asked her to move in with me," Gabe met his partner's gaze.

"You want her to cock block?" Calvin asked scrubbing his mouth with a napkin.

"She's all alone in that big house." Gabe fidgeted in his chair. "She's so small and fragile like this expensive piece of crystal…"

Calvin took a swig of coffee and sat back, "Your Mom looks about as fragile as a bomb, for real."

"But you want to bring a girl over to meet her." Gabe finished the granola bar then took another sip from his cup. "She's the same lady that stood on a chair and fixed your tie when we graduated from the academy."

Calvin beamed. "Man listen, when she fixed my tie, I knew I was sharp. But enough about all that. I'm serious. Your Moms can read people. Maybe if she sees me with a nice girl—Well?" Calvin said raising an eyebrow.

"Well, what? You've been over there a million times. Had dinner, raked leaves, and raided the cookie jar on the kitchen counter. If you want to do this, you ask her," Gabe tossed back the last of the coffee and gathered his trash.

"Told you she doesn't like me, man."

"If she didn't, do you really think I'd be partnered with you?"

"She vetted me?" Calvin asked

"No. I did that. She just agreed with me. She's always been careful with me and Monet and Olivia," Gabe said drawing in a breath that made his chest hitch.

"Olivia?" Calvin questioned.

"What? Gabe asked suddenly distracted.

"You just said Olivia. You didn't tell me you had another sister."

"Olivia and me…we grew up together. She practically lived at my house," Gabe said throwing his cup away before making his way to the elevator, "We'll start with the grunts. Mark is working on getting us an in with Leadership."

Calvin stuffed the last piece of his muffin in his mouth. "Meet you up there. I wanna finish up down here with some of the EMTs and radio in."

CHAPTER SIX

"I think our little patient is allergic to doctors," Olivia said as a warm ripple of laughter filled the hospital room.

She smiled as the infant wrapped her tiny brown fingers around Olivia's finger and sneezed again. "Well, after all the drama it took to get you here little one, I would be allergic to doctors too," she said handing the baby over to his mother.

Olivia scanned the faces of the residents standing a respectable distance from the bed. Some whispered behind cupped hands and stopped when she focused on them. "Almost done here guys. I'll dole out assignments and then you can raid the cafeteria. Christine told me that Ms. Lemon made chili again for the soup of the day," She called over her shoulder.

As a few groans and a sprinkle of laughter rolled through the room

Olivia squeezed the young mother's shoulder. "I'll come back and check on you in a while Rumina. Congrats again. He's a handsome fella."

Tears leaked from the corners of her eyes as she nodded at Olivia. She gave the young mother's arm another comforting squeeze before she waded through her residents.

"She is my angel. You guys treat her right. We wouldn't be here if it wasn't for her," The patient said.

Olivia fished her phone from her pocket, looked at the time and bit down on a curse. She finished scribbling down notes on a pale purple legal pad and handed it off as she hurried down the hallway.

"Okay guys, sorry I ran over. You gave great answers, but some of you are turning this into group think. Your colleagues won't always be around you. That's where your critical thinking skills will shine," Olivia straightened the magnetic white boards that clung to the patient room doors. "Here are the assignments. I've written your names at the top of your page and scenarios are in the student portal," she said before handing her purple legal pad to Rina Oberon, one of her residents.

Olivia glanced at her phone again then faced the group and paused. "I have an elective in a few minutes so make sure you're back and on point by two pm. I'm the only one that can be late."

Christine came out of a room with Olivia's tablet and pressed a stylus pen into her hand. "And she's never late so back here by 1:30," she warned, as she pointed at something on the screen.

Another shorter blonde nurse appeared, and Olivia signed off on more orders over Christine's shoulder. Residents continued to pull their assignments from the legal pad and converse among themselves. Christine took the tablet and closed it before pulling the stethoscope from around Olivia's neck and started working her lab coat off her shoulder.

"We need to get you upstairs, Olivia. Scheduling moved you to another operating theater. Blood Bank is on standby. Systems said the electronic health records will be back up soon. The rest of the downtime paperwork can wait."

Olivia nodded as she continued to flip through a chart at the Nurse's station. "Somebody do me a favor and check on Mr. Ackerman in 325. See if he wants that cup of coffee now. Check his sugar while you're at it," she said continuing to flip through the chart. Olivia scratched out one dose of penicillin and put in another before signing off on the order.

Christine removed Olivia's glasses from the back of her collar and handed them to the unit clerk behind the desk.

"Nadine, can we get a small meal sent up here from Dietary, please?"

She said and the Unit clerk nodded and grabbed the telephone receiver. Olivia reached for her," Oh, and his wife Ms. Lola will be here in a while. Make sure she eats too. Last time I saw them together, he was trying to feed her his meal. Thanks."

Nadine smiled and dialed the number as Olivia looked over another chart.

"Ollie?" a male voice called from somewhere behind her.

Christine continued to pull Olivia's arm out of her lab coat. She nudged Olivia's arm. "Olivia, I think someone's looking for you."

She glanced up at Christine then went back to the chart. "Doubt it. Mr. Ackerman's first name is Oliver. Besides, only one person ever called me 'Ollie' and he's not here."

"Oh? Describe him," Christine replied, as she stopped pulling on the sleeve.

Olivia glanced at her then returned to reviewing another document. "I don't know…tall, handsome, reddish-brown hair, warlock green eyes… granola bars in his pocket," she said continuing to put her scrawl on the paperwork when her pen started skipping.

She tossed it on the counter and then searched her scrub pockets. "Damn, does anyone have a pen I can borrow?" she asked as someone behind her plucked the pen from her messy bun sending her wavy dark brown hair cascading down around her shoulders. Olivia reached for the pen. "Thanks… I always forget about that one."

He wasn't real.

"Sometimes you had two or three tucked in your hair and still asked for a pen," Her residents started backing away as Gabe moved closer. His deep green gaze shifted slowly over her. He leaned closer and took in a deep breath. "I promise not to disappear if you hug me, Ollie."

"Gabe," she managed.

His smile widened as he nodded and slipped an arm around her waist pulling her into his coat. Every pore in her skin opened at once drinking in the raw masculine heat of him. Olivia snapped out of it and threw her arms around his neck. Gabe chuckled and lifted her from the floor.

"Hey, Ollie," he said. His voice was lost in the fabric of her scrub top.

His breath heated the fabric sending another shockwave through her body as he lifted her higher.

"Oh my God. Gabe… but how? I don't understand…… Gabe?" She pulled back and took his face in her hands. She glanced down at the arm still trapped in her lab coat. He reached for the collar.

Christine stilled his hand and finished pulling the garment off. "Alright stop gawking. Dr. Calderone said 'Break.' So, if you're squeamish don't even think about lunch,"

Some of the crowd of residents dispersed.

"A doctor? I should have known," Gabe smoothed her hair out of her face.

"Yes, and an exceptionally good, very busy surgeon who's about to be late for surgery," Christine said before turning her attention to Olivia. "Excuse me for interrupting, but we gotta go get you scrubbed in," Christine handed the lab coat to Nadine who still stood behind the desk.

Christine and Nadine shot each other a look as Olivia focused on Gabe. He was looking at Christine. But then he blinked and tilted his head and gazed down at Olivia.

"You look the same, Ollie," he said in amazement. "After all these years you—" Gabe moved to say something more when he was interrupted.

"G, Max called. He kept his word. He had some findings for us."

Gabe still towered over her only now there seemed to be so much more of him eclipsing the world beyond them. He pressed his cheek against her palm and smiled.

"Precinct? You followed in your parent's footsteps," she smiled "Always figured you would."

The mountainous, huskier man moved around and stood near Christine as he flickered a gaze between them. "Uh yeah. He runs a Murder Squad," he said focusing on Gabe. "Listen G, Max was able to get the victim on the table sooner. We need to get going," Calvin insisted as he stuck out his hand to Christine. "Excuse me Ma'am. I'm Detective Calvin Ford."

Gabe never took his eyes from her as the man beside him continued to speak. If a world existed beyond them, Gabe looked like he'd forgotten it.

"You know Max Caldwell?" Olivia asked still gripping his shoulder.

"Yes, he's the Head Coroner now. Ollie, I can't believe it," he pressed his forehead to hers.

"G, we gotta fly man. He has some information for us," Calvin insisted as he shook Christine's hand.

"Heard you the first time Calvin," Gabe said pushing Olivia's hair back over her shoulder. He blinked and eased his grip around her waist. A sad smile touched his features as he lowered her to the floor. "God knows I want to keep you. Ollie. It's just… Wow, how long has it been?" he asked.

"A thousand years and…" she started, and his eyes lit up.

"A thousand years and a day with eternity above and beneath," Gabe finished. "You still remember that."

"It was how we measured time back then. It was good to see you Gabe," Olivia managed as she hugged him once more then walked a few steps away. She was about to take another step when his hand gently encircled her wrist.

"Ollie wait. I can't let you slip away again. Put your number in my cell," He dug his phone out and pressed it into her hand.

For an insane moment, her telephone number was a jumble in her mind. He glanced down at the phone in her hand and moved closer. He traced her pulse line with his thumb. Olivia almost wept with relief when the digits fell back in line. She put the numbers in and handed it back. He scooped her into his arms again and buried his face in her hair and took a deep breath.

"Olivia, we have to get you scrubbed in. I'm sorry but she's gotta go," Christine insisted with a sense of urgency.in her voice.

Just then, the PA system chimed. "Dr. Calderone you're needed in the OR. Dr. Olivia Calderone please report to the OR," Olivia flinched.

"Go on, Ollie. It's just. I mean wow…," he said before kissing her on the forehead.

Olivia ran her thumb over his high cheek bone before she gave his arm another squeeze and took off down the hallway.

CHAPTER SEVEN

Some crimes scenes smelled worse than others.

Time was little more than slices of death that caused certain chemicals in the body to break down. The absence of life gave the environment a thickness, that made normal colors seem to fade to a dingy grey. Blood hung in that kind of viscosity. It clung to the ceilings and the walls, but the sheer weight of that tear in the human existence made life impractical. Impossible.

The morgues were no better.

Sure, the air was saturated with an ultra-clean bleach smell, but underneath it all, autolysis, the process where the semipermeable walls between cells and organ down and decomposition started breaking down as decay set in and began to spread. Gasses were building which meant the other custodians of death were arriving for the feast.

By the time Gabe and Calvin reached the county coroner's office, Max was already at work rattling off measurements and observations into the Dictaphone above his head. The seafoam green gloves on the medical examiner's hands were the color of the organ he pulled from the girl's body and placed on the scale.

Max looked to one of his technicians. "Millie get them some face masks. On second thought, how about you gents go into the observation room? Calvin forget about mouth breathing. Putrefaction has a distinctive bite."

Calvin gave Gabe the side eye. "You two in the same book club or something?" he asked shuddering in disgust.

Gabe walked over to Millie and accepted the masks from her hand. Once inside the room just off from the examination room, Calvin flipped the red switch on the wall.

"Okay, Doc, what can you tell us?" Calvin leaned on his arm with his head facing the door instead of the grisly goings on in the cadaver room.

"Maturity of the fly larvae suggests that she'd been there four to ten days. Her body just gave out, essentially. Speaking of organs, we're missing some just like I thought," Max said as he scratched some note onto a clipboard holding a generic anatomically correct drawing of a person.

Gabe moved closer to the glass.

"The incision on Miss. St. Clair's side was from a surgery that removed a kidney. The close was appropriate, but she shouldn't have been moved or discharged," Max said as he grabbed a pair of forceps from the table.

"Anything else?" Gabe glanced at Calvin who struggled not to gag.

"Ovaries are gone too. Uterus shows signs of a recent abortion. The guy you found on the road was missing a kidney and a lobe of his liver and his corneas," Max paused and looked over at Gabe through the observation window. "Some sutures were in the last stages of dissolving. Looks like somebody went back for seconds on both of them."

"Idents on the guy? Calvin asked while facing the door as though Max was standing in front of him.

"Only this young lady here. Family is scheduled to ID the girl. Called around to other counties they're all saying the same thing. A couple of them were college students in the same condition." Max waved Millie over and she started laying out the suture kit.

"Can we get a list of the medical examiners you called Max?" Gabe asked as he fished his case book out of a pocket and started scribbling down notes.

"Millie already has a copy waiting. Anything from your side of the fence? Dean, if your glasses fall in my patient one more time, I'm going to glue them to your face. Put your goggles on!" Max snapped at the young intern peering into the body.

Calvin dry heaved and bolted from the room.

Gabe took Calvin's place and pressed the intercom button. "My crew is still canvassing."

"You know, there's a market out there for organs," Max said shoving the clipboard in Dean's direction forcing the man to back away from the table. "They call it Share Cropping now, people will cultivate and sell their organs piecemeal for rent, drugs or video game equipment. Black Market isn't just about sex anymore."

Gabe let the silence between them spread as Max continued to work.

"Agreed. It's an old idea for a new age. People will buy and sell plenty of things that'll keep you up at night," Gabe mumbled, as he tucked his casebook away and left.

CHAPTER EIGHT

"You didn't mention the girl from last night." Olivia sat back on the sofa and removed her glasses.

"Apples and oranges compared to what we're dealing with," Tiana replied.

"It's starting again, Tiana. Just like I knew it would. Now do you see why I had to—"

"Shut up about that," Tiana snapped, "None of that was your fault. You did the best you could under the circumstances."

"Not enough. You know it wasn't enough." Olivia untied one sneaker and then the other.

Her last patient was resting in recovery and her residents were on their floors completing their assignments. Everything was going smoothly even after Gabe's heart telegraphed an ancient message across her breasts and into her very soul.

"You're here. I'm here. The rest of it is icing. Hey you still there?" Tiana questioned as the alarm to her car chirped. "That girl was in a bad way. Body just didn't know it was dead yet."

Olivia dragged a hand through her hair and focused on the phone call.

"The tanker left port on time."

"You sure about this? There were other ways. Maybe something not so public."

Olivia chuckled bitterly as she tugged her hair back into a ponytail and secured it with a stray rubber band. "Kind of a moot point now. Purple. Love the new hair color by the way."

"You know me," she said with a grin, "Annoying all forms of leadership is my favorite pastime. Now, get some shuteye. You're slicing and dicing in a few hours."

As the line went dead, Olivia tossed her blue tooth earpiece on the white fabricated wood table and scrubbed her face with her hands.

"Don't worry. He didn't leave a hickey," Christine said as she came in and sat her coat and her tote bag down the floor next to one of the side chairs flanking the table.

Olivia tugged at her ponytail to tighten the rubber band. "I have no idea what…"

"Girl, stop playing and spill the tea. Who was that walking piece of sex music?" Christine inquired folding her arms and raising an eyebrow.

Olivia still hadn't given herself a chance to unpack the fact that Gabriel Symone -Garrett was actually there. Moving back to Shadow Bay was a spur of the moment decision that took years in the making. Part of her fantasized about the prospect of him still being there in her hometown like a lighthouse guiding her across the dangerous waters of their past. The adult part of her pushed all of that aside.

Gabe was a citizen of the world just like his parents, Cassiel and Alana Garrett had raised him to be. Backpacking across Europe or joining the military wasn't out of the realm for him. Summers abroad meant that a port on any continent could serve as home.

Someone had to leave. One death was enough.

"Chrissy," she warned, cutting off her dark thoughts while reaching down to pick at her shoelace.

"Don't 'Chrissy clutch the pearls' me. He just about shoved all the residents out of the way to get to you. Who is he?" she asked flopping down in the chair.

"Gabriel Garrett. We went to high school together," Olivia confessed with a feeble shrug.

"Did you now?" Christine asked before crossing her legs and folding her hands as though settling in for a long night.

"What's to tell? We've been best friends since third grade." Olivia gripped the cushion on each side next to her knees.

"Annnnd?" Christine waved her hand to coax her to continue.

Olivia glanced up at the ceiling and shrugged. "Nothing. College. Life."

To save us both one of us had to leave.

"What do you mean nothing? If he looks like hot dirty sex now, he had to be something else back in high school," she quipped, wriggling her eyebrows in a comedic fashion.

"It was a long time ago," Olivia admitted with a frown.

The world moved on, but the nightmares still ripped her out of a deep sleep from time to time. The ache of his absence between her thighs tore her from slumber that dissolved into tears that threatened to wash her away. Olivia ran a hand over her belly and glanced at her friend.

"Why do you ask?" she said hoping the question would distract her friend.

Christine rolled her eyes. "Because that man put a finger to his lips and every damn one of those female residents and Nadine got wet, except me. I got a little pregnant."

"Stop it." Olivia covered her mouth holding back a laugh the first one she had in months.

"What? That man hugged you with his entire life and he smelled good too. Girl, forget those books and let him put your back out," Christine said as she writhed in her chair imitating a lap dance.

"Good night, Christine." Olivia covered her face and laughed.

Christine snagged her coat and tote bag and stood. "All jokes aside. I'm just saying it was nice," she said shrugging into her coat.

"What was?" Olivia bit down on her lip before she looked up to find her friend smiling.

"Seeing you like that. You be about your business and you're great at it. Better than all those fossils upstairs. It looks good on you."

Olivia shook her head still confused.

"Happiness, and I think you spread some of that to Officer Hotness. You didn't see the way he breathed you in. Looked like he hadn't taken a breath that deep in a long time." Christine flicked her braids back over her shoulder. "Night Olivia. We pick it all up tomorrow. I'm back on at later in the afternoon. I have to take Cory to the kidney specialist in the morning," she mumbled, with a frown.

"How's my boyfriend?" Olivia asked with a hesitant smile at the mention of the friend's beautiful little brown skinned boy with the gap between his bottom teeth.

Christine blinked rapidly as she worked one of her own. "No word from the Organ donor registry."

"It takes time Christine, "Olivia moved to stand. "I know that's not a comfort."

"Still talks about you, though. How pretty, smart, and funny you are. I think your detective has some competition in my Cory." Christine retreated managing a smile.

Olivia sank back down on the sofa. "Not a chance. Cory had my heart after he sang to me at his seventh birthday party. He's getting good with that guitar," Olivia replied, hoping that the mention of a happier time would comfort her friend.

"Only because you taught him. He takes that thing everywhere he goes, even dialysis," Christine commented with a watery grin.

"Well, you tell him from me that he owes me a serenade or a recital soon," Olivia replied

"He'd love that. Night Olivia," Christine beamed before hurrying out.

Olivia raked a hand through her hair and muttered a curse. She pulled out her phone and thumbed through the pictures and stopped on the one Christine had taken during Cory's last admission. Olivia smiled at the two of them sitting on the colorful carpet in the hospital playroom holding a jam session. Tears pricked her eyes as she ran her thumb over the little boy's image and said a little prayer that an organ donor materialized as the miracle his blood type deemed it to be.

CHAPTER NINE

"And in other news, a tanker was reported missing just outside international waters. Sources say it left the African Port of…"

Gabe sat with his back facing the large flat screen television on the wall. The Murder Boards took center stage in the squad room. As information came in, the detectives, shared the information and made their contributions to the white boards taped off in different areas. His desk was stationed at the back of the squad room against the wall with Calvin's directly across from his. The rest of the floor branched out into neat rows with a sparse number of detectives working at their desks or moving around somewhere downstairs clocking in or out for shift change.

Everything paled in comparison to having Olivia walk out of a hospital room and back into his life. When he returned that evening, he fully expected a repeat of the reunion. Instead, he ran into Dr. Marsden trying to play gate keeper. No sooner had he gotten settled on the floor next to Olivia's sleeping form his phone rang with news of another body found. Gabe grabbed his cell phone and mashed the favorites button and smiled as her name filled the screen. A bubble of excitement filled his belly as the phone began to ring.

"Hello?" Her tongue caressed each syllable making his heart skip a beat.

"You know I can think of at least four other places for you to sleep instead of the Resident's Lounge. That place was a pig pen." He hoped his voice sounded a lot calmer than he felt.

"Gabe," The shuffle of papers in the background made it clear that she was multitasking.

Hearing his name carried on breath while envisioning her mouth forming the word made something in his heart turn over. Picking her up that way was a kneejerk reaction. If the crowd around them wasn't so thick, Gabe wasn't so sure he wouldn't walk up the hallway carrying her. She more than filled his arms and the closer he held her, the more she fit against him like an organic puzzle piece. Rich tropical scent of cocoa butter and hibiscus filled the air around them. Her rich wavy hair felt like cornsilk against his face.

"How'd you sleep?" he asked with his heart slamming against his ribcage.

The question sounded simple enough, but the memory of her arms around his neck with her breasts mashed against his chest, the inquiry had all sorts of connotations to it making the muscles in his thighs ache. Olivia always connected in all the right places when he was a horny teenager. Now, the gentle pressure of her gave him a "thereness" that he didn't know was missing until then.

"Fine, I guess. I mean… you couldn't have gotten much rest," she said.

Even her answer was more intimate as if they'd been together in bed making the kinds of shadows on the wall that haunted his dreams. The comment, he imagined he'd make the next morning as he worked his desire into her skin like an exotic lotion.

"Wasn't trying to. Can you meet me for lunch?" he asked scanning the room to see if anyone was eavesdropping on the conversation.

Lying wasn't a habit for him but telling the truth would tip his hand.

In all honesty, when a nurse named Leslie confided that Olivia was sick with jet lag the case and everything else took a back seat. Seeing her asleep with her lab coat pillowed under her head put his initial concern to rest but then seeing her there all warm and sweet made every muscle in his body hurt. All he wanted to do was climb on the sofa behind her and pull her onto his chest. Instead, he covered her with his coat and parked himself on the floor. When she turned in her sleep and draped her arm over his chest like a seat belt Gabe felt his soul crack open, and then, the phone rang.

"I don't know Gabe. There's a mountain of paperwork on my desk and I have a meeting this afternoon where I'm presenting," she said with a touch of sadness to her voice.

"And your scrub nurses probably organized everything according to priority and you've been studying and preparing for that presentation for weeks. Come on, Ollie- Girl. You have to eat sometime," he said picturing her at her desk chewing on her bottom lip as she worked out some complex problem.

"I haven't heard that name in a lifetime. My nurses like you. Tiana told me you were standing watch over me last night," she murmured, as her low intoxicating voice moved through him like a measure of music.

"Hardly. You looked exhausted, and I didn't want anyone to disturb you. Figured if it was important, one of your nurses would come for you. One did. She had purple hair. Which leads me back to my original question. Why the resident playpen?" he asked as the image of the woman with purple hair and the half sleeve tattoo stood in the doorway studying him.

"Makes sense. I'm there on the floor if my patients or my residents need me," She uttered as her pen plopped on the desk.

Gabe smiled inwardly knowing he now had her full attention. "I can almost see the residents squabbling over your attention. Tommy Marsden certainly is a needy little fishy."

He frowned as the memory of the resident with his pocket protector returned. Every encounter he had with Marsden irked him. The man's bedside manner was mediocre at best, and his interpersonal skills were nonexistent as Leslie pointed out when she shut him down for not answering Gabe's questions directly.

"You still there?" Olivia asked and the smile in her voice radiated the kind of warmth that made his heart skip a beat as he basked in her attention.

"Never left, Babe," he replied, hoping she hadn't advanced the conversation any further.

"You left your jacket won't you be needing it?" she questioned. He hoped she was still wrapped in it or that at was warming her thighs the way he wanted to.

"You were cold," he said trying hard to envision her dressed in nothing but his coat.

She shuffled the papers once more. "You say that like it explains all the mysteries of the world,"

"It doesn't?" He asked with a chuckle. "Meet me for lunch. You can bring it to me"

Her silence on the other end spread between them. If she said no, he'd play it off like it didn't matter knowing full well it would hurt. Another voice intruded on the silence as she asked one question and then another.

"How bad?" The tension in her voice stoked his. "All right. Prep him for surgery. Gabe, I'm sorry. I have to go," she said before hanging up.

"Damn man, you look like somebody ran off with your balloon," Calvin said as he flopped down and pivoted in his chair to face the computer.

"Olivia had an emergency," he mumbled, dropping his phone back in the drawer.

Calvin smiled and turned to face Gabe and folded his hands. "Yeah, about that. So that's Olivia huh?"

Gabe jiggled the mouse to wake up his computer. "I am not discussing her with you," he said, trying to keep the smile from his face.

"I don't understand why? Inquiring minds and all." Calvin's grin was wider than a mile. "Now I understand why none of the women buzzing around you ever stood a chance. Beauty is deadly. Couple that with intelligence and you got something lethal."

"Calvin, what did I just say?" Gabe warned.

Calvin raised his hands in mock surrender. "Okay." He turned back to his computer. Using his two index fingers he punched in the password and studied the screen for a second or two. "Beauty and brains. Wonder if *she's* read any good books lately."

Gabe balled up a piece of paper and threw it at him.

CHAPTER TEN

"You gave a brilliant presentation today," he said as the knock off version of his Cool Water cologne fouled the air.

Olivia felt her stomach sink as the hospital president's voice washed over her immediately making her skin crawl. She sifted through the puzzle pieces in the box and handed one to the little girl sitting beside her at one of the playroom tables. Beacham's shadow fell over them as Leslie came over and ushered the girl away.

She sat back and took in the older man with his perfect platinum grey hair and beard. Those beady pale blue eyes always gave off a feeling of superiority as if only a few inhabited his orbit and even that was an at will residency. The last doctor who fell from his good graces had to leave Shadow Bay Medical Group and move to another state to find work. Even that was tenuous.

"Thank you, Dr. Beacham. Sorry I ran a little behind," she said praying he wouldn't decide to sit beside her. "Oliver Ackerman fell out of bed damaging the central line I put in last week."

Beacham studied her with one hand tucked in his lab coat pocket just over the black cording from his stethoscope.

"Oh, but you made up for it. Why, I could charge admission to your contribution to our bi-weekly Mortality and Morbidity conferences. Most of them are only there to hear you anyway," he commented, sinking into one of the children's chairs and grimacing as both knees popped in protest. "Crickey! These chairs are way too small," he complained, before facing her.

"Hardly the case Dr. Beacham." Olivia moved the box between them as she plugged a squared blue piece into the border at the top of the puzzle featuring a hot air balloon.

"Please. After everything we've been through, I thought we agreed that you would call me Richard or Rick in less formal surroundings," he offered before finding a piece in the box and putting it in place. "And you're being modest. You are the only surgeon I know that can turn a boring conference into a teachable moment every week. Why, if I didn't know any better, I'd think you were after my job."

Olivia sat back and studied the man. For all the money he flashed with his expensive cars and thousand-dollar suits, the man still stank of cheap whiskey and even cheaper morals.

"Never in a million years. I came home to serve my community. Nothing more," she quipped, as she ran a finger over the border of the puzzle featuring the beginnings of a fluffy cloud.

Beacham pursed his lips. "With the world at your feet and numerous prestigious medical institutions calling every week for a consult from you or a member of your team…" Beacham folded his arms and crinkled his nose. "Your time, it seems, is more valuable than mine. Maybe you can help the police solve their little issue," he said smoothing his thumb over the puzzle edge a little too close to her hand. "According to the President over at Shadow Bay U the girl was a lab coat chaser. Got herself killed someplace else and had the audacity to die here in my hospital," he griped, focusing on the television on the wall.

"I didn't know death could be an inconvenience in a hospital," Olivia countered following his line of view.

The volume on the television was too low to hear but the ticker tape running along the bottom of the screen gave an update on the missing tanker. Her heart cramped in her chest as another ship carrying blue and orange tractor trailer containers glided across the shimmering water. Beacham cleared his throat and Olivia angled in her chair to see him studying her with rapt interest.

"Tankers don't often get lost at sea unless they have help," he mused, "I remember having a devil of a time getting our medical and food supplies in, only to discover that the port masters could be bought."

Olivia took another puzzle piece from the box and ran her thumb over the edges. "You know as well as I do that transport, even under the best weather conditions can vary from ten to thirty days."

"True enough. We were fortunate that you were able to speak the dialect of that port master in Jinja Bay to find our wayward cargo. In any case, the girl's death in this hospital makes it our responsibility to be cooperative." Beacham smoothed down his tie. "Police Commissioner Mark Brown called. As a professional courtesy I suggested a point of contact for his detectives and after your little reunion with the detective what was his name? Detective Garrett?" he said sliding his gaze to hers.

Saying Gabe's name made him real. Olivia retreated to the safety of the television screen. It was one thing if she said it and quite another when her boss did. Olivia ignored the audible click her throat made when she swallowed.

"We grew up together," she said. The words felt sticky in her mouth. Saying anything more would have triggered a walk through the ruins of her childhood. A trek she had no intentions of taking with Beacham's eyes crawling all over her.

"You were always good at establishing relationships with the natives. Even overseas, you were the only one that I knew that could walk through a warzone unscathed because both sides loved you like some light skinned Latino savior."

Olivia chuckled as she dusted off her hands and stood. "So that's why people were shooting at me? Because they loved me, right."

Beacham rose from the chair gripping the wall. "Forgive me. It was a bad segue. I remember how close you came to death, and I shouldn't be making light of it. I just meant that because you know the detective you can get him in and out of here quickly so that we can go on with the work of the day."

"You're right. Sorry I snapped at you," Olivia said as she flickered a gaze at the clock on the wall. "I have another surgery in a half an hour. I'll help as much as I can, but if Gabriel Garrett is anything like his parents, he won't be easy to get rid of," she said as a cold chill washed down her spine.

"And who were they, politicians, or something?" he asked, making his way to the door.

Olivia searched her memories for the right combination of words to describe Cassiel and Alana Garrett.

"Our school bus driver missed our stop. Got lost somehow. State, local police and the FBI surrounded the bus. Ms. Alana got us off the bus and locked the door. No one knows what she said to that man. All I know was that he resigned and moved out of the state."

"And that means what exactly?" he scoffed.

"They are the last people on the planet anyone would ever want to mess with, and their son is probably worse."

CHAPTER ELEVEN

Late afternoon blossomed into early evening as Gabe left his mother's house and headed back to the station. As the men and women that made up his night squad filtered in, the white boards situated along the far wall near Gabe and Calvin's desks continued to evolve with new information being added. Roll call signaled a changing of the guard and a chance to head back to the hospital.

Gabe smoothed his hand over the back of his neck and up over his head removing the black watch cap he wore. He stuffed the cap in a pocket. Two young nurses staring at him started giggling to themselves. An older woman scowled at him from the corner like a troll under a bridge. Her muddy brown gaze dropped to the tattoo on his lower arm. Gabe pulled up a sleeve even further so that the blue haired woman could get a good look at what she was disapproving of. The swirling script was Olivia's favorite passage from a Shakespearean Sonnet.

For thy sweet love remembered such wealth brings that I scorn to change my state with kings.

Each room he passed was quiet and Olivia's absence on the floor howled from every corner. He'd thought about asking for directions to her office, but the idea of seeing her in her element warmed him inside. He felt the badge shift against his chest and covered it with his hand. Usually, Gabe kept the thing under wraps until he had to display it. Wearing it in most places gave him an all-access pass. He paused at the room she emerged from earlier and peered inside.

"She's not in there, Detective. That patient and her baby were discharged this afternoon," Christine called from the nurse's station.

Gabe walked over as the woman gave some silent direction to one of the residents behind her before she stood and rounded the counter. The woman was tall with dark brown eyes and braids that were pinned back from her face. Her scrubs were the same seafoam green color that Olivia wore, but her pink shoes reminded him of heartburn medication that tasted like liquid chalk.

"You're Christine, right?" he asked.

She glanced down at her badge and smiled. "Very observant Detective. What brings you out this evening?"

"Please, call me G everybody does." Gabe grinned and waved his hand. "Evening ladies," he said letting his gaze drift to the women behind the desk.

They shared a look before they jumped and scattered to other parts of the unit. Christine stuck out her hand and he shook it once. "Don't mind them. You've been the talk of the whole damn hospital since your reunion with Dr. Calderone. G huh? Hmph. Not everybody calls you that. Olivia calls you Gabe."

"And if my mom is angry with me, she pulls out my entire government name," he joked, as he scanned the area.

The woman in front of him seemed nice enough, but a smile and a warm greeting didn't shorten the distance between them. She looked at him the way all women did when they were sizing up whether a man was good enough for their friend or themselves.

"Is Olivia, I mean Dr. Calderone in surgery? I can come back later if she is," he offered suddenly wondering if coming there unannounced was such a good idea.

Christine rounded the desk "She performed several today. Come on, I'll take you to her," she said walking past him. Gabe watched her walk down the hallway.

She came back and tugged on his sleeve. "Come on, she'd be happy to see you," she said as a warm buttery grin made her eyes crinkle at the edges.

Gabe planted his feet making the woman jerk to a stop and release him. The idea of the woman tugging him long like some wayward child bothered him. "If she's busy, I can come back," he repeated suddenly regretting the whole idea.

Christine tugged on his arm again. "You are just the distraction Olivia needs. Maybe you can get a meal into her."

"Why hasn't she eaten?" a member of housekeeping nodded as they continued to push a mop and bucket up the hallway.

The concern in his voice made her sober up. "I make sure Olivia eats. Sometimes she gets so wrapped up in her cases that food is the last thing on her mind."

The more the woman talked the more Gabe wanted, no needed, to see Olivia. She was already small enough. The thought of her not eating bothered him. "She have anything today?"

"Half a cup of yogurt probably something in her meeting and half of my bagel and that was only after I refused to hand over her tablet until she did." Christine continued up the hall pausing long enough to make sure he was keeping up.

Gabe fell in step beside the woman. Olivia declining his invite to Tassey's filled his mind.

"Well, that hasn't changed. My mother had to take Ollie's homework until she ate a least half of a sandwich or whatever was on her plate when we got home from school. Listen, if she's busy I'll just give her a call."

"Why Ollie?" Christine asked as they rounded another corner.

Where the other corridor was stark with little or no décor. The medical surgical unit on this side of the wing required badge access and the walls were covered in bright colors with comic book themes and superhero emblems on the name plates.

"Excuse me?" he asked, stopping in front of her.

"Everyone else calls her Olivia or Doc. C. You call her Ollie."

Gabe put his head down and smiled. "Mid semester of third grade she walks in the room. Instant crush," he said with a smile before shaking his head.

"She notice you?" she asked with a nudge.

"Not even slightly," Gabe chuckled. "I borrowed a pencil from her every day for a month; and then, one day she looked at me." Gabe stopped and leaned against the wall," First time I called her Ollie she smiled." Gabe took in a breath that shook his chest. "Went home that night and told my mom that when I grew up, I was going to marry her."

You're being selfish Ollie. Why Connecticut, you had a full ride at Shadow Bay U.

His heart cramped in his chest as the memory of her running away from him in the airport that last day. He backed away shaking his head.

"Looks like you still want to," Christine offered, as she reached for his arm once more.

Gabe tried on a smile that ached at the edges. "What, marry her or take care of her?" he joked shrugging out of her grasp.

Christine's smile widened. "Both, now quit stalling."

Gabe opened his mouth to protest. Christine gave him a knowing look then gestured with her head at the doorway.

The brightly colored room was filled with children of all ages sitting on a carpet that looked like a little city with highways and byways that a child would push cars on. In the center of the room, a little girl in a princess hat and matching costume over her pajamas sat on Olivia's lap as she strummed on an acoustic guitar. A little boy in pajama's sat across from Olivia attempting to mimic her finger positions.

"And that handsome fella right there is my Cory." Christine beamed.

Gabe regarded the boy with a hospital band on his arm trying to keep up with Olivia on a guitar. He smiled when the boy turned his body and Gabe spotted his signature on the guitar.

"Pretty mean six string your son's playing." He offered. Christine gave him a watery smile.

"Olivia gave him that guitar for his birthday earlier this year. She was worried that he wouldn't make it to his birthday. Gave it to him early. He barely puts it down. It's his kidneys. He needs a transplant."

"I'm sorry to hear that. Christine." He offered reaching for her.

Christine squared her shoulders and smiled. "No matter how bad he hurts after dialysis. No matter how tired, he sees her and perks right up." She faced him. "It's the waiting that gets to you. Six months ago, he was as healthy as an ox. Now he moves around like an old man."

Cory turned to the doorway and his face lit up. He struggled to his feet and ran to her. Christine stooped down and swept him into a hug.

"Mom, did you see me? Olivia says I'm getting better with my finger placement." He chirped before facing Gabe. Cory dusted his hand off on his shirt and extended it.

He shook the boy's hand shocked by how frail it was. "I'm Cory T Watson. Who are you?"

Gabe stooped down to the boy's level and shook his hand. "I'm Gabriel, Olivia is a good friend of mine."

"Mine too!" the boy chirped. "Isn't she great? She came to my school for…" He squinted. "Mom what's it called again?"

Christine put on her best smile. "Career Day. Go grab a cupcake, sweetie Glam Ma will be here soon."

Cory shifted the guitar on his tiny shoulder and stuck out a hand once more. "Nice to meet you Mr. Gabriel."

Gabe nodded as he caught a glimpse of the children wearing party hats and a cluster of adults snapping pictures with their phones as the children sang Happy Birthday off key.

He leaned against the door and watched as the little girl put her head on the guitar body and rocked along with the music. The blinding white bandage made the pink glitter cone with the even darker piece of tulle sit askew on the girl's head.

"Christine, he's wonderful. I'm sure Olivia is doing everything she can to help."

Christine sniffled then focused on the activity in the room. "We have a whole department of surgeons, some of the best in the country and out of all of them, she is the only one that will come in and do something like that," Christine said proudly gesturing with her head.

Gabe glanced at Christine. The woman was smiling as she folded her arms across her chest. He must have made a sound because she looked at him and added, "For real, for real? This place would run a hell of a lot better with her at the helm. She cares for her patients like they're family,"

Gabe glanced back at Olivia. The little girl was facing the group as the song ended. Olivia took one of the treats from the three-tiered cupcake stand and she tapped the little girl on the nose leaving behind a tiny bit of frosting. She took her cup cake and dabbed Olivia's cheek with frosting as one of the parents snapped the picture.

"When Cory took a bad turn, she stayed with him all night holding him. She'd already worked 18 hours but stayed through another shift so that I could work so he wouldn't be alone."

Christine said. "Olivia may miss a meal here and there, but you see the results."

Gabe watched as Olivia extricated herself from the girl and made her way to one of the groups of parents. She was backing away from the festivities and Gabe stood up from the wall and caught her.

"Hi Gabe! What are you doing here?" she asked, throwing her arms around his neck.

"Rescuing a fair maiden from starvation and an army of kids hopped up on sugar," he said turning his face into her hair.

The confusion on her face as she stepped back made him smile as he reached up and straightened the pink and purple crown. Olivia smiled and reached for it.

"No, keep it on. It suits you. Matches your blush," he grinned.

Olivia looked back and forth between the two of them. Christine grinned and pointed at her cheek. Gabe ran a finger along her cheek drawing her attention back to him. He sucked the icing from his finger. "Butter cream…. Nice. But a half a cup of yogurt, a bagel and a cupcake aren't dinner,"

"Gabe how…" Olivia eyed him with more than a little suspicion.

Christine winked at him as Cory ran out and grabbed her hand then started walking down the hallway, "She's land locked but there's a decent café downstairs that does carry out," She called over her shoulder. "Bring me back a bag of chips while you're at it."

Olivia's mouth fell open. She folded her arms and looked back and forth between them, "Are you two ganging up on me," she asked, before shifting the guitar strap on her shoulder.

Gabe erased the last of the icing from her cheek with his thumb.

"My new BFF tells me your poor eating habits are still in full effect. So, what is your majesty in the mood for?" he gave her a clumsy bow. "You gotta eat sometime Ollie," He raised an eyebrow as he moved to suck the icing from his thumb.

"Hey that's my blush," Olivia protested as she grabbed his thumb and licked the icing from the tip. "What are *you* in the mood for?" She asked raising her own neatly arched eyebrow.

Gabe backed away from the door pulling her with him. "Right now, I need an entire can of buttercream cake icing in my life."

"Plenty in there," Olivia said waving a hand in the general direction of the playroom.

His mind filled with images of her in the backseat of his truck covered in cake icing and little else. "Soup and a sandwich," he said, "Anything else?" he asked clearing his throat.

"Your company. Can you stay for a while?" she asked.

For the rest of my life.

The words were there. Right there. Gabe felt his heart cramp in his chest. Maybe it was the way she was looking at him or what her scrub nurse had said. In that instant, he was ready to drop to a knee like a knight in some corny romance and pledge his life to her cause. Instead, he hugged her and breathed her in.

"It's the only reason I'm here. Meet you back in your office." he managed before holding her back from him.

"What's wrong with the resident lounge?" she teased, pinching his side.

"Ugh smells like corn chips and stale coffee in there," He chuckled as he grabbed her hand and kissed the back of it.

"Flatterer. It could have been me smelling like dirty socks," Olivia giggled as she put her hands between them and pushed gently at his midsection.

"Hardly. When you were a little girl, you always smelled like soap, bubble gum or butterscotch disks,"

"And now?" she queried with a squint.

Gabe shrugged. "You smell like home."

Olivia put her hand on his shoulder and smiled. A nest of papers sitting on a computer station on wheels caught her attention and her eyes widened.

"Beacham assigned me to help with some case that you're working on. Something about the girl that came in here last night," she said with a frown.

Gabe touched the back of her hand and marveled at how warm she felt. "Ollie please. Not tonight. Stay here in the moment with me," he pleaded.

Olivia nodded, "My office then. Christine can show you after you drop off her chips."

CHAPTER TWELVE

The first time Gabe planted a kiss on the inner aspect of her right thigh, Olivia's orgasm came faster than a mail delivery service. The thick mane of soft red curls on his head and the fine sprinkling of stubble on his cheeks wreaked havoc on the sensitive skin between her thighs. Every swipe of his tongue posed a question that a series of feather light flicks answered.

"I wasn't quite sure what you wanted so I took a chance. Ollie are you okay?" he asked. The rich deep cadence of his voice summoned her from the past into the raw masculine heat of his presence.

If a five-hundred-year-old Scottish malt were a man, it would look like the one sitting across from her. Gabe hadn't so much as touched her when they made it back to her office when the first orgasm rippled from the apex of her thighs to the top of her head. The phone call from Christine gave her the reprieve she needed to reign herself back in. Turning to see him arranging their dinner on the coffee table sent a wave of nostalgia washing through her.

Shadows of the little boy who always had an extra peanut butter and strawberry jam sandwich in his Captain America lunchbox made her large corner office cozier by the second. Even as a teenager, Gabe swept off the space at the lunch table directly beside him before sitting her tray next to his. On dates, he often held up their glasses and pushed the one with more water or soda in it over to her.

I'll spend the rest of my life taking care of you if you let me.

The sincerity in his voice, back then still poked at a raw place in her. Olivia settled on the sofa beside him, he held out a Styrofoam cup of soup with a napkin wrapped around it.

"Careful Ollie," He warned before grabbing his own cup.

She peered in his cup he caught her peeking and showed her the contents.

"Beef barley. Want to trade?" he asked holding out the cup.

"No. I'm being nosy," she quipped before peeling the lid off and tossing it on the coffee table.

"Take a few sips of that soup and I'll tell you what else is in the bag," he said pointing with his head.

***

Olivia resembled a little girl sitting on the sofa with her legs folded. Every sip she took of the chicken noodle soup added a little more color to her cheeks. She barely touched the sandwich, but her coloring was getting better.

"Mom would make a deal with you. Eat half of that sandwich and I'll give your notebook back."

Olivia smiled. "Take two more bites of that spaghetti and *maybe* I'll let you borrow a book from my library, she'd tell me and that was a true privilege. How is she?" she asked

He took in a breath that made his chest hitch. "Still keeping her feelings close to the vest as always." Gabe smiled and pointed at the sandwich in front of her.

Olivia put down her cup and unwrapped her sandwich then clutched it to her chest. "You remembered."

"It was all you ate when we were kids. Well, that and the second granola bar I used to carry in my coat pocket. Still do actually," he quipped, as he sat his cup aside and reached in his coat. He pulled out two green and silver foil packages. He placed one granola bar on the table then grabbed his cup of soup and sat back.

"That's for later. When do you go home?" he asked hoping he didn't sound intrusive. And then it dawned on him. What if she had a husband and kids waiting for her? He searched the third finger of her left hand and sighed with relief.

Olivia shrugged as her cheeks hollowed from scraping the roof of her mouth with her tongue. "Not 'til the weekend," she replied taking another bite of her sandwich as she gestured with her head toward her luggage in the corner. "Came right in from the airport. Attended a conference in Miami for Continuing Education Credits. Ended up delivering a baby during rounds if you can believe that."

Gabe eyed the luggage tags and grinned. "You never could pass up a chance to learn something new. Remember that night we almost got locked in the Shadow Bay University Library?"

"That was all you. Nobody told you to go upstairs and fall asleep in one of the conference rooms," She mumbled around a mouthful. "Almost lost my job over your foolishness."

"What? I was tired. Goofing off all day is hard work," he joked as she inched closer into his space and nibbled on the corner of her sandwich. Gabe held his cup out of the way as she settled with her back against his side. He heard her sniffle, and he sat his cup of beef barley aside and attempted to turn her to face him. Olivia buried her face into his bicep.

"If I knew peanut butter and strawberry jam was going to make you cry…" Gabe pulled her closer. "Ollie, what's wrong?" he asked, breathing in her scent.

"Memories like that saved me many days when I was away." Her words heated the fabric on his arm as she spoke. He sat there holding her in a comfortable silence, but the question hung in the air.

Why didn't you come home? Why didn't you come back to me?

The words burned at the back of his throat. It was enough that he was thinking them. He had no intentions of saying them aloud for fear that the elephant in the room would charge. She was home with her sweet body resting against his. In that warm quiet space in her office, time stopped, and the world fell away.

"Take another healthy bite of that sandwich and maybe I'll tell you what else I got for you," he remarked as the memory of their parting resurfaced.

Olivia tried so hard to be mature and careful and to think things through logically, but something else colored every word she spoke. He even resorted to kissing her in an effort to sap the poison from the words and discern the truth beneath the surface. Their arguments seemed to swim up out of nowhere like summer squalls loud violent and then the clouds would part, and the world was still there, no worse for the wear.

Gabe pressed his face into her hair and breathed her in. Without even realizing it, she had run her fingers over a wound in his soul that even he wouldn't touch. The questions engulfed the back of his throat, but the more he breathed her in, the more it just didn't matter. She was there. Right there in his arms. The living breathing version of the woman who plagued his innermost thoughts, made the one he'd conjured over the years seem foolish. He was about to pull her closer when he noticed that she was trembling. He snagged his coat from the floor and covered her with it.

"First day I met you was the hottest day of third grade. You sat at the back of the classroom shaking like a leaf," he said as she looked up at him.

"Mrs. Cowling made Hilary Snowden responsible for me, but you took over," she murmured half laughing and crying a little.

"Had too. Hillary liked to pick her nose and eat it. She's an attorney now," he said with a shudder that made her giggle.

"Eww. Does she still pick her nose?" she inquired taking another bite of her sandwich.

"No, thank God. She's a Pitbull in court though. Gary hooked up with her and they got married. You remember Gary?" Gabe asked and reached in his pocket to extract the photo.

Olivia snuggled closer and smiled. "Oh my gosh! I remember this." Olivia ran her thumb over the picture, as she pointed at Gary, "He was so bashful; I remember the kids used to tease him about his size." She sat up and faced him.

The sudden loss of her made him groan as he reached for his cup of soup. "He thinned out, married Hillary and they've got four kids. He's the District Attorney."

Gabe moved to sit back and felt something digging into his back. He dug down behind him and pulled out the book and held it out to her. She ran her finger along the spine.

"Spent a lot of time overseas doing missionary work. We learned to function on less, but this? Spent hours in bookstores when I came stateside. Found this last week."

"Now there's a classic," he said with a smile sitting the cup aside. "Not a well-known poet by any stretch but man oh man could this guy breathe emotion on the page."

"Read to me," she asked still studying the photo.

Gabe opened the book and started reading aloud. Olivia settled against him once more and he read through several pages. He was about to move on to the next chapter when he noticed that she'd gone quiet beside him. He flexed an arm enough to send her sliding across his chest. Olivia was sound asleep with the photo of their small group of friends clutched to her chest.

Gabe put the book down and slipped his arm under her knees to move her onto his lap. Gone were the tremors that wracked her body as her breathing evened out. She filled his arms perfectly, but it surprised and scared him that she was so light. Gabe scooted down on the sofa so that she was resting against the middle of him. From somewhere deep in her sleep, Olivia whimpered as she snuggled closer to him. "Stay with me," she said with a watery sigh.

"Shh. Baby I'm right here," He whispered as he brushed his lips over her forehead.

And the world fell away.

CHAPTER THIRTEEN

"Damn man, you having a fake snowball fight over there or something?" Calvin asked before he sank into his chair and folded hands behind his head.

The wads of paper steadily grew as Gabe attempted to file his case reports. Olivia's words poked at a raw place inside him.

We learned to function on less.

The fact that Olivia lacked anything bothered him, but the way she said it haunted him. She was so matter of fact about it as if needing even the basics was too much to pray for. Sure, he heard the stories and saw things firsthand when he was in the military traveling the world but hearing her say it brought a lot of his own memories of wounded or starving men women and children back.

Sometimes the newspapers got it wrong.

What sounded like politics boiled down to basic human rights. While men and women in suits argued over giving taxpayers the bare minimum in economic relief, men, women, and children dressed in rags searched for clean drinking water in the sweltering heat. Where lawmakers rattled on about humanity from the convenience of a clean safe office in Washington, children as young as nine were crouching in the mud cradling assault rifles for the promise of food.

We learned to function on less.

Gabe thought of Olivia cradled in his arms and the purple rings of exhaustion around her eyes and suddenly he couldn't hold her close enough. She was home and he didn't care how or why after all those years, but he had no intentions of wasting it. Here was a chance to make good on all of the promises he made as a boy and the blood vows he made as a man if he ever had a chance to see her again. His apology would be one for the ages. He took in a cleansing breath and brushed the wads of paper in the trashcan by his desk.

"Idents came back on the dead guy in the street. He was a doctor out of Delaware. Same place your cousin, Shawn, works. Transplantation Centers of Delaware. I put in a call to him. All they could tell me was that he was out of contact." Calvin leaned back further as the chair creaked under his weight.

Gabe nodded as he minimized the screen on his computer and keyed in the name of the center and frowned at the manicured lawns sculpted flower beds and the nondescript brown building sitting in the background. "Which probably means he's out of a job again."

"What the rest of the world calls a gambling addiction he thinks is a lap dance from lady luck. Recovery is a joke he only stays long enough to pay off his debts. Frankly, I'm amazed he still has the use of his hands."

"For sure. Surgeon or not, Regulus Chastain, Georgia Mai and people like him have no qualms about showing up on a job to collect their money one way or another," Calvin replied, as he sat up and jiggled the mouse to wake up his computer. "That Optometrist out on Route Forty still claims he lost his eyesight in a hunting accident. They found him wandering around the Pine Barrens. No gun, no hunting gear, but evidently, he's out hunting grouse with two gaping holes where his eyes should have been."

Gabe shuffled the papers into a neat pile then gave them a light tap on the desk. "People think that just because my mother came up with Regulus Chastain and Maji Speaks and Georgia Mai, and Bobbi Raye Bennett that everyone in her orbit is protected. It's why my teachers at the academy busted my chops so much. Alphabet City was no better. Headhunters from the CIA, NSA and the FBI tapped me for organized crime back at the academy. Everyone figured I had an in or needed to be sitting somewhere pushing paper instead of doing real police work."

"Yeah, you had to get shot to prove them all wrong." Calvin rolled his eyes.

"Pretty much," Gabe said with a chuckle as he tucked the papers in a grey Shadow Bay Police Department Folder.

"How is your Moms? Figured you went to check on her at some point between last night and today," Calvin said as he scanned the murder sheets.

Gabe snagged the plastic shopping bag from his top drawer. "Calvin look alive," He cautioned before tossing the bag to him.

His gaze fell on the copy of the old photo Alana had unearthed from one of the many photo albums she kept squirreled away. The way Olivia had the picture clutched to her chest made his throat ache. The expression on her face when she woke up in his arms, the muted wretchedness filled his chest with a strange pain.

Calvin buried his nose in the bag and inhaled deeply. "Your Mom *does* like me," he beamed, before opening the bag and grabbing a cookie. He took a bite and groaned in ecstasy. "You know I'm not sharing right?

Gabe held the picture under the lamp on his desk to examine it. Olivia had her back pressed against his with her shoe untied. Calvin raised an eyebrow and Gabe handed over the photo.

"She was a tiny thing," Calvin remarked. "Strong wind could have knocked her over."

Gabe nodded and held out his hand. "She was strong though. My God she was smart, blew past everybody in high school, even me. I was too busy being the class clown."

"She looks haunted G," Calvin said as he handed the picture back.

Gabe put the picture in his breast pocket and worked at a response. "Her parents sold her for a hit of crack cocaine," he said before meeting his friend's eyes. "She had a right to be haunted, angry or bitter, but it didn't stop her. We both skipped a grade. Even then she soared past our classmates."

"Figures you wouldn't fall for an ordinary girl," Calvin teased, "No wonder you never settled down."

"How could I? Olivia was the one I was supposed to grow old with." Gabe cleared his throat and stared at the blank computer screen. "And I drove her away."

***

Gabe grabbed the receiver and made several phone calls. By the time he looked up again lunchtime had come and gone. The sizable dent in his reports kept part of his mind occupied while the other half returned to the warm cocoon of Olivia's office where the pressure of her resting against his midsection made everything right in his world.

"Taming the paper dragon, I see."

Gabe smiled as Commissioner Brown's voice and the scent of fresh tobacco steeped in cherry juice washed over him. He twisted in the chair to see the old man take up residence at a night shift detective's desk.

"Uncle Mark, what are you doing down here instead of on Mount Olympus," Gabe asked as he ran a hand over his beard.

"Rather be here any day then over there at City Hall watching the mayor and his cronies tell us how to do our jobs in Law Enforcement. I know you two are already working a case, but I need you to head out to Towson to look at a scene," Mark swiveled in the chair so that his back was to the rest of the room. He crooked a finger in Calvin's direction.

"Any particular reason why?" Gabe asked as he closed the file on his computer and snagged his coat from the back of a chair. Calvin grabbed his coat and stood.

"Yeah, Max called me personally. G, he asked for you by name," Commissioner Brown said as he tied the belt to his trench coat.

CHAPTER FOURTEEN

Cutting through the city removed fifteen minutes from their drive through rush hour traffic, but little else. By the time they reached the scene the last rays of light were painting the skyline in purples and pinks. The lookie loos behind the yellow crime scene tape jockeyed for position with their cellphones held high. From where he sat in his truck, Gabe viewed the uniforms performing crowd control around tents that glowed and eerie white from the CSI lamps.

Calvin waded through the crowd to one of the uniforms while Gabe walked the perimeter a few feet behind. A young man with a guitar looked on along with the others. Once he'd made a complete circle, he jogged over to Calvin, and went into the tent.

Again, Gabe was a few feet behind his partner taking in the colorful artwork tacked to the refrigerator and the cups and paper plates with smears of paint in the sink. He stuck his hands in his pockets as he made his way past the island.

"Calvin," he called out and at once his partner was at his side. Gabe gestured with his head as Calvin followed his line of view to the cutlery set that was missing a butcher knife.

He watched Calvin search the island and the sink before he looked up at him.

"Not in the sink. Where the kids at?" Calvin gestured to the refrigerator. "Two pictures two different names,"

"Gentlemen?" Max called softly.

Both men rotated to see Max standing in the doorway in a white Forensics suit. As they made their way over to him, one of the technicians walked up and held out two pairs of green latex gloves and some paper booties that reminded Gabe of shower caps. Gabe covered his shoes and hands before stepping onto the makeshift path of linoleum tiles that were strategically placed on the floor. Four steps and a sharp left led them to a small den where flashes from a camera illuminated the arterial blood spray on the wall.

Gabe inched over to see the body being photographed from different angles.

"G, there's blood on the ceiling," Calvin whispered.

"Cast off," Max said dismally. "The body is still fairly warm which places the time of death around two thirty maybe three this afternoon. Gentlemen, I know this man."

Gabe surveyed the room before he focused on Max. "Has the house been checked for children? There's fresh artwork on the fridge and palates in the sink."

Max gripped Gabe's arm to make him pay attention. "This was called in by the victim's wife. She took the grands for ice cream before taking them home. They had to get *her* out of here. Started having chest pains. She found him."

Gabe nodded as he scanned the area once more. "Mark said you asked for me by name."

Max nodded as he pointed to another room. Gabe stepped on a few more tiles before they made into what looked like a family room and stopped in his tracks. Calvin almost bumped into him before he stopped.

"Jesus H. Christ. Are those words?" Calvin whispered as they all looked up at the walls and the ceiling.

"The strokes are too fine to be made with a fingernail or fingers. Near as I can tell, it looks like a fountain pen," Max said studying the ceiling.

Gabe stepped on a series of tiles that led over to the wall near the fireplace. He leaned closer and started reading aloud. "The mission of this center is to…" Gabe took in a sharp breath and backed away from the wall. Calvin came over and looked for himself.

"G what's wrong?" Calvin questioned.

Before Gabe could get the words out, Max pointed to a list further up on the wall. Calvin looked back and forth between the two men. "Somebody want to clue me in?"

"It's the mission statement from my mother's center. Look, there's a list, Calvin. My mother's name is there. Who's the victim, Max?" Gabe asked as he looked around for Max.

"Eagan St. Clair. Abra St. Clair's father. Family pic confirms it." Max said pointing to a picture frame.

"Wait, how do you know? I mean how do you know Doc?" Calvin shrugged.

Gabe looked around at the walls once more, Max walked over as Gabe carefully retraced his steps across the blocks of floor covering.

"Insulin pens in the fridge with his name on the box. Gabriel, one look at this man's skin and the smell of his breath tells me he was a brittle diabetic. He would have been a candidate for transplantation, sure, but never a donor."

Calvin moved closer to the men. "So, what you saying, Doc?" Calvin looked back and forth between them.

Max was staring at Gabe. "All of the organs housed in the chest and abdomen, the central cavity organs are gone. All of them."

CHAPTER FIFTEEN

"Protective custody, G the whole nine. Mark is probably already working on it," Calvin said as they walked to the truck.

Gabe swallowed hard as he tried to get his breathing under control. He ran a hand over his mouth before he fished in his pocket for the keys. "She won't accept protective custody. You don't understand." Gabe felt one of the granola bar wrappers and his heart cramped in his chest. He sat back and willed himself to go still, then swallowed again before he stabbed the key in the ignition of his triple black pickup truck. "You don't know my mother."

"G, look around man." Calvin secured his seatbelt before he dug out his phone and thumbed his contact list into view," She don't have a choice."

Gabe leaned forward and rested his forehead against the steering wheel as he gunned the ignition. "She won't hide Calvin. You don't understand." Gabe reached for the gearshift and sat back. "My mother took two cop killer rounds to the chest. She has endured things that would have most people locked up in a psyche ward somewhere. She won't run."

***

No sooner had Gabe put the vehicle in park he was out and taking the steps by twos.

As he reached the hall leading to her office he was running. He burst in to find Alana sitting on the sofa with his Aunt Myra sitting close by trying to work some warmth into his mother's pale hands. Mark was sitting across from them.

"I'm fine Gabriel," Was all she said as she stood and went to him. She took his face in her hands. He gripped her wrists and pressed his forehead to hers. "Je vais bien… Wo hen hao…. Estoy bein… ana bikhayr."

He nodded wildly each time she spoke the same words, 'I'm fine' in French, Chinese Spanish, and Arabic before he hid his face on her shoulder. "Never should have gotten you involved. This is my fault."

"It's fine son. I'll go home with Mark and Myra." Alana gripped the back of his neck and simply stood there.

Gabe lifted his head from her shoulder and pressed his forehead to hers once more. Alana smoothed a hand over his cheek, and he kissed her palm. He pressed his trembling lips to her forehead then took a step back and looked at Mark.

"Uncle Mark…. Her mission statement was on the wall. The list of names."

"We've seen the list, Gabe. They are pillars in the community that serve on the board here," Myra said as she held out a yellow legal pad filled with the names.

Gabe stepped back far enough for his mother to smooth down his shirt. He took the legal pad from Myra and tore off the top sheet, then carefully folded the sheet of paper in fours before he tucked it into his coat.

"Uncle Mark, we both know what names on a wall could mean. Eagan St. Clair was Abra's father."

"I know son. Apparently, she was a match. The girl's mother confirmed it. The surgery was all set when she went missing. Listen we already have units dispatched to cover the others and you know we have your mother." Mark held out an arm to his wife. Myra walked over and stood by Mark with her hands clasped between her breasts.

Gabe reached for Alana, and she took his face in her hands.

She tilted her head slightly so that only he could see her eyes darken with a steely resolve. "Ve a atraparme un monstruo."

Gabe stepped away from her and walked out the door. From somewhere behind him he could hear Mark talking to Calvin. "I only speak a little Spanish and even I got that one. Go on, Calvin before he leaves you," Mark warned.

"What did she say?" Calvin asked.

"Go catch me a monster," Gabe called over his shoulder.

CHAPTER SIXTEEN

Peace was relative in the morgue. Pain and suffering were at a merciful end and to those that believed, death was a complete healing. Even if grief hovered in the corners, death continued its peculiar rhythm and rhyme that shaped silence into symphonies and loss into sound.

After her stint overseas, Olivia toyed with the idea of going into Pathology. At least there she didn't have to worry about a prognosis or diagnosing despair. But then Bimbi was there digging her head under Olivia's chin needing so much. Needing her.

Even when the doors to the elevator slid open, the afterhours front office looked like any other. Positive affirmations hung on the walls. Half deflated mylar balloons from someone's birthday party twisted lazily in the breeze consisting of recycled air from the vents near the ceiling. Olivia waited at the desk for a moment, hoping that someone was still there tapping away at a keyboard or putting their scrawl on some last-minute paperwork, but the silence seemed to grow.

Olivia made her way past the desk clutching the personal effects bag to her chest. The lack of life persisted, and it didn't matter how nicely the front office was decorated with neutrals and warm colors. The further she ventured to the back the colors seemed to fade, and a prevalence of grey became a shade darker until all that remained were the cold stainless-steel slabs lined up in two rows and a wall with small doors served as a marker for the eventual. She took in two deep breaths to acclimate herself to the subtle stench that seasoned the air.

Breathing through her mouth was never an option. She remembered one of her classmates from medical school doing just that before they were dragged from the decomposition room. "Tastes like day old raw hamburger! Smells like it too!" The girl kept shrieking as they dragged her down the hallway.

Olivia sat the clear drawstring personal effects bag aside. She ran her fingers over the name once confirming the information in black permanent marker was correct. In the morning, the large docking bay doors would swing open with a mechanical yawn. The hearse, marked with the lettering from the funeral home, would wait silently to take the departed to another set of cargo bay doors or some other place where the families could say their last goodbyes to a casket full of remains or a box of ashes.

From where she stood, Olivia could see the neatly packaged body bags and other accessories of death stacked according to purpose on shelves that reminded her of the skeletal remains of some exotic animal.

The filing cabinets beside the wall unit sat silently waiting for the next report. She noticed that the lock was sitting open, and she moved closer. Olivia ran her fingers over the tabs until she found the neatly typed lettering for Organ Procurement. A quick look in the electronic health records software gave her access to a directory she printed out and placed in a manila file in her desk. Upon even closer inspection, she found another directory listing a hard copy in the basement in the morgue.

Olivia pulled the drawer open and thumbed through the files. She pulled one of the files to the top of the drawer and walked over to one of the slabs. She ducked past the long hose with the shower head on the end and spread out the papers.

Metal on metal made a soft shriek as a door to one of the refrigerated drawers slid shut. Olivia searched the dark areas of the room as her heart thumped sickly in her chest.

" Hello?" she called.

Her voice echoed back to her. Olivia flipped a page as she ran her fingers across the names and case numbers looking for dates and times. The soft scrape of metal against metal made her stand straight up. Olivia snatched some of the pages from the prongs at the top of the folder before folding and stuffing them in her pocket.

"I was just dropping off some patient personal effects. I'll be out of your way in a second. I didn't realize anyone was down here. Dr Caldwell? Are you there?" Again, her voice echoed back only now there was breathing, shaky breathing and footsteps moving toward her. Olivia eased back into the shadows by the cabinet as the footsteps got louder. She flattened herself against the wall as she made her way back toward the front office.

By the time she reached the receptionist's desk she was in a full run back to the elevators. Olivia made it halfway down the corridor before falling to her knees. She staggered to her feet and took off around one corner and then another still looking behind her searching the dark for the rapid footsteps that echoed beneath her own.

She rounded another corner and slammed into a hard wall and an even stronger pair of arms. "No," she screamed as she slapped and kicked at the person struggling to trap her arms down by her sides. Olivia wriggled free and planted her feet on the corporate artwork and proceeded to run up the wall. She was almost up and over the man's shoulders, when he grabbed her by the waist and fell back against the far wall.

"Ollie! Ollie stop it! It's me, Gabe," he roared "You're safe, babe, I got you."

The world greyed away a little. She fell against him as he struggled to hold her up.

He grabbed her face and made her look at him. "Are you okay? Answer me, Ollie," he demanded.

Olivia snatched away and looked behind her. Gabe swept her behind him as he pulled his gun. She slid down the wall trying hard to catch her breath and stop the convulsive tremors racking her body. Gabe took a step forward and Olivia grabbed at his ankle. Her fingers scrabbled along the top of his boot as he moved forward.

"Gabe it's nothing. I just… It's nothing really."

"Stay here," he commanded, in a murderously low voice.

Gabe moved down the corridor with his gun drawn in the direction she had come from. After what felt like an eternity. He came back around the corner stuffing his gun down the back of his pants and he stooped down to her. "Are you okay? What just happened down here?"

Olivia licked her lips as she tried to catch her breath. She reached for his shoulder, and he slipped an arm around her waist and stood. He pushed her hair back from her face as he examined her.

"Olivia what happened?" he repeated.

She shook her head wildly as she tried to get the tightness in her chest and throat to subside.

Gabe caught her cheek in his hand. "Stop shaking your head at me and talk. What happened? Why are you down here by yourself?"

"Nothing. I just got spooked. I was dropping off… It was stupid. This place gives me the creeps." She tried speaking slowly but the words tumbled from her in a horrifying stream.

"Are you hurt? What did you see?" he questioned moving closer to her as his eyes swept up and down her body.

"I just thought I heard something. It was just my mind playing tricks on me. I was just being stupid," She tried to move away, and he blocked her in with his arm.

"Stop saying that." He cautioned. "Now, what did you hear?" His eyes flicked over her.

"This place is closed after hours and I was just dropping off some paperwork It was stu…,"

He tilted his head almost daring her to say the word again. Olivia licked her lips as she drew in a cleansing breath filled with him. When she opened her eyes, he was still staring intently at her waiting for an explanation.

After another eternity, he blinked and drew her to his chest while tucking her head under his chin. "One of the residents or your nurses could have taken care of this errand."

"We were backed up and I've been down here before," she squeaked, hating that she sounded so small and scared.

He pulled her back from his chest. "Not at night, I gather. Not alone like this," Gabe wasn't asking so much as he was telling her and all she could do was shake her head as the fear that choked out all reason gave way to embarrassment.

Olivia tried to turn, but the way he was holding her left little room for her to do anything but face him. She craned her head in the direction of the elevator. He pressed his forehead against the side of her head and took in a breath then sighed, bathing her in concern.

She tried not to notice the way his chest was pinning her to the wall. His heart thumped against her breasts as if in communication with her heart rapping against her ribcage. He took in another breath practically willing her breath to match his.

"Come on," He mumbled as he grabbed her lab coat sleeve and pulled her to his side. He put a possessive arm around her as he walked, half carried her to the elevator.

Olivia cringed at the soft ding as the elevator arrived on the floor where her office was. She was walking, but his stride was urging her to move faster until they reached her door. She pushed her way inside. From the reflection in the window, she could see him close the door and put his back against it. His gaze still raked over her features as the muscle in his jaw clenched and unclenched. For an insane moment Olivia was sure he intended to stay there all night assessing her, stripping her of all pretense or modesty. But then his gaze drifted to something distant, and his countenance changed. He thumbed the lock then moved past her to flop down on her sofa.

"Gabe?" Olivia moved closer.

He flinched at the sound of his name then reached for her arm and pulled her down in front of him so that she was sitting on the coffee table.

"Haven't seen an evasive move like running up a wall since we were kids. Are you sure you're, ok? Are you hurt?" He asked fixing the lapel on her lab coat before he checked her hands.

"I'm fine really. Gabe what is it? What's wrong?" Olivia hooked her fingers under his chin and made him look at her.

The second he did, she dropped her hand. The concern she saw there evaporated as his gaze grew hard. "My mother is in protective custody because of the case I'm working on."

Olivia moved to put her hand on his shoulder, and he shot a look at her that made her lower it.

"I dragged her into this and now…. There's been another murder. Family member of the girl I brought in here."

Olivia sat back on the table and watched as he tried to concentrate on her hand by lacing his fingers through hers.

"There was blood on the walls and names. My mother's name and others," he said quietly.

She could feel her spine stiffen as he spoke. What little resolve he had was fading fast and his anger hardening his features was maturing into something darker, more frightening than rage. "Gabe maybe I—"

He took in a breath that shook as he sandwiched her hand between both of his. "Got called to another murder. If I didn't know any better, I'd swear I was looking at you. Even my partner pointed it out. Another name from the list and her mission statement from her center on another wall. More blood all over the place. I get here, and nobody knew where you were. Thought I'd lost you."

Olivia leaned forward, and Gabe breathed her in and brushed his lips over her forehead. "I'm home Gabe, right here with you. You won't lose me, I promise."

"I lost you before," He mumbled.

Olivia snatched away as he reached for her. She easily ducked out of his grasp and stood.

"Olivia, I'm sorry I didn't mean— Can't imagine what kind of man you think I am." Gabe stood and headed for the door. "It was a mistake to come here. I'm sorry for what I said."

"A good one," she called after him.

Gabe put his hand on the doorknob. "What?"

Olivia came to him. "You just asked me what kind of man I thought you were, and I said a good one."

"You don't know that." Gabe snatched the door open. "How do you know? That could have been me down in the basement."

"Perhaps you're right because the person I knew never ran from a fight he started." Olivia raked a hand through her hair as she nodded.

Gabe thumped his head on the doorframe. "Didn't come here to fight, Ollie."

Olivia walked over and put her hand between his forehead and the surface of the door stopping him. "Why did you come here, then?" Olivia pulled him from the doorway and put her back against the surface closing it, "Why?"

"I don't know. Just forget it. I was wrong and I'm sorry. Just forget I said anything." Gabe reached for the doorknob and Olivia blocked his hand with her body. He reached for the door again and she covered the doorknob with her hand. "Ollie, please just—"

Olivia took his face in her hands and gave him a shake. "The person I knew never lied or blew me off either."

Gabe brushed her hands from his face and reached for the doorknob and paused. "Didn't know where else to go." He ran a hand over his head and looked away.

"So, what am I? Something to do, or keep you from wallowing in self-pity, what?" She said taunting him.

"Look, I said I was sorry." He snatched the door open.

"So am I, never thought of myself as damaged goods or second choice," She spat. "Whole town thought so, but not you." She laughed bitterly. "Or so I thought."

Gabe closed the door and took a step toward her. "You were my *only* choice. Then and now. I needed my friend." He bit down on a curse and looked up at the ceiling "I needed you."

Olivia leaned on the back of one the chairs stationed in front of her desk. "I'm right here Gabe. Standing right in front of you. I can't give you back those years Gabe." She shrugged and showed him her hands. "I can't. Don't know that I would *even* if I could. All I have is now. If that's not good enough for you then maybe you should leave." Olivia pushed at his midsection and tried to move past him.

Gabe planted his feet as he gripped her wrists lightly in his hands.

"Ollie wait. Please. I'm sorry." The hurt and longing lay naked in his eyes. Gabe leaned against the door with his hands stuffed in his pockets. "Kept thinking if I could just get someplace quiet. No that's not true, "he admitted "I thought if I could just get to you. I'd have proof that the world wasn't crashing down around me." He stuffed his hands in his pockets and hunched his shoulders.

Olivia tugged one of his hands from a pocket and pulled him to the sofa. He flopped down and she cleared a space on the coffee table and sat in front of him.

"The one thing my father made me promise to do was shield my mother from the darkness they spent years fighting. Never asked me to finish school or go to college or anything else. I had *one* job Olivia. Just one." He bit down on a curse and looked away.

"Shh don't," Olivia whispered as she kissed the space below his left eye.

Gabe moaned as he slipped his hand behind her neck and pulled her closer. His lips trembled against her cheek. A thunderous knock at her door made them both jump. Olivia pivoted to see Christine's figure through the frosted glass trying the doorknob before swiping her keycard and barging in. Olivia rose from the table. She could feel Gabe assuming his full height behind her.

"I'm sorry to interrupt. We got multiple gunshot wounds coming in and they need you to scrub in," Christine blurted out before stepping back through the door.

Christine's gaze drifted to Gabe. Whatever the look was on his face made her retreat a step or two pulling the door part of the way closed. "I'm really sorry Olivia, but we need your help out here." Christine shot her a pleading look before she closed the door.

Gabe smoothed her hair down and planted a kiss on the back of her head. "Go on. It's fine."

She turned as he gave her a smile that broke her heart. "They need you," he said shakily. He gestured with his head. "Go on Babe.,"

Olivia wrapped her arms around his neck. He crushed her to his chest so hard she took in a sharp breath. For all the strength she knew resided in him and the sheer wall of muscle that made him a fortress around her, Gabe was clinging to her, trying to draw what sustenance he could from her.

She took his face in her hands and she pressed her lips to his eye lids making him close his eyes before she kissed him on the mouth. She dragged her open mouth across his cheek and over to his ear. "You need me, Gabe," She whispered.

Gabe breathed her in as he smiled against her neck. "Never stopped, Ollie. Now go do what you need to," He whispered as he mouthed the words into her skin before kissing her shoulder and releasing her.

She pulled away as he smoothed her hair back over her shoulder. "Stay here Gabe. In the meantime, take a look at this." She dug in her pocket and pulled out the papers. "This was another reason I was downstairs. I don't know if any of this helps but I'll come back. There's more in my top desk drawer. Maybe that will help too. I was going to call and meet you somewhere to talk about it." Olivia leaned up and kissed him on the corner of the mouth and rushed out the door.

CHAPTER SEVENTEEN

"What the hell happened to her?" Gabe snapped, as the blood stain on Olivia's pale green scrub top spread.

Purplish red bruises continued to form on her upper arm. Gabe sank to the edge of the table in front of her. Olivia blinked owlishly at him sending tears spilling over her cheeks. She reached for him. "Are you all right, Gabe?" Olivia asked cupping his cheek in her hand. "I'm sorry I left you."

Gabe looked over his shoulder at Christine. "Somebody better start talking. She didn't leave me like this."

Christine's face contorted in agony as tears leaked from her eyes. She raked at the wetness on her cheeks and struggled to regain her composure. "Shooting. Some kids were beefing. One kid was DOA. Somebody saw her working on the shooter. We lost that kid too. When she came out to deliver the news all hell broke loose. Took four security guards to pry some guy off her."

Gabe reached over and grabbed a wad of Kleenex and dabbed at her nose. Olivia blinked again sending more tears cascading down her cheeks. "Sorry I left you, Gabe."

He moved from the edge of the table onto the sofa next to her then coaxed her into his arms. Olivia pressed her face into the side of his neck and went still. Gabe looked at Christine biting on her lips trying not to cry. "This happen a lot?" he inquired accusingly before lifting Olivia onto his lap.

"Healthcare professionals get hurt and cursed out more often than people realize. Sometimes we get spat on…,"

"That's not what I meant Christine," He warned. "You know it's not."

"Her first day here we were chased up the hallway by an irate father. His child fell off the moped they were riding. No helmet. He felt like Olivia didn't try hard enough to save his child. She nearly broke her arm getting me out of harm's way. Its why we keep her separate from the families and out of the ER as much as possible. Tonight, we had no choice. We followed every precaution," Christine offered as she wrung her hands.

"Then why is she the only one bleeding?" he snapped cradling Olivia's head to his chest.

Christine looked up at the ceiling and threw her hands up. "Happened so fast. He came out of nowhere, cornered her and slammed her against the wall. I couldn't get to her."

Another nurse and a doctor rushed in with Tommy bringing up the rear. Gabe took one look at the young man trailing behind the others. "No. Not him. You can get anyone else in here to look at her. Anyone but him."

"Detective this is Dr. Rina Oberon. Can she have a look at her?" Christine asked reaching for the doctor walking in.

The tall brunette moved past Christine and the nurse and reached for Olivia. "Her only thought was getting back here to you. Now, I know you want to help Detective, but we need to assess her condition," Dr. Oberon said as she settled down on the sofa near Olivia.

"Please G. Let her help," Christine pleaded.

Gabe shot another pointed look at all of them before he arranged her on the sofa.

"Anyone but him," Gabe said repeated swallowing at the rage burning the back of his throat.

Everyone glanced at Tommy standing near the door. Christine and Dr. Oberon ducked under Gabe's arm and started checking Olivia over. Gabe stood near the sofa with his arms folded across his chest as they checked her vitals and cleaned her face and hands. Christine held a white blanket out to Gabe, he snatched it and wrapped it around Olivia's shoulders.

When the doctor started cleaning up the first aid supplies, Gabe came back over to the sofa and sat down.

"How bad is she?" Gabe slipped his arm under Olivia's legs and swept her up against his chest and stood.

"With a mild concussion, and a possible sprain to her arm, she's probably better off here under observation, Detective," Dr Oberon said quietly.

"She's in shock," Christine offered before fixing the blanket around Olivia's shoulder. "We can rehydrate her and make her comfortable."

Gabe took a step toward Olivia's desk. "Besides the IV is there anything you're doing here that I can't do at home?"

Christine moved forward reaching for Olivia, "Wait what are you talking about? You can't just take her. No. Do something Evans!"

The security guard coughed in his fist then took a step forward.

Gabe backed away. "Evans. Not a good idea," he warned.

"You don't even know where she lives, G," Christine muttered.

"Well, she's not exactly safe, here is she?" Gabe said his tongue heavy with sarcasm. "I'll take her to another hospital before I leave her here with any of you."

In all honesty, he hadn't thought any further than getting her away from them to some place quiet. That way, he could assess for himself whether Olivia was okay or not. He took a step toward the door and Christine, blocked his way.

"Detective Garrett—G, Olivia wouldn't want to be carried around like some doll."

Olivia wasn't moving. He looked down into her face. The color was draining from her skin the longer he stood there. Gabe cradled her head to his neck and moved once more for the door. Christine looked at the others and blocked his path again.

"Like you said I'm a detective. It's not that difficult to find out where Olivia lives. You work the 11th precinct, right Evans, right? Southside?"

The security officer blanched then nodded as he bowed his head.

"Be useful Evans. Bring her briefcase and her handbag to my truck," Gabe spat.

He watched as Christine's face fell. Gabe hoisted Olivia higher against his chest. The woman in front of him looked like hell. Each time he moved, Christine moved and reached for Olivia. Gabe pulled her out of reach.

"I have no intentions of dropping her if that's what you're thinking. I mean where was all this concern when she was down in the ER?"

"She's not a doll and you have no right to take her out of here!" Christine shouted.

In the years since he'd joined the force, Gabe had seen his fair share of workplace violence. As a Homicide detective, he worked several cases where the victims only crime was clocking in.

Gabe looked down at Olivia sleeping against him as the overwhelming urge to push Christine out of the way made his gut burn. He looked around at the group. None of them were looking at Gabe. Their eyes were glued to Olivia. Even Tommy who spent most of the time just outside the door ventured closer. Gabe looked down into Olivia's silent, pain stamped face. He pressed his lips to her forehead and sighed. "Fine. Take me there."

Christine shot a look at the others as if to confer silently with them.

"Christine, you're her friend, right?" Gabe questioned as he clutched Olivia closer.

"Yeah. I'm her friend," Christine looked up at him and nodded.

"And I'm her *family*. I've known her, loved her longer than any of you. Help me take care of her. Help me get her home." He started for the door and Dr. Oberon stopped him.

"She needs a sling or something," she said as she tentatively reached for the blanket.

Gabe blocked the woman's hand and drew Olivia closer. "I'll make her one," Gabe said brushing his lips across her forehead. "Evans, clear a path."

CHAPTER EIGHTEEN

It was obvious the women had a relationship, but how deeply hadn't occurred to Gabe until he caught a glimpse of Christine rocking Olivia and praying over her in the rearview mirror. Once he carried her into the bedroom and put Olivia on the bed. Christine ushered him out of the bedroom.

"I can take it from here," She insisted, before closing the door in his face.

Gabe walked out toward the living room taking in Olivia's place as he went. Everything about her condo was warm and welcoming. Even the chairs in her living room looked like arms reaching, welcoming the weary traveler.

Gabe tapped the dimmer switch on the wall in her living room and a gallery accent wall appeared out of the darkness. Each panoramic frame held pictures that featured Olivia in various countries working with patients. Some pictures were taken in hospitals while others were filmed in the bush near army green tents with red crosses emblazoned on the sides. He was so lost in the photos that he barely heard the floor creak. Christine stepped up to look at some of the pictures.

"I see the toll her job takes on her day in and day out. Her work overseas took even more. There was joy there. You can see that on the walls, but I think something bad happened over there too." Christine pointed to a picture of the woman Gabe encountered with the purple hair, "Tiana the scrub nurse on days was with Olivia and even she won't talk about it. Most of the surgical team we have is because of Olivia. They followed her here. Dr. Prescott too. Not that he'd ever admit it."

Gabe glanced in her direction. "Wait. Did you say Prescott? As in Shawn Prescott?"

"Yeah, you know him?" she asked.

"Too well. He's my cousin," Gabe said biting down on a curse as his blood began to boil. He scanned the photos for his cousin and folded his arms. "He's not in any of these. You sure he was there?" he asked trying to keep a civil tone.

"Tiana said so. He worked at the hospital on and off for a long time before Olivia came on board I remember because the military kept coming to visit her," she said folding her arms as she pointed at the pictures with her head.

"Whatever happened must have been really bad even the hospital president Richard Beacham is weird about her. He was with her the longest I think," Christine said before looking to him "Olivia would have been pissed if I didn't tell her about the shootings. She was On Call."

"All the more reason to have her away from that place tonight," he said scanning the photos of smiling children and adults. "Let somebody else be on call for a while."

Christine nodded as she walked over to her coat and tote bag. Gabe leaned on the door as she moved into the hallway. "Let me just say this. You just came back in her life, but she's my best friend. You be careful with her. I know I fucked up. You can't."

Gabe leaned his head on the door and smiled at the woman. Christine was shorter than him by an inch or two.

She tapped him on the chest with her finger. "You can't," she repeated.

She moved to turn away then thought better of it and looked at him.

"If it makes you feel any better the police have the man in custody G."

"It doesn't. I should have been there," he said glancing back at the photos, "You headed back to the hospital?" He asked leaning on the door.

"Have to finish the shift, but I'll be back at 9am." She bit down on her bottom lip. "We would have kept watch over her tonight. We're her family too."

"Thanks for getting us here," Gabe said as he closed the door and pressed his head forehead against the surface.

His cousin? She stayed away all those years, but his cousin never so much as said a word. Never told anyone anything about having found her or even being in contact with her. He thumped his head on the surface of the door.

"Gabe? Are you okay?" Olivia leaned against the wall leading to her den. She was dressed in a grey tank and a matching pair of pajama bottoms and white socks. Her hair was in a braid that hung over her left shoulder.

"Ollie what are you doing out of bed?" as he twisted the knob for the deadbolt and came to her.

Olivia took a step forward and her feet tangled together. Gabe easily caught her and carried her back to her room. As he moved to lower her to the bed, she gripped his shoulder and he sat down. He looked down into her face as she settled into the crook of his arm. Tears leaked from her eyes as she struggled to stay awake.

"Never should have left you," she whispered, "We were dying. Someone had to leave."

"Shh Ollie don't. You had patients. I understood," he said.

Olivia shook her head softly. "Got lost Gabe. So lost," she said with a watery sigh.

"Should have come after you a long time ago Babe. I'm the one that's sorry," he said as he steeled himself against the shudders that racked her body as she lapsed in and out of consciousness.

***

Gabe was in a light doze when his phone buzzed in his pocket. He ignored it as she snuggled deeper into his embrace. Again, his phone started buzzing. He finally reached between them and dug his phone out of the front pocket of his jeans.

"Speak."

Calvin's voice flooded his ear.

"You gotta come downtown G. Labs are back from the blood on the walls. Handwriting analysis too, G you need to know something."

"Tell me when I see you." Gabe thumbed the disconnect button and looked down at the way he was holding her.

Olivia was on her stomach against his chest and her hips were wedged tightly between his thighs. He took in the way one of his hands was resting against the bare skin at the small of her back. He smoothed a hand over her bare skin relishing the feel of her. Then his fingers found the first, then a second and third thickened raised area. Gabe pulled up her shirt long enough to see one of his fingertips fit into the small sunken circular scar.

He smoothed down her shirt and wrapped his arms around her as he stared at the ceiling. "Jesus, you got shot," he whispered.

CHAPTER NINETEEN

Gabe took the last steps to his department by twos. The minute he reached the top the usual conversation stopped as all eyes fell to Gabe. Calvin stood up from his desk and came over to him. He gripped Gabe's arm and started for one of the interrogation rooms. Once inside Calvin leaned against the door and looked at him.

"Where were you?" Calvin asked

"At the hospital. You said the labs came back."

Calvin started pacing the room. "I had them run it three times and the results were the same. The signatures were the same and I made them go back and check that because it didn't make sense."

Gabe stepped into his friend's path.   "And right now, you're making even less sense Calvin. What did they find?"

"The blood on the walls, the words— on one scene the blood was a match to your Mom man."

Gabe took a step back momentarily rebuffed. "No that's impossible. Check it again."

"I just told you I did all of that." Calvin grabbed his arm. "Even the handwriting results were checked. Same result. Now I can argue that someone might have used an electronic signature pad. Maybe they swiped a carbon from her checkbook at the center. Forging someone's signature is easier than you think. She had an iron clad alibi for Abra and her father, but the fact remains."

Gabe stepped back even further from him, "What facts remain? She didn't do this Calvin. What motive would she have? She's not a doctor. She wouldn't know how to even begin an organ extraction."

"I've seen your mother's library G, but true that. She has no motive so far as we can tell. Your uncle Mark confirms that she never left his sight, and his wife will attest to that, but…"

"But what Calvin? Finish it."

"The there was another blood type found at another scene. Had them run that again too. It was Dr. Calderone's."

"Impossible. I was with her all night. She was bleeding yeah, but not enough to paint the damn walls." Gabe put his head down as he struggled to remain calm. "Somebody assaulted Olivia at the hospital last night," he said as Calvin gave him a side eye. "It wasn't like that. She was pretty banged up, but I got her home and stayed with her. Her friend is with her now. Saw her arriving as I was leaving."

"You said you needed a break. An hour sure, but we had work to do, G," Calvin said.

"I know Calvin. Went over there to—Ollie had a bloody nose and some bruises. Maybe a sprained shoulder. Happened not long after she gave me this," Gabe said as he reached in his coat and grabbed the paperwork and tossed them on the table in front of Calvin.

"What's this?" Calvin asked, spreading the papers out on the table.

"Organ Procurement keeps a list of donors and recipients living or otherwise. There's also a list of who performed the procedures dates and times. Robert Beacham is a cardio thoracic surgeon. He did organ transplants. Same guy now runs Shadow Bay Hospital. But take a look at the names, Calvin. They match at least half of the list we saw on the walls at the crime scenes."

Calvin spread the papers out and compared the names to the photographs.

"Your Mom's name isn't on any of these lists. Neither is Olivia."

"My mother is not a donor, or a recipient and she damned sure wasn't scrubbing in to perform a procedure no matter how extensive her library is," Gabe snapped.

"Olivia know any of these people?" Calvin asked as he lined the documents up next to the photos.

"Most of them. We both worked at my mom's center over the summer growing up. Mom never mentioned Beacham,"

Calvin continued to scan the paperwork with a frown. "You sure your head is clear for this one?"

Gabe came away from the wall. "What are you insinuating Calvin?"

"We have bodies dropping like flies and you go on a date?" Calvin interrogated rising to his full height.

"Excuse me Detective," Gabe said taking a step closer. "Who do you think you're talking to? I don't have to justify myself to you or anyone else in this place."

Calvin chuckled bitterly. "That's rich, you're pulling rank. I'm not one of those detectives out there that idolize your crazy ass. This is basic stuff. Everyone is a suspect until they're not. Suspects inject themselves into investigations all the time, man."

Gabe had seen his fair share of overly helpful people trying to steer a case throughout his career. Shock couldn't be faked. Olivia's injuries couldn't be faked. She had the same look he'd seen in domestic violence cases where the women detached from reality or fixated on the smallest detail to keep them sane.

Gabe stepped back momentarily rebuffed squared his shoulders. "Ollie got shot Calvin. She has scars on her back and——" Gabe ran a shaky hand over his beard. "You don't know them. Mom or Olivia. You don't." Gabe warned as Mark lead Alana and Myra through the room back to his office. He snatched the door open and followed. "Mark you gotta know this is a set up."

Mark showed Myra and Alana to the chairs in front of his desk. "Do I strike you as the least bit stupid G? Of course, it's a set up."

Gabe walked up and stood behind Alana's chair. "Then why'd you bring her in for questioning? Mom didn't do this. You know she didn't,"

Alana twisted in the chair and grabbed Gabe's arm. "I volunteered Gabe and fix your tone. Mark is not the enemy, and neither am I."

Gabe bit down on a curse then looked up at Mark. "Sorry Uncle Mark."

"She wouldn't allow me to take her statement at home. She needed to go on record. She had to see the murder boards, G," Mark said as Myra grabbed his hand.

CHAPTER TWENTY

From the moment she stepped into the squad room the usual hum of activity fell away and a gaping growing silence filled the air. Alana moved with the grace of a dancer as she navigated through the desks to the crazy quilt of murder adorning the white boards.

Gabe stood back with his arms folded as she took in the carnage that towered above her. Myra pushed past Mark and sidestepped through the row of desks. "Alana is my best friend and if she can endure it so can I." Mark tried to put an arm around his wife, and she shrugged him off.

Alana weakly waved her hand over her head and behind her and shook her head. Myra stopped, and Mark drew her back into his arms.

"It's not a greeting." Alana's voice was quiet and steady. She moved closer to the photo with the bold black letters. Her fingers trembled slightly as she traced the letters in the air above the photograph. "It's not… Good Night, Doctor. It's a name. Needle men or Night Doctors are responsible for some of the biggest medical breakthroughs and atrocities in the world. We had some on the strip. They worked off the books cleaning stab wounds or bullet wounds. Some even altered crime scenes."

Alana focused to another grisly photo on the wall and stuck her hands in the pockets of her grey dress slacks. "During the Season of Sacrifice, Cabalists believe that from March nineteenth through May first, the world should be bathed in the blood of innocents to ensure a fruitful harvest. Night doctors didn't hold such lofty ideals their season of the blood was around the clock, and we were the crop."

Gabe walked over and looked at the pictures on the white board. Alana faced him.

"The faces always changed. Men. Women. These people stuck the Hippocratic Oath in their back pocket. There was always a harvest. 'The harvest is white.' I remember now. It's what you said if you were willing to sell your blood or organs. The shadow lilies knew the code."

Gabe looked briefly over his shoulder at Mark and Myra. His uncle pressed his face to the back of her head as tears leaked like blood from his aunt's eyes.

"The poor, the homeless... people no one would miss. Throwaways like me, Valerie Phaedra, Maji, Georgia, Regulus, Raye and yeah even Toby." Alana folded her hands behind her back in a pose of tranquility.

"Mom, you don't have to do this," Gabe said as he reached for her.

She shrank back from him. "The Pimps or the Dealers would summon them, and they'd do the work. Some sold dreams. Others only nightmares. All of them collected money or body parts and whatever else could be salvaged and sold to anyone with a large wallet and no questions," she said running a shaky hand over her mouth. "We were nothing more than blood cattle sold for parts."

Gabe took a step forward reaching for her and Alana put up her hands as if to ward off a blow. He stepped back and showed her his hands. She was there, right there in front of him and yet, he could see her stumbling over the jagged stones of memory reopening wounds that festered and wept as she spoke. If there was a healing at one point, speaking the words, cut through the scars that led her to the back roads.

"There was one... No, two that came to the strip one season. One had a fondness for boys. The other...'The younger the girl the sweeter the pearl.' He said that a lot. He was the one with the spray on tan and capped teeth. He couldn't be so bothered with paying for his pleasures unless he could collect in other ways first."

"Collect? What… organs? Mom was he harvesting organs?" Gabe asked as his stomach cramped.

Alana ran a shaky hand over her mouth as she stepped back and bumped the whiteboard. One of the pictures floated to the ground and she winced. "Everything we had was for sale, even our screams."

"Mom…. Did they hurt you?" Gabe asked dreading the way the words felt in his mouth.

She was back there in that place that only his father knew about. That place where the walls grew thin. The howling place that threatened to pull her beneath the surface. Only once had he seen her like that huddled in his father's arms sitting on the floor in the middle of their kitchen rocking her back and forth.

"Mom… did they hurt you," He repeated, already knowing the answer.

Alana stooped down to get the picture. "They hurt all of us. Toby only hung around them for the money. By the end, I think he knew what they really were and just wanted out. He didn't show at the extraction point. Neither did the ones he hung with," she said before pinning the phot back into place with a bubble Shadow Bay PD blue bubble magnet.

"Alana…," Mark came up to stand beside Gabe.

"Made September take me to them…. Wasn't even a lot of money maybe a couple grand stuck to the floor and three bodies. All of their organs were gone…even their eyes," Alana sighed and reached around for a chair.

Calvin jumped up and pushed his chair behind Alana's legs and she flopped down. She patted his hand before she looked around at the desk. "You have to stop by the house more often, Calvin," She pinched the seal closed on the plastic bag that held the last peanut butter cookie. "You're running low. I'll be sure to make some more."

Gabe kneeled beside her, and Calvin walked over to the boards. Alana placed a hand on Gabe's shoulder. "You're not sleeping Gabe." She ran a thumb under his eye. She patted the side of his face, and he kissed her hand.

"Mom, I'm sorry. I had no right to drag you into this."

Alana slid her thumb over his lips to silence him. "I don't know why my name is on the wall or why Olivia's blood is all over the place. You saw my arms Gabriel. I haven't had bloodwork done in months. In any case I didn't write my name anywhere. Maybe one of them is still alive. Maybe both. I heard they traveled overseas sometimes. I saw a few of them in the brothels. Word has it that sometimes men like them would glean from some of the villages. I don't know maybe one of them remembers me or thinks I know something."

Mark came over and pulled up a chair and sat next to her. "All the more reason to keep you in protective custody. We're going to get this on paper and get you home. "

CHAPTER TWENTY-ONE

"Time of Death," Olivia said softly.

The nurses and surgical tech began to clean the teenage boy's body and prepare him for the morgue. Tiana stripped out of her gloves and went to Olivia.

"There was nothing you could do. He was already halfway there when he arrived," she said unlacing the ties on Olivia's blue surgical gown.

"Doesn't matter. He's fourteen Tiana. He should be home playing video games not some gang banger," Olivia said as she ripped the stained gloves from her hands and threw them in the biohazard bin near the door.

Tiana worked the gown off of one arm and was about to pull the other sleeve down when the double doors swung open. Shawn and his team breezed in

"Okay people let's move like we have a purpose," Dr. Shawn Prescott said as his team fanned out around the room. Olivia's team glanced in her direction, and he looked around.

"Am I missing something here? You just called Time, right? The mother gave consent. Neely show her the papers," He commanded. The young red-haired nurse walked over and held out the paperwork.

"Has she been told that her son died?" Olivia asked taking the paperwork. Without reading it she handed it over her shoulder to one of the Surgical Techs standing close by.

Shawn chuckled as one of his nurses held open a blue surgical glove. He shoved his hand in and flexed his fingers. "That's where you come in Doc C. You get to deal with the screaming and crying. I'm here to save another life if I can," he said before looking over at Olivia's team still standing around the patient. "We're on a time crunch Ollie."

Olivia took a step forward. "Don't ever call me that," She warned as her people closed rank around the boy's body. Olivia gestured with her head and her people stepped aside.

"Whatever Dr. Calderone." He snapped. Shawn glared at his staff still congregating in one small area near the double doors to the operating theater. "Well? What are you standing around for? We have work to do. Gates get the coolers ready," he said before turning to the patient.

***

Olivia was tugging a fresh scrub top over her head when she heard the door to the locker room open. On a good day, Shawn's aftershave hung in the air burning the eyes and the nose of the unsuspecting. Being forced to sit through the remedial trainings on minimal body scents in a hospital environment, Shawn still reeked of a mixture of patchouli and day-old sweat.

She walked over to the full-length mirror to fix her hair and he leaned in the doorway and studied her with his muddy brown eyes.

"General Roth said you were more dead than alive when I found you. He spent hours digging shrapnel out of that beautiful body of yours." His gaze crawled over her as he folded his arms, "He wouldn't let me anywhere near you to help. Even afterward his nurses wouldn't let me anywhere near you."

Olivia faced him. Shawn's gaze drifted slowly up her body and paused between her midsection and her face. He ran a pasty tongue over his lips and continued his once over.

"I have a family to inform. If you will excuse me," she said heading for the door.

Shawn stuck out his hand to block her. "The organs are on their way in case you were wondering. Kid in Delaware has a new lease on life because of me." He towered over her by a good two feet. Stale sweat rings peeked at her from under his lab coat.

"You're standing in my way Shawn," She warned as she took in a breath and instantly regretted it. "Last time you tried that. I nearly broke your nose. Maybe this time I'll get lucky."

He blinked rapidly and dropped his arm. "Why is this so hard? We were friends once," he said slipping a stray lock of her hair behind her ear. Olivia batted his hand away.

"Gabe was my friend. You were a confused little boy that couldn't keep his hands to himself, until I made you," Olivia said giving herself enough space to deliver a roundhouse kick to punctuate her request to leave.

"Gabe was no different than me," Shaw spat.

"Gabe and I were the same age. You were twelve. Gabe and I were going to get married after high school," Olivia said planting her feet. Even if it meant she was on suspension for a week or three, seeing him crumpled on the floor would be money well spent.

Shawn inhaled deeply and leaned in once more "Well my golden child cousin wasn't your first. I was. Remember that."

Olivia looked down the hall and smiled. "Don't flatter yourself. That horror belonged to the crackhead my parents sold me to." Olivia shoved him out of the way and started down the hall. "You were nothing more than a preemie that left a stain on the front of your pants."

His labored breathing as he jogged to catch up to her made her stop and turn on him. Shawn stumbled to a stop.

"Your services are no longer needed here, doctor." Olivia stepped closer. "You can go back to the muddy hole you crawled from."

His smile faded as he studied her. "Something ought to be done with that mouth of yours." He reached for her then stopped. "Be a shame if someone closed it permanently.

"Somebody already tried. Remember?" She quipped.

Shawn's smile faded as he gazed up the hallway.

"Have you been watching the news? The Harbor Master in Jinja Bay managed to lose an entire ship. How is that even possible? Imagine the paper trail and the money lost. No one has seen or heard from him or his family since."

"Perhaps he's on holiday" Olivia said inhaling slowly while praying that her voice sounded normal. "His job allows that from time to time."

"Millions of dollars' worth of cargo just gone. I'm sure they'd do just about anything to get it back. Anything." He fixed her stethoscope and traced her collarbone with his thumb.

Olivia smiled and stepped closer. "Children shouldn't play with scary people like them. Sometimes they let you live." She took another step and Shawn backed up.

"You the doctor that was taking care of my boy?" A female voice said accusingly behind her.

Olivia watched as a short dark-skinned woman with tears leaking from her eyes approached them. Tears creased her cheeks as she clutched a football with streaks of blood on the seams to her chest.

"They said you left my son to take care of that boy that shot my Joshua. Is that true?" she asked her voice breaking. The man standing beside her towered over both women. Olivia caught a glimpse of Christine running up the hallway with the security guard.

"I am sorry about your loss. Here's let's go sit down so we can talk."

"It's her. She did it. She let our boy die." She said as her face dissolved into a mask of rage. She closed the space between them. "I remember you from the village. We paid good money for the merchandise. Where is it?" Olivia glanced over her shoulder as Shawn retreated to the locker room. And then Olivia wasn't on her feet anymore. Male fingers bit into the soft flesh between her elbow and her shoulder as her head made contact with the wall.

"Where is the shipment?" a male voice snarled as he slammed her into the wall again and again.

The scream froze in her throat as Olivia bolted upright in the bed. Sunlight bathed her bedroom in soft yellows as the fragrance of fresh coffee and bacon filled the air. Olivia frowned as the events of the night before settled over her. She didn't recognize the man's voice. English wasn't his first language. She rolled onto her stomach and reached for her landline telephone and pressed the number nine.

Olivia moved to sit up and pain shot through her arm making her yelp. She waited for the world to settle again when a fresh bolt of pain settled behind her left eye.

Great, busted arm and a migraine to sweeten the deal.

"Olivia, are you ok?" Christine yelled rushing into the room.

Christine dried her hands on the dishtowel and came over to the bed. She eased an arm under Olivia's shoulders to help her sit up.

"Last thing I remember was being at the hospital." Olivia looked down to see a sling draped over her shoulder. She fingered the pink floral print that matched the duvet in her water closet. She moved to drag her hand through her hair. Her fingers grazed the lump on the side of her head stoking the already growing migraine like a fire. A fresh bolt of pain shot up her arm making Olivia double over.

"What are you talking about?" Olivia pushed herself into a seated position.

"Some lady and her husband were lingering in the lobby after they found out their son died. She must have seen you when she came out of the bathroom. You got hurt in the ER. We brought you back to your office and your friend went ballistic. He wasn't satisfied until he got you out of there. Looked like he planned to walk over us to make it happen," Christine said as she untangled some of Olivia's hair from the sling.

"He was already upset when I left him. Is he here?" Olivia asked as she eased herself to the edge of the bed and reached for the Tylenol on the nightstand.

"G 'voluntold' me to bring him here. When I got here this morning, he was leaving," Christine said as she came over and shook the pills into her palm and handed her the glass of water perched on the nightstand.

"Did he say where he was going?" She asked before taking the pills and chasing it with a sip of water.

Christine grabbed the icepack, ruptured the cooling agent, and shook the bag. "No, but he looked pissed, though. We probably should get you in for an x-ray. The way you're tossing that pain medicine back, you probably need to have your head examined too." Christine smoothed a hand over her back and Olivia smiled.

"Definitely need my head examined for a lot of things," Olivia said trying on a smile.

Christine's chin began to quiver as she flopped down beside her. "Olivia I am so sorry. Everything happened so fast. Did you know that guy?" She asked. "He looked like he said something to you."

"Never seen him before in my life," Olivia said peeking inside the sling at the ring of bruises on her arm.

Where is the shipment?

Olivia shuddered and glanced at Christine.

"Tiana looked like she wanted to punch me in the face when she found out. She called like four times this morning. Every time I answered, she hung up."

Olivia tried to push the thoughts of her friend with the purple hair out of her mind. The last time Tiana got off on a tangent, the four-foot nine woman flipped over a gurney and threw a table filled with surgical equipment across the room.

"I'll call her. And smooth things over," Olivia said grabbing Christine's hand. "You are not responsible for any of this you hear me?" She hooked a finger under Christine's chin.

Christine nodded wildly as she buried her face in Olivia's shoulder. "I understood why G was mad. We've been so careful with you since your first day here. I took my eyes off you for a second." She sat up as more tears spilled down her cheeks. "You looked like a rag doll dangling from that guy's fist. Just kept slamming you against the wall and whispering in your ear. I don't even think he cared that his son was dead. Not even sure if it was his kid. Some other people came in asking about the same boy."

Olivia squeezed Christine's hand. "Of course, it was about his son. Grief makes some people angry. I mean what else could it be?" she gazed out her bedroom window that looked out on the Inner Harbor.

The sun shined brightly with rumors of a false spring while the blue grey waters churning below told another tale.

CHAPTER TWENTY-TWO

"She didn't do it," he snapped before straightening his tie and picking a bit of link from the military ribbons on his uniform.,

"Do what exactly?" Gabe asked as he locked eyes on Calvin.

"Whatever you people are investigating. You saw the Top-Secret listing on her file. That should have been enough to leave her alone. Look who is your supervisor?"

Gabe settled back in the chair and let the quiet spread between them. Calvin scratched a date at the top if his ragged legal pad before focusing on the man seated across from them.

General Harley Roth had the same size and build as Calvin only older. The General's salt pepper grey buzz cut hair and weather worn face spoke of years on European shores fighting for God country and whatever agendas the men and women in Washington deemed appropriate.

Calling the man was the only thing keeping Gabe on the case. After getting his mother out of there, all eyes fell to him. He thought of Olivia curled up in bed and the prospect of waking her and demanding answers made his stomach hurt. Instead, he volunteered to call the number on an email demanding to know who they were and why they were requesting information on her.

Seeing the scars on her back that morning was more than enough. Asking her point blank was out. How would the conversation even start? He slept with her sure but asking Olivia to pass the sugar before explaining away the scars on the small of her back wasn't happening. He wanted to wait until she felt like sharing.

Hell, he wasn't even supposed to know they existed, but his hand was under her shirt. It felt right having her there in his arms. The intimate way she rested between his thighs made him think of all the times they sat in the back seat of his car listening to music or reading. Everything in his life clicked into place when she was resting against him. No feeling, no woman ever came close to replicating the thereness of Olivia Calderone.

And then he saw the reports and a new pain spread in his chest. The words he had spoken with such conviction when he taught at the academy from time to time came back to haunt him.

Everyone is a suspect, until they are not.

It didn't matter that he'd given his virginity to the shy quiet girl he loved more than his next breath. Memories were just that and reality washed in like a tide. Her absence over the years was like a scar healed over.

"Dr Calderone's blood was found on scene at a murder investigation," Gabe heard himself say when the General barged into the precinct demanding to see the man in charge.

Roth unbuttoned his uniform jacket and reared back in his chair. "And that means what to me? We all had blood preserved in the event any of us got injured. She wasn't true military, but I insisted on it after she got hit the first time." Roth tapped his ring on the table then rolled his eyes. "She was given the highest commendation a civilian can receive from the United States Government. Her reputation is above reproach."

Gabe glanced at Calvin 's legal pad to see him writing down the award. He'd forgone grabbing a legal pad and a pen when the man stormed in demanding to speak to someone in charge about Olivia. With Mark and Myra taking Alana home Gabe gladly assumed his role and led the man into one of the interrogation rooms instead of his office he still refused to move into.

Roth reached into his coat and extracted a black box. He opened the navy-blue box and pushed it across the table. Gabe studied the Medal for a long time before tracing the ribbon and the medallion set in the crushed velvet.

"Presidential Medal of Freedom. They don't give those out easily." Gabe ran a finger over the medal and pulled the box closer.

"Had she been enlisted a purple heart would have been pinned to her uniform. Like the ones they pinned to yours. I read up on you Detective Garrett. Medal of Valor and a Purple Heart. You could have made a career out of the Marines. Arturo Blades said you were the best of the best," Roth said with a hint of admiration.

"Ancient history, sir," Gabe mumbled trying hard not to fidget in his chair.

He thought of his medals tucked in his sock drawer and the days he spent flat on his back at a military hospital in France as some dignitary pinned it to his hospital gown with his parents standing at his bedside. He closed the box and put a hand over it.

"You know we only give these out for people of a certain caliber." Roth glanced at Gabe and stuck out his chin. "People that put their lives on the line for someone else. If you knew her, you'd know that."

"Doesn't explain why her blood was found at a murder scene where the victim had most of his organs removed," Calvin said before giving Gabe a pointed look.

Gabe glanced at Calvin then back at Roth.

"You've got to be joking. That woman barely takes a day off. When would she have time to go spelunking in someone's body for some organs—" The incredulous look on the man's face made Gabe seethe, "She's gifted enough, and her hands are perfect for the procedure, but we're about saving lives not some Frankenstein grave robbing crap."

"How would you know that?" Gabe asked as he patted the box.

Roth stared at Gabe for a long time. The tight smile plastered on the man's face became a sneer.

"I trained her. Her work ethic is better than mine. Look, whatever evidence you think you have is bogus. Somebody planted it."

"Why would somebody do that to her? If she's such an angel of mercy? Did she have enemies?" Calvin asked as he scribbled something else down.

"Everybody loved her," Roth snorted.

"Not everybody," Gabe said as he tilted his head. "Somebody wanted her dead or she wouldn't have this." He patted the box once more.

"In case you haven't been keeping up with current events detectives, we're not liked overseas. We've been run out of a few places with more than sticks and stones. Being part of a MASH unit didn't make us immune. Sometimes they take us to care for their wounded before they kill us off. Happened to Olivia more than once."

Gabe gave a mirthless chuckle. "True enough. What don't I understand is why all the animosity? We're running an active investigation into some murders here on American soil where the bodies are turning up without their organs."

"There were cowboy surgeons over there that harvested organs for profit. I can guarantee that none of my people were involved, and Olivia Calderone *is* one of mine," Roth snapped.

Gabe's thoughts filtered back to the pictures on Olivia's walls. Roth was featured in several of them wading into a sea of children or somewhere in the background as Olivia did the same.

"What about Shawn Prescott? Is he one of yours?" Gabe asked as Calvin shot a look at him. Gabe glanced over at him before focusing on the general again.

"Absolutely not. His paperwork said Shaw, but he changed it to Prescott for whatever reason. I think it was to hide from somebody. Stuck with it overseas and back here in the states. Prescott was too busy playing grab ass with the nurses and some of the younger village girls. He was part of the same missionary church group Olivia came from." Roth cringed at some memory before looking up at them. "Followed her around like some lovesick schoolboy until he made the mistake of stepping on one of her patients." The man's grin grew wider. "She leveled him with a right hook. I made sure he got put on a boat back to Bumfuck, Wherever ASAP. Showed up in a few more places attached to other missionary outfits, but never military. He had skill but so does a chainsaw."

It took everything not to laugh as Gabe rubbed the bridge of his nose. A hot spurt of pride warmed his insides even more. The general settled back in his chair and studied Gabe with a keen interest as if seeing him for the first time.

Roth's gaze dropped to the box and at once he became sober. "A village fell to the local militia. She managed to get the children and four of our people and me on a stretcher out on foot through the bush. How old is the blood you found?" Roth asked before folding his arms across his barrel of a chest.

Gabe thought of the picture he'd given Olivia and smiled. She'd done the same when his Scout Troop got turned around when the roads were washed out. Gabe got the troop to safety, but in the panic to get the other children to their parents, Olivia abandoned her Girl scout troop to find Gabe. By the time Gabe's parents reached the high ground. Olivia and Gabe were sitting in the tree above with his troop below. Her face was as muddy as Gabe's.

A knock at the door drew Calvin's gaze as Gabe studied Roth. "According to the coroner the blood found the on scene had an anti-clotting property for long storage."

"Well, there's your answer detectives. Like I said everyone on my team gives blood for storage. Did you even bother to ask Olivia or is all this cloak and dagger behind her back?" Roth said as he stood and held out his hand. "She's a real nice lady. I'm sure she'd tell you all of this if you asked her," Roth said. His familiar mask of disdain and arrogance descended once more.

"When she's not performing surgeries back-to-back at Shadow Bay General, Olivia Calderone is in Washington giving lectures to doctors from all over the world or in Miami taking classes for CEUs to keep her skills sharp. She's a surgeon gentleman, and a damn fine one; not some Slicer or Cowboy in it for the glory." Roth extended his hand for the dark blue box once more and Gabe slid it across the table. "Olivia… Dr Calderone never asked for this medal or any of what she endured."

"Why?" Gabe asked as Roth went to the door.

The general turned as if disgusted by the question and the man asking it. "She was too busy being thrown in a mass grave."

CHAPTER TWENTY-THREE

"Who the fuck put their hands on you?" The southern drawl filled Olivia's ear and heart with a smile.

"Mary, I'm fine," Olivia said as she looked around the empty classroom.

"You are the only one that insists on calling me that. Everybody else is fine with Maji Speaks," the voice countered on the other end of the line.

"But Mary is your name," Olivia replied as she reached for a stray purple crayon.

"Sounds too female and we both know I am not one or the other. Names are petty and mine never fit no how." The voice drawled as the sound of papers rustling signaled that they were multi-tasking. "It's enough that I exist. Maji Speaks works well enough. Profound and profane is good enough for me."

"You missed your mammogram. I was expecting to see you—"

"And my prostate appointment too. Stop changing the subject. Why am I hearing you got hurt from Tiana instead of you?"

"It was nothing Mary. Some grieving father just—"

"Name, Olivia or do I need to come up there? You remember the last time I did that shit. Security named a standard op after me."

"Mary stop it! You're not some avenging angel charging into some hollow cause of mine," Olivia said as she planted an elbow on her thigh. She picked at the sling then and rubbed her eyes as the silence spread on the other end of the line. "I'm sorry. I didn't mean to yell."

"Like I give a hell. Being your avenging angel was easier. This shit you have me doing now has Alana Symone written all over it."

"I am what you two made me." Olivia said.

"Yeah, two demons raising a child. You more like Alana than her own kids. You could have stayed gone; you know." Maji hissed

"Some families are birth made and others are Earth made. Shadow Bay is my home. My family is here. You're here Maji." Olivia smiled into her phone knowing her old friend with the startling grey eyes was palming the moisture from them as her platinum gray dreadlocks sprouted out from her scalp like snakes.

"And you can quit that shit. You know I'm allergic to all that compassion you be waving around."

"How are they?" Olivia asked as her friend took a drag from what had to be the first cigar of the day.

Maji exhaled slowly and Olivia imagined the usual fine tendrils of smoke curling from the nightclub owner's nose. She took in a breath longing for her old friend's beard oil and the familiar telltale bite of Marijuana and tobacco steeped in the Jamaican rum that permeated every inch of fabric in the nightclub owner's lair.

"You already know they're all right," Maji hissed. "Worrying the hell out of me."

"Ms. Mary I—"

"Profound and profane is good enough for me." She snarled, "Maji Speaks works well enough for the bill collectors. Putting handles on it don't make it mine anymore. We both know I am not one or the other."

"And I love you more because of it. The hearings are in a couple of weeks. If we can get them there the government will take over. Just a little longer Mary, please," Olivia said as the silence on the other end grew.

"Why I put up with your little narrow ass is beyond me," Maji said taking another hit. "You lucky I love you. Now get off my phone," she said as the line went dead.

Olivia took in a cleansing breath and pulled her earpiece from her ear and stuck it in her pocket.

"Hey Ms. Brenda."

"Olivia what on earth do you think you're doing?" She said as she grabbed a purple plastic box on her way to Olivia.

Brenda brushed the crayons from her hand into the box and showed Olivia to a chair.

"I'm fine, don't fuss."

Brenda rolled her eyes and sucked her teeth.

"I can fuss over whoever I want to. You're not the boss here. I am," She chuckled as she sat beside her.

Olivia watched as the older woman picked at the sling and pinched her lips together.

"How long you out for. Beacham say?" Brenda asked.

Olivia smiled and shook her head.

"Merely a formality. Had to make it appear legit in front of the stakeholders. He sent me home with plenty to do including a paper to finish for a medical journal. I can still teach."

Brenda peered into Olivia's eyes then sat back.

"And instead of having yourself a lie down for that migraine you have brewing, you came here,"

"You called me, Ms. Brenda," she said meekly.

"To check on you," The older woman insisted.

"Are you sorry I came?" Olivia sat up and looked her old friend in the eye.

"Your hands were made for better things than this," Brenda said as she waved a hand dismissively over her head.

Olivia grasped Brenda's hand and gave it a squeeze. "My hands are put to good use whenever I can help someone."

"You know what I mean Olivia. Your grandmother Elsy would be proud. After losing your Mamma to drugs. Seeing you graduate with an

MD well; God restored," Brenda said patting her on the leg. "My Antoine Sebastian always said you had a brain on you." Brenda's blinked rapidly as she cleared her throat and looked around the small room.

The empty classroom was decked out in primary colors with book bins and large soft building blocks stacked in the corner. Snack time was in full swing down the hallway with a children's movie soundtrack playing over the chatter of small voices.

"Tell me more about this man you said was hanging around here," Olivia sighed as she looked around the room. She made of mental note of the crown carpets and the board games in dilapidated boxes knowing full well that the replacements she ordered would be there later on in the week.

Brenda straightened her back. "Well, it was like I said. His clothes looked right but something about the man was off. He worked the room like a politician handing out matchbooks." Brenda fished around in the breast pocket of her blue denim work shirt and pulled out the small colorful square and handed it over.

Olivia thumbed the flap open and read the number. "You try it?"

Brenda nodded. "Man said the dead girl's name; Abra. Might have been her father. Sounded worried. Begged her to come home. Said he was sorry about their argument."

She nodded slowly. "You should go to the police with this, Brenda."

"I don't blame them, but I don't talk to them either. You know that" Brenda cleared her throat and looked off toward a window.

Olivia reached for the older woman's shoulder. "I know you don't trust them after Antoine died in custody, but Gabe and his squad are good people."

"You mean the Brooder? He was good with Abra that night. Calmed her down when Tommy folded." Brenda dapped at her eyes with the hem of the shirt before she focused on Olivia.

She took in a shaky breath as her body ached from his absence. After the debacle at the hospital when Beacham put her on temporary hiatus, the urge to call Gabe was unbearable and so was the shame. He needed her last night and she left him there in her dimly lit office. Christine's account of her condition when she returned made it ten times worse.

There was no reason to get him involved in a mess she created. The man already had his plate full with his murder investigation. Olivia had no intentions of shoving her baggage on his plate.

He looked pissed Olivia. He looked like he would have walked over all of us to get you out of there.

"He does brood," Olivia agreed with a frown. "He has reason to these days."

Brenda shook Olivia's hand to get her attention, "You still don't look right. If you want, I can drive you…"

Olivia straightened her back as a little boy stood in the doorway. Brenda held out her arms and he ran over and hugged her.

"Hey Nate, what's going on?" Brenda asked as he hid his face in her meaty arm. He held out a chocolate chip cookie wrapped in plastic wrap to Olivia.

"Thanks Nate," Olivia said taking the cookie.

"Tell your Brooder he better watch out," Brenda said as Nate leaned up and whispered something in her ear. "Nate here gets all the ladies," she said while leaning over so that the boy could whisper in her ear. The smile on the woman's face faded as she looked over at Olivia.

"Brenda what is it?" Olivia said rising from the chair.

"He said he can't wake his father up." Brenda stood and hauled the little boy up on her hip.

Olivia followed Brenda down the hallway to the Family wing of the shelter. Brenda handed the boy off to one of the other workers and continued to move to the door at the end of the hall. Brenda gave a soft knock as she eased the door open.

"Roger? Nate said you were feeling poorly," Brenda said as she palmed the light switch over the dresser. "Roger are you alright? Now, you know the rules about alcohol."

Olivia grabbed Brenda's arm and jerked her to a halt. She gestured with her head and Brenda looked down at the floor as the stain on the floor continued to widen.

***

Gabe tossed his coat on his desk as he thumbed through his contact list. He tapped the letter O and smiled as the phone connected and started to ring. He was still waiting for his ear to fill with her voice when Calvin walked over and grabbed his coat.

"Come on G we got another one."

"Where?" Gabe muttered a curse as he hung up and grabbed his jacket.

"Some shelter down on Biddle Street," Calvin called over his shoulder.

***

Gabe shouldered his way through the crowd with Calvin on his heels.

"Look can ya'll do something about these people? Clear this hallway!" Calvin yelled. "This ain't no fucking reality show. Get gone!"

Gabe was about to say the same thing when the crowd thinned out and Max walked over to him. "Hey, Max. Same scene. different cast?" Gabe said grimly.

Max walked overreaching for his arm. Gabe looked up to see Brenda talking with another detective. Gabe looked in the room at the EMTs packing up. In the far corner, Olivia sat in an overstuffed plaid chair with her legs crossed. Her blood-stained hands were folded neatly in her lap.

"Gabe listen to me, "Max shook Gabe to get his attention. "Are you listening to me? She tried to resuscitate him, but he bled out."

"Max what is she even doing here? He questioned as he glanced at Max and then back into the room at Olivia staring straight ahead. The pink floral pillowcase he swaddled her arm in that morning was gone. The blue and while sling she'd been wearing was in an evidence bag stained being carried away by a man in a black jacket with the words Forensics in reflective letters on the back.

A paramedic walked up and held out a fresh sling wrapped in plastic, "Doc. C. will be needing this. Brenda Mabry over there runs this place. She works with Doc C. over at Shadow Bay," he said quietly as he pressed the plastic bag into Gabe's hands and leaned closer. "She used her sling to try and stem the bleeding."

Calvin walked up and thumped Gabe on the shoulder. Suddenly the world was filled with sound once more.

"Locard Exchange," Max said quietly.

"Wherever she stepped, whatever she touched. I know Max," Gabe said trying hard not to yell. His heart cramped when he zeroed in on the streaks of red on her face.

"It's why she won't leave the room Gabe. She's waiting for Forensics to exclude her."

"Can I go to her?" Gabe moved toward the door and Calvin thumped his arm and pushed some latex gloves into his hand.

Out of the corner of his eye, Gabe saw two uniforms move from their station on either side of the door. Gabe shot a look at Max.

"Max, I can't stand in this hallway. She could be hurt. Her arm." he raised the sling.

"I know son, go on," Max put a hand on the back of his shoulder.

"Ollie," Gabe pulled on the gloves as he made his way inside.

She blinked slowly and looked at him. "Twenty-Five Grand," She whispered.

"What?" Gabe stooped down near her chair, and he tried to smooth her hair back.

"No!" she said blocking him with her arm. The movement caused her to yelp.

"I know Olivia. I'm sorry," he whispered. "Let me help Babe, please?"

Olivia looked at him.

"Let me try," he said as he reached for her again.

Olivia clutched at her arm and gestured with her head. "No Gabe…. The wall,"

He looked from the body covered with a sheet to the wall above the twin sized bed. Gabe took in the child's artwork clinging to the wall on a small patch of tape. The yellow smiling sun in the upper left-hand corner shined down on two stick figures standing by a house. Scrawled beneath the drawing were the numbers she's spoken aloud.

"He sold his kidney to buy a home for his little boy," she said as her voice broke.

CHAPTER TWENTY-FOUR

Gabe glanced down at his scraped knuckled and made a fist. As he studied the camera men and the reporter milling about in an ocean of spectators.

"You alright man?" Calvin asked before looking down at Gabe's hand. "Never did say what the General said to you before he left."

Gabe continued to study the reporters congregating around his mother's center. Calvin started the ignition and pulled into traffic. Gabe was heading out to his truck to gather his thoughts. From hearing the horror story from his mother to dealing with the general, his head was buzzing. Every hour that passed meant he had no idea how Olivia was.

"You're him," Roth said as he handed in his visitor's badge.

He joined Gabe as he walked out to the parking lot. The late afternoon sun was deceiving as the frigid temperature made him zip his coat. Roth popped the collar on his own Black camel hair coat before planting his black fedora on his head.

"Him? What are you talking about?" Gabe scanned the area. The discussion upstairs didn't necessarily exonerate Olivia.

If anything, it spawned more questions that he had no intentions of asking the man standing beside him. The fact that the man knew more about Olivia than he did stuck in his craw. And while Gabe knew he should have been thanking the man for saving her life. The question hung between them.

Why weren't you there?

"Thought it was Prescott the way he kept crowding into her space until we moved her and her scrub nurse into the barracks. Gabe, right? She cried for you," Roth said as he extracted the box for his coat and handed it over.

Gabe opened this his box and pulled out the ornate container that held Olivia's medal and opened it.

"Never seen you hit a civilian before. If Mark hadn't pulled you off him, I think you would have killed him."

"My cousin is a lowlife. Hardly what I would call a civilian. If Mark hadn't pulled me off my dear cousin. You're right, Shawn would be in the morgue, and I would be behind bars," Gabe finished for him as he snapped the box shut.

It happened so quickly that Gabe barely had time to think. One minute he was closing the door on his truck and the next his cousin Shawn was barreling across the street near the precinct parking lot hurling insults.

"First your mother and now Olivia? It's all over the hospital and the news." He took a swing that Gabe easily side stepped as Calvin hooked an arm around his cousin and hurled him back a few steps.

"Easy Dr. Prescott. What's your hurry?" Calvin asked as he restrained Shawn.

"Let him go Calvin. Just what is it that you think I've done?" Gabe said, taking a defensive stance.

Shawn staggered away straightening his tie. "She isn't even home good and here you are dragging her into your nightmares. The only reason she's probably on, mandatory leave because of you. Even when we were kids, if you were in trouble, she ended up in it too."

Gabe still hadn't processed the idea that she was on leave of any kind when he called the hospital to check on her. "How do you know about anything going on with Olivia? You don't even work at Shadow Bay

General."

"Shows how much you know. I serve as a locum from time to time,"

"And that means what to us, Prescott? "Calvin quipped as a crowd began to form.

"A locum is a substitute doctor that helps out when—"

"Oh, you mean like a temp. Like rent a Doc?" Calvin teased causing a ripple of laughter through the group.

"Your mother's center is crawling with cops and reporters. No surprise there, but now you pull Olivia into it. Wasn't enough for her to leave you all those years ago. You had to go and do this?"

"I think you better leave Shawn." Gabe took a step toward his cousin.

Shawn looked around at the group of men and women pausing at their vehicles before coming closer. Gabe looked over to see Mark coming over and groaned.

"Why? You know it's true. You and your mother are worse than plutonium. Everything dies around you two. It's why Uncle Cass is dead."

Before Gabe knew it, Shawn was on the ground with his hand clapped over his nose. The crowd swirled around him as someone helped Shawn to his feet. Mark stepped between them, and Gabe backed off. He pressed his back against the driver side door of a police cruiser and pulled up his sleeve.

"What the hell is going on outside my house?" Mark roared.

Gabe shook the ache of an unused punch out of his arm. "Technically, Uncle Mark it's my house now," Gabe said amazed that is voice was still calm. "And Shawn was just leaving."

"Acting like a bunch of kids out here I have to wonder." Mark snapped his fingers to get his attention. "How many times I have to pull you two apart when you were boys? Three guesses who this is all about."

"He came at me Mark," Gabe said pulling up his other sleeve. "Keep my father's name out of your mouth, Shawn."

"And you punched a civilian out in front of God and everybody." Mark crowded into Gabe's space.

Some of the men and women from Gabe's squad backed away as

someone from the group muttered. "I didn't see anything you guys see anything?" someone asked.

"Naw I didn't see shit. I was just heading to my ride for shift change." Someone else cracked.

Gabe stood up. "Stop it. All of you. You will not compromise yourselves for me. Commissioner Brown is right," he said as he looked at his detectives one by one, "Not for me or anyone else. I assaulted this man and you all witnessed it."

Gabe faced Shawn still pinching his nostrils with a handkerchief. Mark wedged himself between the men and eased Gabe back a few steps.

"Shawn, are you pressing charges against Lt. Garrett?" Mark said looking warily back and forth between the two men.

"I should, assaulting me in front of all these people. I could have your badge and your pension." Shawn removed the cloth from his face and folded it in half. He scanned the faces of the few cops that remained from the scattering crowd.

At last, he looked at Mark and sniffled before rolling his eyes. "Are you kidding Uncle Mark?"

"I assure you we take assault very seriously." Mark said using his own weight to force Shawn into distancing himself. "Now LT. Gabriel Garrett just admitted causing you bodily harm. Will you be pressing charges?"

"It was a love tap and I deserved it. It was a low blow bringing Uncle Cass into this. Detective Garrett was defending himself, Commissioner. I threw the first punch. Sorry Gabe," Shawn said extending a hand.

Mark blocked him. "And you are the one bleeding. Are you pressing charges because I don't want to look up and see paperwork later on because you had a change of heart?"

"No, Uncle Mark. There won't be. Olivia Calderone was always a sticking point between us. Hearing that she got suspended and then hurt on top of that made me see red. I was out of line. I'm sorry Gabe," Shawn said directing his conversation to Gabe. "Really man, I apologize. Olivia has always been a sticking point between us."

Gabe eased his uncle aside and stepped to Shawn so quickly that he bumped into Calvin. He grabbed his hand and shook it once.

"You've had like three Mondays in one damn week," Calvin said giving Gabe a shove snapping him out of his thoughts.

"None of this is easy. First your mom as potential witness and now Olivia hurt, suspended, and found on a murder scene. You may not drink but I feel like having some scotch for you!" Calvin chuckled as he circled the precinct and headed down another street.

"Hospital. I got copies, but the originals need to go back where they came from. That and I need to check on Olivia."

"Your girl was a big help with those lists, man and for what it's worth nobody thinks she's involved with this."

"Olivia doesn't belong to me," Gabe settled back in the chair and sighed, "Not anymore."

"Says the man with her name tattooed across the back of his shoulders. You are not exactly objective when it comes to her," Calvin said sliding his gaze to Gabe's.

Gabe cleared his throat and looked out the window. So much was unfinished between them. After she gave her statement, Olivia effectively cut him off at the knees when he offered to take her home preferring to have Rhonda Young, one of his detectives do the honors. Even then he wanted to hold her to his heart. He rubbed at the knot of tension between his shoulders.

"I'm just saying. You looked like you wanted to kill your cousin in that parking lot," Calvin said quietly.

"I did. When we were kids, Shawn always had this weird fascination with Olivia. I mean we were younger than him by four years, but it didn't matter." Gabe felt his jaw tightened as he fixed his sleeves. "Shawn cornered her in my tree house one day when we were playing hide and seek with some other kids at a cookout. I came around the house and she was on the ground, broken again. He was staring at her from the tree house with this strange look on his face."

"G, we don't have to do this right now." The concern in his friend's voice poked at that raw place in Gabe.

Gabe took in a shaky breath. The air was suddenly too thick as the remnants of the rage he felt back then threatened to bowl him over. "Shawn tried to explain it away. He said it was an accident," he said focusing on the traffic rushing by.

"I went after him with a baseball bat. Tried to bludgeon him with it. It took my dad and uncle Mark to get me off him. I knew what he was. Mom did too. Heard rumors about other little girls in the neighborhood where he lived," Gabe cleared his throat. "She'd already been through enough. Olivia deserved better. You're right. I'm not objective about Olivia."   He looked at his friend and worked at a smile. "I wanted to hold space for her last night. After everything she went through, I wanted—" Gabe struggled with the emotion crowding his throat.

Calvin paused at a traffic light. "She thought enough of you to distance herself." He finished for him.

Gabe met his friend's gaze and nodded once.

"Like I said man, figured you wouldn't go for a regular girl." Calvin said as he made a left and continued a four-corner circuit that put them several blocks away from the precinct.

Gabe bit down on his tongue hard enough to draw blood as he backed away from the memories. "We always held space for each other. I was supposed to grow old with her, Calvin."

"What happened?" Calvin inquired.

Gabe snapped his head in Calvin's direction. The bitterness on the tip of his tongue dissipated as the memory of her running from him in the airport as a teenager melded with the vision of her huddled in his seat behind the desk swimming in his old sweatshirt filled his mind.

"I thought it was college, but now…"

I can't give you back those years… all I have is now.

Her words were so clear in his head that Gabe sat up. "Same as before. I screwed it up."

CHAPTER TWENTY-FIVE

Olivia rolled over on her back as the tears spilled back into her hairline.

It wasn't shock.

At least she could be clear about that as she sat there waiting for the forensics technician to take her fingerprints and have her strip out of her clothing and hand everything over.

While he finished shift change, Olivia sat at his desk staring out the window. The remnants of ink on her hands reminded her of the soil she dug through searching for Bimbi's stuffed Giraffe.

Gabe kept watch through the glass window that separated his newly vacated office from the rest of the squad room. She was swimming in his gray police sweatshirt that Rhonda, one of his sergeant's gave her. Even with the sling in place, her bare shoulder slipped into view, exposing a blood-stained, pale blue bra strap. She didn't even ask why they asked if she would submit to a body search. She'd been through customs enough to know a refusal raised red flags.

Rhonda drove her home, but by the time she emerged from the shower, Gabe was there marveling over the oceans of people pulsing around her on the gallery wall. He ran his thumb over one of the images of Olivia sitting amidst a group of children.

Even now after all these years, his smile warmed her from the inside out. His masculine energy rose like heat filling the room, touching off a firestorm within her. The one thing that haunted her dreams was there, finally in the flesh. Every instinct told her to run hard and fast just like before. She crossed the floor instead.

In several of the pictures, a little girl dressed in a red jumper dress with a yellow top, and flowers sprinkled across the collar stood nearby with the tail of her lab coat clutched in one hand and a thumb firmly screwed in her mouth.

Perhaps if I start slowly. Maybe if I explain why I stayed away...

"There were more bodies in the water than fish after a while. Same river many of the villages used for cooking and drinking. They thought we were devils. That maybe we brought the sickness and death. They threw things… sticks and rocks. Stopped wearing lab coats and scrubs for a long time," Olivia swallowed hard as she searched the pictures. Her heart crowded into her throat.

"Tell Detective Payson I said thank you. I'll get this washed up and back to her as soon as possible,"

Gabe moved closer, "Ollie," he breathed.

Her hand trembled as she touched the wall beneath each frame. She traced the images of a little girl dressed in a white tee shirt and pink overalls.

"Malawi. Cambodia. Uganda. We never went where we were wanted; always where we were needed."

"Looks like you were her favorite person," he said slipping an errant lock of her hair behind an ear.

"Bimbi loved music. Whenever I'd sit down to play, she'd wedge herself between me and the guitar you made for me when we were kids," Olivia reached for another picture of the two of them. She cried out in pain as she gripped her arm and staggered back from the wall and fell to one knee.

Gabe gathered her into his arms and carried her to the sofa. And then it was all too real. The things she'd done. Nathan's father wasn't the first she'd see or even the worst. But Gabe would understand. He knew her since third grade. If she couldn't tell anyone else, surely Gabe would understand. And then her eye fell on the picture of Bimbi and the children surrounding them. Their laughter was like music. Their screams… all of the screaming.

Olivia struggled in his arms. "You shouldn't be here." She wriggled in his grip and Gabe held her tighter.

"Ollie wait. I don't want to drop you." He sat her on the sofa and flopped down beside her. "Where else would I be?" Gabe asked half-jokingly as he fixed the sling strap.

Olivia sat back from him. She thought of the picture back at the crime scene. "Not here. I'm a suspect."

He reached for her again and she cringed. No, the answer was clear. She'd made a promise. It was all she had back then and on the strength of it they lived.

"I was on scene covered in blood, Gabe. Rhonda told me my blood was found at another crime scene when she asked for my clothes. I am a suspect."

"You are not! Stop saying that." He grabbed her by the arms and shook her softly.

Olivia blanched as she choked back a scream.

Gabe dropped her as if she were hot. "Ah Jesus. Ollie, I'm sorry. I didn't mean to hurt you."

Olivia backed away and stood. "My boss drafted me to help, but I wanted to help—tried to," she said as she backed away. "I can't do that now. He'll assign someone else. You have to go." She tiptoed around him making sure no part of her body touched his.

Gabe followed and she bumped into the wall and slid down. He went to her, and she pushed herself to her knees just as Gabe's hand fell to the small of her back. Olivia jerked away and fell flat on her stomach. Gabe put his arms around her midsection and sat back against the wall.

Olivia struggled in his arms. "It was a mistake to come here. Never should have come back here. Let me go."

Gabe pressed his face against the back of her head.

"Babe stop. Just stop fighting me. What you saw tonight—"

A mixture of a sob and a laugh spilled from her as she warred with pulling away and no longer denying herself of his touch. "It's not the worst I've seen. People inject themselves into situations all the time. I thought I could help and… and… and "She continued to struggle as her throat closed around the memories and she began to hyperventilate.

Gabe folded his arms and legs around her until she stopped fighting and broke down. "You functioned on less. I get that. But not anymore. I got you. Hear me? I got you." Gabe unfolded his legs and brought her to his chest.

"Shouldn't be here Gabe," she said as she pushed at his shoulder.

"Ollie, I don't care about the scars or Shawn." He released her.

Olivia sat further back. "My scars? Shawn?"

"I've seen the scars on your back, Ollie and I don't care if…"

Olivia scrambled away from Gabe and stood. "What does Shawn have to…"

Gabe stood up and dusted his hands off on his jeans. "Is he the reason you wouldn't come home?"

Olivia chuckled, "You of all people know that could never happen."

"Ollie, it doesn't matter. I didn't mean…," Gabe scrubbed his face with his hands.

Olivia sidestepped around him until she reached her front door. She snatched it open barely missing her face.

"What's to talk about, Gabe? You already have it figured out. I wasn't home making love to you so I must have gone for the next best thing and fucked him instead? Tracked me down like a runaway slave. Tried injecting himself into everything I did. He wouldn't go into the villages though. Too scared to get sick."

"Ollie…I'm sorry. I saw him today and we——-" He sighed and put his head down. "I punched him,"

She jerked the door open further biting back a scream as her arm thumped the heavily ornate wooden surface. The world greyed away, and she slumped against the door. Relief and sickening waves crashed through her.

Shawn Prescott was the one man she hated most in the world just managed to give her an out. "Fine. You won't go then I will," Olivia said releasing the doorknob. She started down the hallway and stopped.

"Olivia I'm sorry. I never meant—" he ran a shaky hand over his mouth and looked away.

"You're absolutely right Gabe. He's exactly why I stayed away. You know it's funny. You called me selfish back then and you were right. All I ever thought about was us. What a beautiful mistake that was. Lock the door on your way out," She took the last few steps to her bedroom door and slammed it.

CHAPTER TWENTY-SIX

Gabe sat down against the wall inside the bouldering center. He'd seen his fair share of them over the years, but most were used for play dates for children and amateur climbers. The jingle of the carabiners as they loosened and tightened reminded him of keys in a pocket: loud and intrusive when the world needed to be quiet. The Zone out on Ruxton was just right. The old factory had been gutted and revamped floor to ceiling with finger and toe holds spaced so far apart you needed to really know what you were doing before you even came through the front door. Novice classes were held in the mornings. Elite Hour was by appointment only and Gabe had a seasonal membership that afford him plenty of time to climb.

Hand over hand then balancing nearly upside down to grip the toe hold Gabe made his way up the wall. Only once had his finger grip failed and dangled some 30 feet from the floor below and that was when he thought about Olivia slamming her bedroom door.

With a few choice words, Olivia managed to stich their past together. Gabe shook the thoughts from his head and looked up at the ceiling. Everything had gone left so quickly that even as he stood outside her front door trying the knob to make sure it was locked, a tumble of confused thoughts assailed him.

She was giving him an out, but it felt more like a slap in the face. Never once had it entered his mind that she was a suspect. For her to say the words aloud made it ten times worse. He knew the drill. How many times had some helpful witness turn out to be the prime suspect?

Every time her phone went to voicemail, Gabe put his face in his hands as he tried to quiet his breathing. Every time her phone went to voicemail, it loosened the bridle on his anger.

"Don't give me that crap. My nephew's truck is outside. Just tell me where you think he'd go." Mark's familiar bark echoed across the room.

"G! You in here? Gabriel? G, where the hell are you?"

Gabe scrubbed his face with his hands before he leaned over and looked down. Mark was standing in the middle of the floor in a grey sweat suit that matched what little hair framed his brown scalp. The old man scratched the top of his head before he put his policeman's baseball cap back on.

"What's up Uncle Mark? You climbing today?" Gabe teased.

Mark smiled up at him. "Boy get your ass down here. We gotta talk." The look on the old man's face left little room for debate.

Gabe made his way more than halfway down the wall before he glanced behind him. He crouched down low then took in a deep breath and pushed hard with his legs until he was away from the wall and his legs were up over his head. He landed a few feet from his uncle crouching down on one knee.

"You and your mamma acting like a bunch of goddamned spider monkeys. You two ever do something normal like bowling or jogging? "Mark rolled his eyes before scanning the room once more.

Other climbers continued to slowly make their way up the walls while two men dressed in climbing attire were descending or talking quietly amongst themselves.

"Mom knits. She taught me how. If we ever end up in the Zombie Apocalypse, and all else fails I can make us all blankets. She'll have to do the sweaters," Gabe quipped "You know you shouldn't come in here yelling like that. You could break somebody's concentration."

"If they're paying attention and not ear hustling it shouldn't be a problem. You and Alana ever race to the top?" Mark asked as he walked over and handed Gabe a towel.

"She wins every damn time. Is my mother, okay?" Gabe asked as he scrubbed his arm with the white terry cloth towel.

Mark mopped the bottom of his face with a shaky palm. "You're not going to like it no matter how I tell it. Gabe your mother is in jail."

"What?! On what charge?" Gabe roared as he started walking toward the exit. Mark jogged after him.

"Stand still for a minute. She's not there on any charges. She asked to go," Mark said glancing at the wall.

Gabe scrubbed his face with the towel and backed away. "And you let her?" He studied his uncle. The man looked away from Gabe. Gabe tilted his head and squinted at him. "Ah Jesus Uncle Mark. You took her there?"

"Gabe, she told me to," Mark replied. "She thought she could help."

"You could have said no. Why would you think any part of this shit would be, okay? How could you even think—" Gabe stormed through the lobby heading for the locker room. Once they were inside, Mark grabbed his arm. "Get off me. You should have stopped her."

Mark snatched Gabe closer and shook him into a gasping silence. "Excuse me, have you met your mother? She just does shit." He released him and fixed his sweatshirt.

"When I told her about Olivia at the shelter, your mother got it in her head that she needed to talk to some woman named September Dade. She wants you to see Maji," Mark stepped back against the wall as two climbers walked past.

Gabe snatched a towel from the pile near the door and scrubbed his arm. "Why? Maji can't stand me What makes you think they'll talk to me?"

Mark shrugged "How should I know? I'm still baffled that your mother chose that creature as your godparent after you were born."

"Maji Speaks would burn the world for my mother. Me? I'm sure she'd toss my ass on the bonfire and dance around it."

"Why?" Mark asked.

The question hammered at Gabe as the memory of Olivia slamming the door in his face flooded his mind. Gabe glanced at Mark before walking over to his locker.

"Let me guess. Olivia?" Mark said taking a seat on the bench. "Your mother suggested it, so she probably called to get you an audience. Maji has a pulse on the underground: here and overseas."

Gabe stared at a bouldering wall poster featuring Cathedral Rock and a clear blue sky as the backdrop taped to the wall above his locker. "Mom wasn't supposed to be involved in this case, remember? She's a civilian isn't that what you told me? Neither one of them should be involved." Gabe swiped at his arm with the towel once more.

"But you didn't listen and it's a good thing you didn't. Alana put a lot of things into context. Olivia finding that man at Biddle Street helped too."

"You saw what it did to Mom, Uncle Mark. You didn't see Olivia."

Mark took off his cap and rubbed the top of his head. "I saw enough."

"Olivia tried to resuscitate… Fuck! Why now huh? As if I don't have enough shit to deal with!" he said ripping his locker open.

"I know, G. Now Alana is safe. The Warden himself has eyes on her," Mark cautioned, and Gabe glanced over his shoulder.

"You're making this sound like it's the most logical thing in the world. My dad would never… You know what forget it." He snapped before pulling his sports bag from the locker

"You're right. Cass wouldn't, but he trusted Alana even when it made more sense not to." Mark tapped Gabe on the arm. "Look, I've known your mamma a long time. I've never been able to follow her fucked up logic, but her compass ain't broken."

"Denied territory Uncle Mark. She was never ever supposed to go back inside. Not for anything," Gabe flopped down beside him and searched the floor. "I had one job." He snagged the towel and scrubbed the top of his head then draped it around his shoulders.

Mark put a hand on Gabe's shoulder a shake. "Alana's not there to stay, son. I'm going back for her this evening. "

"No, I'm going," Gabe snapped as he leaned over to unzip his bag.

Mark grabbed Gabe's arm "I took her there and I'll bring her back home to Myra who's about as shook as you are. Called Robert Beacham over at the hospital. Now he's assigned Olivia as our go between."

"Ollie won't do it. Something happened and—" the words stuck in his throat. He planned to talk to her about the body search, but everything happened so quickly.

"What else is new? Seems the closer you two got as kids the more you squabbled. You be about our business, and she'll be about hers. She's the golden child right now, administrative leave or not." Mark said with a grin.

"Well, that's out. She wants no parts of me, and I don't blame her." Gabe replied sharply as Mark poked Gabe in the shoulder with an envelope.

"What's that?" Gabe questioned before turning back to his gym bag. Mark poked him again and he snatched the envelope and opened it.

The swirling script and gold filigree made Gabe frown. "You've got to be joking," he said handing the invitation back.

"Calvin told me about the general. Said he sounded more like her man than a commanding officer. Beacham sounded the same." Mark whistled and removed his Shadow Bay Police Department ball cap and chuckled. "That little bit of a thing has all of you rattled. She's probably not thinking about any of you. None of that shit matters. Put your feelings in your back pocket. Take Calvin and go pick up some tuxedos. "

Mark reached in his coat and pulled out another envelope. I have to go to this thing as part of my new duties as commissioner, but you and a couple of men from your team may be able to listen in on some snatches of conversation or float a question or two. You know how rich people like to talk when they have their drink and a twostep."

Gabe picked the invitation up and turned it over in his hands. "I'll make the call. Calvin, Rhonda, Artemis, and Becca can do it. I'll get back to the office and continue tracking down leads." Gabe said handing the envelope back.

"It's an awards ceremony and a fundraiser for Organ Donation Awareness. You don't even have to stay the entire time although you may want to. Olivia will be there. She sorta has to be there. They're honoring her for her Relief Work. Maybe you can apologize to her."

"How do you know it was me?" Gabe asked. "She can be hard to get along with, you know."

"I highly doubt that." Mark said with a knowing look. "If Shawn is being more of a dick than usual and you're knocking him on his tail is any indication. You were probably a whole ass."

Gabe muttered a curse and rummaged through his bag for some toiletries. "She started it," he said turning to face his uncle.

Mark folded his arms and raised an eyebrow. "Do tell."

"She thinks she's a suspect. Some asshole nearly pulls her arm out of the socket and— and"

Mark put his hand on Gabe's shoulder. "Everyone is until they're not. How many times have we seen a helpful citizen turn out to be the murderer or an accessory? Plenty of people try to steer the case under the guise of helping."

"Ollie's a trauma surgeon, Uncle Mark. The only thing she is attempting to do is save somebody's life and she's not even safe doing that." He thought of the blood stain on her scrub top.

"And she's a good one I hear. Listen it's been a while, G. People change," Mark said clapping him on the shoulder.

"Not Ollie," Gabe mumbled as the wall of pictured filled his mind. "She always had someone's baby on her hip when we were kids. Always had her guitar, the one I made for her slung over her back. Helping wherever and whenever she could. Her staff loves her—" he glanced over his shoulder and sat back.

"You don't sound objective about her," Mark said. "I remember you grieved for her like a death when she left for college. Don't sound like much has changed."

"All I've ever known was that we were supposed to be married. How could I have settled down with anyone else when I knew Olivia was The One? We should be raising our son and his sister and maybe working on another baby by now. It's what we both wanted so badly and then. Everything changed that night she almost—" Gabe winced at a private thought and busied himself looking through his bag once more.

"Black history son. Stay in the present. Now, Olivia called it Gabe. Your Mom even submitted to exclusionary testing. If you can't be objective and see this case through tell me now," Mark said as he plucked the invitation from the bench.

Gabe snatched it back. "I'll go if only to prove she didn't do this anymore than my mother did."

CHAPTER TWENTY-SEVEN

Olivia shifted the guitar strap so that the instrument rested against her back. She reached for her glasses tucked down the collar of her shirt before running a finger over her tablet.

"Your arm is never gonna heal if you don't keep it in that sling," Tiana grumbled as she handed Olivia the stylus.

"Stop clucking around me Mother Hen," Olivia said as she lifted her gaze. "Besides if it helps Cory through… I don't think he can deal with another false alarm. Chrissy can't. He's running out of time."

"I know Olivia. Cory's counts are still off. The dialysis treatments should resolve some of that." Tiana said as she pulled a sheet of paper from the printer.

Olivia took her glasses off and rubbed her eyes before tucking them back in her collar. "Dialysis is a stop gap measure Tiana. He needs a new kidney."

"Organ Registry do what it do Olivia," Tiana said as she scribbled down some notes.

"Yeah, just not as fast as it does for others with large wallets," Olivia said from the crook of her arm.

"How hard did you hit that wall?" Tiana hissed as she fingered one of the bruises.

"Hard enough to see stars and have some assholes ask me about 'a shipment'," Olivia said raising her head to see Tiana staring at her.

"I knew it. I fucking—" Tiana threw the clipboard on the Unit Clerk's desk and folded her arms.

Olivia gripped her arm. Tiana tried to jerk away, and she gasped. Tiana came around the nurse's station and took the guitar and replaced it with a sling. "Sorry Olivia. Look just keep that thing on, will you?"

"It's almost over Tiana. We agreed after Erin," Olivia said as she pressed her forehead to Tiana's.

She pulled back from her. "Not fast enough for me. Leave my dead wife out of this. She made her decision and I made mine. Promised her I'd take care of you, and I will. Besides. It looks like somebody else is vying for that position." Tiana looked past her and frowned.

Olivia shook her head in confusion.

"Father Hen in this case." Tiana pointed with her head once. "Might as well talk to him. He's been blowing up the line here at the desk for damn near a week." Tiana smiled. "The one day he brought lunch and you were away he asked me to give it to Mr. Ackerman and his wife."

Olivia put her head down again and groaned. She wasn't exactly avoiding Gabe. Her suspension freed her up to take care of some things she'd been neglecting and the mountains of paperwork at the office. If she were more honest with herself Olivia would have to admit that the fight was a reprieve that she needed. It didn't stop Gabe from walking through her mind at the most inopportune moments during the day.

Every time she replayed the scenario the answers were the same. Telling him wasn't an option and wouldn't be until it was all finished.

"Just tell him to fuck off. It works for every other swinging dick that comes after you," Tiana quipped

Olivia took in a slow breath and straightened her back. The exhaustion set into his features propelled her forward. She put her hand out and he took it. "Gabe what's wrong?"

"Oh, hey G. "Chrissy chirped as she exited the hospital room. "She hasn't eaten just thought you should know."

Olivia shot a dirty look at Christine.

Tiana rounded the desk and snatched a chart from Christine. "Stop snitching all your life. If you're gonna tell it tell it all. She only came up here to make your son comfortable. She should be in occupational therapy or at home resting that arm."

"Enough ladies. Tiana apologize, right now," Olivia called over her shoulder.

"My bad Chrissy. I'm sorry," Tiana threw her arm around Christine's shoulder and pulled her toward the other side of the nurse's station.

Olivia finally faced him. He looked as if he hadn't moved or stopped looking at her. She brushed the melting snow from his shoulder relishing the feel of the moist leather beneath her hand.

"You need to eat something Olivia," Gabe cautioned as he fixed the guitar strap on her shoulder.

Olivia felt her face flush under his scrutiny. "Is Ms. Alana, okay?

"She's fine," he hesitated, measuring her for a moment.

"Was there another murder?" she countered moving closer. As much as she hated to admit it, her body craved the heat that radiated from him.

"No, Ollie."

"Are you sick?" Olivia put her hand on his forehead and then moved it to his cheek.

Gabe pulled her hand from his face and licked his lips as a tight mirthless smile whispered across his features. "Yes. I mean no—" he muttered a curse and looked over her head.

"Then I don't understand…" she took a step back from him. She looked down at the way Gabe was holding her hand to his heart.

"What if I told you that I need you, huh? What if I said I needed my friend?"

Olivia looked back at the way he was pressing her hand flat against his heart. Something disturbing replaced his smoldering look making her pull away. "You have me Gabe."

"Do I? Look can we talk somewhere?" he asked as something caught Gabe's attention and he bit down on his bottom lip.

Olivia glanced over her shoulder. Christine and Tiana back at the desk hovering over Olivia's tablet ear hustling.

"Anywhere but here," Gabe whispered.

Olivia looked back over her shoulder to see Tiana and Christine looking down at the desk as if the ink blotter calendar they were both staring at held the secrets of the world. Olivia turned back to him and nodded.

Olivia moved to follow him, and Christine walked over and plucked Olivia's glasses from the back of her collar. "I'll just take these." She smiled shyly before returning to the desk.

Olivia nodded and started off with Gabe again then thought better of it and grabbed her guitar.

***

Olivia closed her office door and leaned against it. His body heat radiated like invisible arms around her.

"Maybe we'd both feel better if you hit me hard enough to break my nose again. It's not like I don't deserve it," he said with a lopsided grin.

Olivia scoffed as she walked around him and went to her sofa. "As I recall you pushed me off the swings trying to prove to your buddies that you didn't like me, and we're not kids anymore Gabe."

Gabe took a step forward. The hope in his eyes flickered and then died as the muscle in his jaw tightened. "What's wrong with Cory?"

"He's dying Gabe. He needs a kidney transplant and we're fresh out. Now, I'll ask again. Why are you here?" her mind congested with doubts and fears as she tried to put an edge on her voice. But seeing him, knowing that he was safe made staying angry difficult.

"I wanted to apologize. You'd know that if you'd pick up your phone." He said choosing his words carefully.

"My phone was stolen, Gabe."

He squinted as he glanced around the room. He came to her. "Wait. Did you report it?"

"It's a phone Gabe." she snagged her coat from the sofa and pulled out a cell phone in a new case with blue flowers all over it. "I got a replacement the other day. New phone, new number haven't had a chance to do anything but turn it on and charge it. Not that it matters because I've—"

"Yeah, functioned on less. I get it. But that doesn't explain the nurse's station." Gabe snapped and gave her a narrowed glance.

"Excuse me, did I make love to you last night?" clapped a hand over her mouth.

"What?" he moved closer his eyes glittered with a hint of amusement and genuine shock.

Olivia quickly tried to recover. "Unless you woke up in my bed this morning, I don't owe you an explanation about anything that I've done. Scratch that. I don't owe you an explanation about anything that I ever do; and you can call off your guards. I can take care of myself, or do you think I'm headed out to kill somebody?" she said grasping at straws, because his eyes grew darker making the pearl at the apex of her thighs throb. "Rhonda doesn't even live in my neighborhood. Why was she there buying sandwiches chips and sodas? Looked like stake out food to me."

"Stop it. I never said that" he said in a sharp whisper. "And I sent my people over there to protect you," he said pacing the room "And for the record. I don't have to explain how I allocate my staff. How do I know that the person that attacked you at the hospital won't try it again or send somebody else?"

Olivia blanched at the prospect. Of course, there was a chance that whoever came after her in the hospital would try again. She rubbed her arm sending a fresh bolt of pain to her shoulder. "Thanks for the concern but, like I said. I can take care of myself. I managed all these years without you." She said tonelessly while she looked at the stack of paperwork on the desk. Olivia navigated past him being careful not to let any part of her body touch hers. "If there's nothing else then I won't keep you."

Olivia reached the door and pulled it open. Gabe's put a hand on the surface of the door and slammed it shut. "I didn't run away like some sad scared little girl!" Gabe blinked as he reached for her.

There was a knock at the door. The administrative assistant poked her head around the door. "Dr. Calderone is everything okay?" she asked as she pushed her way in and looked around until she saw Olivia.

She raked her free had through her hair. "Yes Ms. Sittler. This is Lt. Gabriel Symone we were just having a discussion. Sorry if we got too loud."

The woman nodded and before giving Gabe a pointed look as she left.

"It may not matter to you Gabe, but this is my job. You don't see me coming to where you work, and—" Olivia chuckled "Oh wait My bad. I did invade your sandbox soaked to my underwear in another man's blood."

Gabe sat down on the edge of her desk. "Stop it, Ollie. I mean it." He warned.

"No, you stop it Gabe. One thing we always had was trust. I never lied to you, never you or anyone else for that matter until—"

"Shawn." He finished for her.

"He followed me to Seattle and then to Connecticut after my grandmother died. I ditched him and got lost overseas." Olivia walked around the desk and flopped down in her chair. "I don't know how, but one day I'm in a village delivering a baby and the next, he's there telling anyone that would listen that I was a doctor not some donut dolly or ass wiper."

"Ollie," Gabe slid to the chair in front of her desk and ran a finger over her name plate.

"Shawn had a gift for twisting the truth into a lie. Halfway decent surgeon but a pathological liar none the less."

"Ollie, I didn't,"

"You didn't want to know Gabe,"

"He was in love with you."

"And I loved you with every fiber of my being. Had you asked me on that senior boat trip I would have gladly said yes to being your wife and raising our kids while we went to school,"

"Then what happened? Why didn't you come back to me?" he asked.

"In the middle of a murder investigation you want to do this?" Olivia said pushing herself up to the desk. "Fine. Why didn't you come after me Gabe? I was in Connecticut not off world."

Olivia took off the guitar and laid it on the desk. "We were fighting a lot those last few days before I left. You were so convinced that I was sleeping around because I couldn't meet you after school. Babysitting kept me in clothes, but I needed a real job to cover whatever my grandmother had pissed away at the casino. She ran into Shawn's father enough out there."

A soft knock at the door made them both jump. Olivia pulled the file from black document bin marked Outgoing. Gabe was tracing the fingerboard on the guitar.

"I remember when I made this for you," he said before looking up at her. "Olivia I—"

Another knock at the door drew her gaze to the frosted window. She could just make out the receptionist's halo of grey curls

"Dr. Calderone, there's a patient headed to the OR Car accident. Beacham wanted you in there to observe."

Olivia handed Gabe the file. "More information I could dig up. Not sure if you can still use it with me being a suspect. Maybe I can get someone else to take over for me," she said as her eyes drifted to the guitar. "It kept me safe and sane while I was away from home. Helped me lull Bimbi to sleep some nights. Take it." She said pushing the guitar closer to him.

Gabe blocked her hand. "This was my birthday gift to you. It wasn't my best work." He said with a sad smile. "I make better ones now. Cory, Christine's boy has one."

"My birthday gift to him a few months ago. Didn't realize it was your company." she said before pressing the file against his chest, "Take it. Maybe it will bring you peace like it did for Bimbi."

"What if you go back to her homeland? You can still play it for her," he offered still staring at her fingers on the strings. He tried to lace his fingers with hers.

"Bimbi's dead Gabe." Olivia said snatching away. "She died in an attack that should have killed us both."

CHAPTER TWENTY-EIGHT

Gabe stood near the entrance to the ballroom with his head down as he listened intently to the cross chatter emanating from the earpiece in his left ear.

The dining room level was decked out in soft candlelight that made the crystal drinkware and the chandeliers above cast a warm glow about the room. Round clusters of pink and white roses were perched on glass pyramids at the center of each table. The raffle area off on the left was filled with artwork, swag bags and attendants accepting tear off ticket stubs.

He opened his eyes in enough time to see Calvin walking up with a plate of appetizers.

"They got everything over there," Calvin said around a mouthful of shrimp

Gabe looked at his friend's plate and declined.

"What? I was doing recon. You didn't eat dinner either," Calvin countered before popping a crab ball in his mouth. The saucer overflowed with shrimp and prosciutto spirals and stuffed olives. Calvin extended his plate to Gabe.

"Last thing on my mind is food," Gabe declined as he looked out onto a vast dance floor below as it filled with men dressed in tuxedos and women glittering in colorful gowns.

The live jazz band was already into their second set of classic smooth jazz by the time Gabe's men secured their locations and pinged him.

"So, what if a couple of doctors from leadership ducked our calls? We would have caught up with them eventually. The minute Mark found out this shindig was going on you were dragging my ass into a shop to try on tuxedos."

"Problem?" Gabe asked with a tired smile.

"For you nah. You the only cat I know that looks like you were born to rub elbows with the elite but look just as comfortable in a night club getting his rope pulled by Big Titty Tina or her sister Big Booty Trudy with their Daddy King Ding-a-Ling proudly looking on."

"I don't even know what to say to that Calvin," Gabe said with a smile.

"You know I'm right," Calvin said before biting into a stuffed olive. He winced and swallowed. "She's here. General Roth too, and a few other big wigs are over there shaking it up."

Gabe straightened to his full height and searched the room. He took a step closer to the banister, "You saw her?"

Calvin looked out on the dance floor continuing to snack on the finger food. "No, but she's sort of required to be here along with our favorite Police Commissioner. She's getting a Sphere of Excellence award for some Humanitarians work she does. Here," Calvin dug in his pocket and extracted the program and handed it over.

Her beautiful dark eyes stared out from the program with the same compassion and warmth he'd grown up with. In all honesty, he'd forgotten about her grandmother's gambling addiction. Sure, he knew about her taking babysitting jobs and little part time jobs at the local grocery stores, but it never occurred to him that they could be lacking. More than once, he spied Maji in one of her big black vehicles while someone left packages on Olivia's doorstep.

"We won't be here long. We'll ask a question or two then get back to the precinct. As much as Beacham talked about transparency, but he lied so here we are," Gabe tucked the program in his chest pocket as he shrugged deeper into his triple black tuxedo jacket.

"You mean Olivia wasn't answering her phone," Calvin countered

"I don't know what you're…"

"Don't even go there, Gabe. You found her in that room on Biddle Street. Came back to the precinct the other day taking everybody's head off. Next time let me go get the paperwork if you two are gonna fight." Calvin cautioned.

"There won't be a next time. Beacham reassigned Olivia," He said as he scanned the room.

Gabe snatched his earpiece out and turned off the battery pack. He pointed at Calvin's ear. Calvin handed over his plate and turned off his battery pack and pulled his earphone out before he took his plate.

"Look, I came here for the case. I did. Mark's idea makes sense. But I also came here to see her." Gabe looked up at the ceiling.

Bimbi's dead. She died in an attack that should have killed us both.

Olivia dropped that bombshell and walked out of the office looking like she was picking up the burdens of the world once more.

I brought her to that. I did that.

"She still won't answer her phone, and maybe it's because she's back in rotation for surgery or maybe she's teaching or something. All I know is I'm tired of leaving voice mails and text messages that she won't answer. I'd settle for a slap in the face right now."

Calvin scrubbed his mouth with a cocktail napkin. "Girl like her probably never raises her voice let alone her hand to anybody. All she gotta do is look at you and you feel like shit."

Gabe chuckled bitterly. "And that's exactly what she did. She's got a mean right hook, though," he said massaging the bridge of his nose. "Mark asked me if I was objective."

"We both know you're not, but you wouldn't throw a case," Calvin said shifting a prosciutto roll around on the saucer.

"I'd request off before I did that." Gabe leveled his gaze on Calvin. "My word on that."

"Then what are we talking about? Sounds like she stepped back to spare you. You gonna punish her for that?" Calvin asked.

Gabe glanced down at the dance floor and his heart almost stopped. Calvin bumped into him as he looked over the railing.

Olivia was moving slowly through the crowd. Every so often, someone would draw her into a group photo. Gabe looked up at his friend.

"People almost never get a third chance. Go make that right man."

Gabe nodded once and took off down the steps. In an instant she was gone, He caught a flash of red from her gown as he waded through the throngs of people. He was about to give up and move to the perimeter when the crowd thinned out some. Olivia was standing with her back to him, but it didn't matter.

The quickening in the core of him spread through his blood like wildfire. As he took in a breath to still himself, he felt his chest shake with unshed tears. As before she was so engrossed in the people, she was talking to that she wasn't aware of her surroundings. Christine looked up at him and smiled as one of the nurses nudged another and whispered something. Gabe moved closer taking Olivia's hourglass shape and the way her red spaghetti strap crushed velvet gown put the sequined numbers he saw moving about the dance floor to shame.

***

"Ladies, I'm beat. I'm going to head back to the hospital."

Christine smiled and shook her head.

"For someone that practically got the keys to the city you sure don't seem happy about it."

Olivia shrugged softly.

"I never wanted an award. I'm just doing my job. If another person asks me to dance, I think I'll scream," Olivia said

Christine shook her head as she stared at Gabe. "Start screaming."

Olivia smiled and shook her head in confusion. "What?"

Rina Oberon pointed with her head and smiled. "Warlock green eyes right behind you."

She turned slowly to face him and took in a sharp breath. Some men were born for tuxedos. Even in jeans he was devastating, but the cut of his suit and the way his broad shoulders framed his body made her mouth go dry.

"Good evening, Olivia. Evening Ladies would you mind if I stole your boss for a dance? He asked extending his hand to Olivia.

"Maybe you can get a smile out of her last few guys asked got a hard no."

Gabe smiled at the group and watched as they turned to talk to one another. Gabe ventured a look into her eyes. The exhaustion hovered around him making the poisonous words on the tip of her tongue fade.

"If I let you break my nose again, can I call you?" he said as shades of regret dampened his voice.

An older woman dressed in a purple gown walked by and kissed Olivia on the cheek. She greeted her hoping the ache in her cheeks didn't show in her smile. Gabe slipped an arm around her waist as he took her hand and placed it on his shoulder. As her face came to rest against his neck, he almost wept. He swayed softly, and Olivia followed.

"Gabe, hurting you is the last thing I want to do." She took in a breath filled with the scent of him.

He turned his face down against her cheek. "First time you said my name on the unit my heart almost stopped. Every time since has been an answer to a prayer. Not hearing you say it hurts worse than that day in the airport," He took in a shaky breath and her heart broke.

"Gabe, don't." She tried to pull away and he held her closer.

"Ollie wait. Please hear me out. I know how things look, but I know you are not a suspect. Okay? I know it. And the last thing in the world I want to do is hurt you. But it seems like It's all I've done."

Walk away. Set him free. You did it before.

In her head she knew she needed to. The muscles in her arms locked. Even if she wanted to release him, she couldn't. When he stopped moving, she endured the tremors rippling through him.

"Olivia, I'm sorry. I hurt you—doubted you." He pressed his face to the side of her head and sighed.

"I deserve your mistrust." She admitted as tears pricked her eyes.

"What? Ollie no. Just hear me out."

Trusting Gabe with her life and her secrets as children was as easy as breathing. The secrets binding her together now were not simply hers alone. If that were the case, she would have gladly placed them at his feet and accepted the consequences. Olivia swallowed hard and faced him.

"I got accused of a lot of things when I was a kid. My parents were drug addicts with wrap sheets longer than robes. Apple couldn't have fallen too far from the tree, right? Every girl that wanted you accused me of cheating on you…. Stealing things. No matter what. You said you knew me." The painful memories threatened to choke out all reason as she basked in his warmth.

"Ollie, I do know you. None of that was in your make up," Gabe said in a harsh whisper. "You were the only one that understood what I was up against living in the shadow of my parents." He paused. "Every move I made was scrutinized. Every mistake I made everyone had a comment about. Mom couldn't live down what she was, and neither could I."

"We are strangers Gabe." Olivia said planting her feet and making him stop.

"No, we're not. I know you'd never…" Gabe insisted

"How do you know? Fifteen odd years is a long time. A lifetime really," Olivia said.

"Then why does it still hurt, hmm? "His eyes probed her entire soul. "Why after all these years does the idea of you being anywhere but, in my arms, or bed hurt like this. I got shot too and you know something? This hurts worse, a hell of a lot worse."

Olivia stepped back so quickly that Gabe stumbled into her. "It's easier being strangers."

"How in God's name is that easier, Ollie?" he asked in a harsh whisper. "So, what are we then, friends? Enemies?"

"Let go Gabe. It's easy. I showed you how years ago," she planted her hands on his chest.

Gabe released her and stepped back. He looked off into the crowd as he struggled to regain his composure.

Olivia smiled and nodded at someone she knew before she looked up at him once more. "Friends…. I can live with that," she said hating the way the words felt in her mouth, "You don't know who I am… what

I've done."

"Then tell me. Tell me about the pictures on the wall. Tell me about the scars on your back. I want to know more about Bimbi. Obviously, she means something to you. How did she die," He asked, dreading the fact that he was hurting her by bringing it up again? "Let me help you carry the weight of your grief. At least let me try."

Gabe was about to say more when he his gaze shifted to something behind her. She turned and caught a glimpse of a heavy-set man moving through the crowd. Several other men and women made a beeline for the front door.

He smoothed his hand over her shoulder pushing her hair back in the process. Olivia snapped her head in his direction as her eyes fell to the spiral cord that hung over his collar. She put the earpiece in his ear as he reached into the back of his coat and plugged in the battery pack. Immediately the cross chatter filled his ear. Olivia searched his eyes as she tried to back away.

"I'm on my way." Gabe drew her closer as he studied her.

Olivia took another step back. "Sounds like you have to go," Olivia smiled softly as she cradled his face against her palm. "Go on, it's important."

"You are important. This… us. It's important. At least let me apologize if I ever gave you any doubt."

"Just did, now go. It's ok. Go," Olivia turned to walk back to her table, and he grasped her wrist. When she turned, Gabe reached into his coat and extracted an envelope.

"You had every right to run from me in the airport. I said things; hateful hurtful things and none of them were true. I was jealous and angry and—Never thought about what it was doing to you," Gabe said as he pressed the envelope into her hand. "My parents gave me airplane tickets to come to you in Connecticut for my high school graduation. So that I could give you this." He reached into his pocket and pulled out a necklace and draped it over her head.

Olivia lifted the fine silver chain to see the clear octahedron shaped diamond in a platinum setting. She tried to take the necklace off, and he stilled her hand.

"There are only three stones like it in the world. One is on my mother's hand. The others she gave to me and my sister for protection. My plan was to give this to you when I asked you to marry me on the night you almost drowned."

"I can't accept this Gabe." She tried removing it again then stopped.

" I got scared, Ollie, " he continued as a wrinkle appeared between his eyebrows. "I was afraid I'd hurt you so much that you wouldn't want to see me." His lips trembled as he planted a kiss on her forehead and left.

CHAPTER TWENTY-NINE

"Casket sharp for a murder scene aren't we, gentlemen?" Max asked as he walked over to Gabe getting out of his truck.

"Just left a stakeout. Port Authority said you asked for me." Gabe waded through the crowd of investigators with Calvin a few steps behind him.

It wasn't an argument. Neither one of their voices rose above the music and the revelers surrounding them and yet Gabe felt raw and broken as he pulled himself up into the driver's seat. He wanted to stay. He knew on some level he needed to stay and hear her, but she stepped away and the world came crashing in.

"Max what do we know?" He asked cutting off his thoughts.

"Not much more than what I told you over the phone. I'll know more once we get the bodies downtown. Judging from the conditions and the extent of autolysis the container shipped this way. There were organ coolers in the cargo bay. Hearts, livers and what looked like corneas, but they weren't stored properly for transport. Days passed so the organs aren't viable."

"Manifests?" Gabe asked.

Max pointed to one of his assistants. The woman jogged over with the ledgers wrapped in plastic. "Seals are like I said. Jinja Harbor, Uganda. A lot of relief workers arrive at that port and travel inland."

Gabe turned and looked at Max. "Relief workers?"

"Yeah, Robert Beacham head of Shadow Bay General and a few others would spend summers over there getting aid and medical help to the civilians trapped in war torn countries. I've been on a few worked some joint missions with the military. Olivia Calderone was there."

Gabe tried to ignore Calvin's gaze as he focused on Max.

"That young lady has a brilliant future in medicine. She's being honored tonight for her work." Max gave a silent direction to several technicians moving toward the Shipping container

"We just left the awards ceremony," Calvin offered.

"I'm surprised they got her to come. Shindigs like that are her worst nightmare. She's about the work not the accolades, "Max said while putting his hand on Gabe's shoulder. "Her prints were nowhere else in the room at that shelter Gabe. She went in to save that man."

Gabe looked up at the sky and breathed in the frigid air. Max patted his arm. "Her blood on scene at the other place had all the markers of being frozen for long storage. It wasn't fresh so it had to be a plant."

Max stepped away and snagged an evidence bag before waving over another attendant.

"As for the bodies here, I can get the photos of the manifest and the autopsy results to you within a few hours. Heartbreaking really. There must have been a child aboard." Max held up an evidence bag with a blood-stained stuffed giraffe in it.

***

"G you look worse than you did before you saw her. You guys talk?" Calvin asked as he tucked his hand between his chest and the seatbelt.

Gabe, I'm sorry.

Gabe ran his thumb over the text and put his phone back in his pocket. "Should have taken her someplace quiet to talk," he mumbled.

Calvin turned to question but Gabe gestured with his head.

Alana made her way across the pavement to Mark's SUV she paused before she got in and looked off in Gabe's direction. Gabe breathed a sigh of relief as he gripped the steering wheel in his truck. Calvin took a swig of his coffee.

"So, you not gonna drive over there and check on your moms?" Calvin asked as he unbuckled the seatbelt.

Gabe turned the ignition and pulled out along one of the side streets. "She knows I'm here. If she found something she'll give it to Mark."

"Which brings me to my next question. The Commissioner, our boss. Your uncle helped your mom *break* into a prison?" Calvin quipped "How does that even work?"

"My mother isn't exactly a civilian Calvin," Gabe coasted a few feet before turning on his headlights.

"Naw she ain't Clair Huxtable either. What do you think she found in there?" he said peering through the driver's side window as Mark pulled off in another direction.

"Your guess is as good as mine, man," Gabe mumbled as he started back toward the precinct.

CHAPTER THIRTY

"Wow, your Mortality and Morbidity scorecard keeps getting hit. How many bodies is that now?" Shawn teased. "We got us a good thing going here. You set them up and I knock them down."

The air was thick with blood. Soon housekeeping would be in to clean away the last remnants of their battle to save a life.

Tiana stopped wrapping the body and walked up on him. "Now that's some ignorant shit you just said."

"Ignorant? I'll have you know I just saved more lives than she has in one night. Me. Not the golden child sitting on the floor having a temper tantrum. "He sneered

Tiana shoved the surgical instrument tray on wheels with such force that she backed him into a corner. "Call off your dog Ollie," Shawn yelled.

"Enough! Both of you. A man is dead or have you two forgotten that? If you're going to have a pissing contest, take it outside," Olivia shouted as she attempted to stand and slipped in the blood and fell on her arm. She cried out and rolled over onto her side gripping her arm.

They both rush to her side and reached for her Olivia cringed. "Don't touch me!" she screamed, as they both backed away and Christine walked in.

"What the hell is going on?" Christine yelled.

Olivia did an awkward sit up as she scrambled back against the wall leaving swatches of blood everywhere she moved. "All of you just leave me alone, please."

"I'm not leaving you Olivia. Not in here and certainly not with him," Tiana rages as she ripped her paper surgical gown away from her chest. The tattered blood streaked remains still hung about her waist like a gruesome apron.

Olivia reached for Tiana then noticed the blood on her hands and inched further into the corner. "I'm fine. I'll be out in a minute,"

Tiana's face dissolved into a mask of rage as she shoved past Shawn and Christine and left the room.

"Go after her Christine. Make sure she's okay," Olivia gestured with her head.

Christine looked back and forth between Shawn and Olivia then reached for her. "I think I better stay."

Olivia shook her head and pointed at the door. "Please check on her."

Christine looked back at Shawn nodding in agreement. "We're practically family Christine. I'll take care of her. Go on like she said."

Once she was gone, Shawn stooped down. "I am you know. Family, I mean. I've loved you as much as Gabe did, more even." He sat down beside her and rubbed his temples. "Why him?"

Olivia moved to stand, and he gripped her knee. "I'd have you. Even now if you so much as looked in my direction. On your back or your knees, I'd have you. If for no other reason than to rub it in Gabe and the good general's face. He was at the precinct with Gabe. Wonder what he told him about you?"

"Not nearly enough if we're both still alive," Olivia turned with a soft grunt and faced him. Know this, Shawn. I'd rather be Gabe's mistress than your wife any day."

"You'll come to me, and I'll make you sit and beg and—"

"Why didn't you just let me die in the village with the others? I know you tipped off the militia. No one else knew we were there." She said with a tired laugh. "Your secrets would have been safe. No one would know about your little human trafficking operation."

He dragged her to her feet and gave her a savage shake. "Believe me I would have, but they wanted the merchandise you stole from me." He hissed. Spittle rained on her cheek with every word he spoke.

Olivia let her head roll back on her shoulders as she took a slow breath and faced him. "You lied to them. Told them they would find work. Women and children." She bit back a sob. "Some were no more than three or five years old. Bimbi's age."

"They were starving. I gave them a purpose." He narrowed his eyes suspiciously. "You know where they are don't you?" He gave her another savage shake sending her hair into a storm around her face.

Olivia moaned as the world greyed away. She thumped her head on the wall behind her to wake herself up. "If I didn't tell Adewale when he put a gun to my head, why would I tell you?"

Shawn chuckled then reared back to slap her. Olivia took advantage of his stance and drove the heel of her hand into his nose. He fell on the floor knocking the instrument tray over in the process. Christine rushed back in, and she moved to help him up.

"Don't worry about him Chrissy. All he knows how to do is take care of himself."

Olivia blinked away the memory and pushed herself up to her computer. The soft crinkle of the envelope made her reach for the breast pocket of her scrub top and stop as she caught a glimpse of her red gown tied in a clear trash bag on the floor near her feet. Even if she could take the gown to the cleaners, Olivia knew she'd never wear it again. Too much had happened in that dress for her to ever feel like wearing it again.

Olivia read through the resignation letter once more and sent it to the printer. She turned her face into her shoulder and rocked back and forth. The movement from the general vicinity of the hallway made her fill up as she pushed the tears threating to run down her cheeks up into her hairline.

"Christine, you go on ahead. I won't be here too much longer. You go on ahead I'll lock—." Olivia looked up and froze.

CHAPTER THIRTY-ONE

Gabe's face was half hidden in the shadows, but his gaze cut through the darkness. He leaned in the door as if he'd been there forever. Gone was the tuxedo and in its place, he wore a pair of jeans and a light grey long sleeve shirt. His dark skull cap matched his coat. Olivia slipped her hair behind her ears and searched the desk for something, anything that would offer the safety his presence in the doorway denied her.

She swallowed hard as she unfolded herself from her chair and stood. "Sorry I didn't hear the phone. They've been announcing people these last few weeks and…"

Gabe moved from the door into the lamp light. "So, it's like that now? I need to be announced," he replied sharply.

"Of course not!" she shouted just above a whisper. Olivia looked in his direction wiped at her mouth. "What I meant was." She swallowed hard and prayed she looked steadier than she felt. "Your mom. Is she okay?" Oliva asked before biting down on her lip and looking away.

"She's fine," he said before closing the door and leaning on it. He shot her a penetrating look as she rose.

Olivia nodded as she dropped the blanket in her chair and rounded the desk. "Then what can I do for you detective? There's no need to finish our conversation. I accepted your apology, but I have no intentions of accepting that necklace. I sent it and your jacket by courier. I sent some contact info on some clinics and Tissue Matching facilities. I also put in names of Department Chairs that can answer any other questions you have."

"You know my name Ollie. Use it" his voice was oddly gentle but barely containing his fury.

"Then what do you want, Gabe? Any of the names I gave you can answer your questions. There's nothing holding you to me." She said as her mood veered sharply to anger.

"Love holds me to you Ollie and maybe that doesn't mean a whole hell of a lot to you, but it means the world to me." He paced the room. "You know it's funny. I went into the military to distract myself. Travelled the world. Went to some of the places we dreamed about backpacking through trying to exorcise myself. Even after I got shot, I kept wondering what's it going to take to make me stop loving you?"

She wiped at her top lip with the heel of her hand. "You got the paperwork. I forgot about a call I put into Organ Procurement the head of the department was already gathering information and I put in a call to some friends and…"

"Did you hear anything I just said? Do I get a say this time or were you just going to roll out?" He said in a low tormented voice, as he dug in his back pocket and dropped the resignation letter on her desk.

Every muscle in her body drained of energy. In her mind she knew she needed to walk back around her desk to put some distance between them, but it hurt. Everything hurt and standing there in front of him, basking in his anger was still far warmer than the cold world that resided behind her desk. Olivia squared her shoulders and raked her hand through her hair.

"I thought it might be best." She mumbled as the guilt spread in her gut.

"You thought." The words seemed to stick in his throat as he moved closer.

"And yes, I can think and make decisions on my own. Who knows?

Maybe you think I slept around to get the job,"

"Don't put words in my mouth, Ollie," He warned.

"Then don't put words in mine," She whispered "Glad to see you still think so highly of me. Back in high school the talk was that I was the town whore. Hell, maybe I was,"

She was horrified by the poison filled words flowing from her mouth. She moved around him to the door, and she opened it.

"That is not true! You didn't lose your virginity you gave it to me, and I gave you mine. You told me that the mere thought of giving yourself to anybody else actually hurt," the anguish in his voice made her throat ache.

"How good of you to remember and take me at my word. Now is a different story. I'm a stranger to you. Maybe I've gone through the doctors in leadership or one or all of my residents. After all I did lie to your cousin's captors. I told them he was my fiancée to get him, Beacham and others out of harm's way. Did Beacham tell you that? Did Shawn? Of course, not. They always made sure they came up smelling like a rose."

"No, you didn't." he said simply "You'd never sell yourself so cheaply."

"How can, you be sure? It's been a while. I've changed. Maybe I did let Beacham, or the other docs run train on me. Maybe I killed that man at the shelter. Twenty-five grand is a lot of money,"

Gabe closed the space between them so quickly that she fell back against her door.

"Don't you ever say that again. Do you hear me? Don't," he warned.

She was too surprised to do more than nod.

Gabe backed away from her visibly shaken. "You'd never welcome a man like that to your body so stop saying that"

"Why? Maybe I did. If not here, then maybe in some foreign country."

The image of the old man rutting against her flooded her mind and made her gag, but she refused to stop. For every vile thing she imagined Gabe was thinking and for the images that made her wake up at night screaming or crying in her shower under scalding hot water she was going to say it even if it killed her.

She took in another breath. She opened the door wider, and he reached past her and slammed it shut. Olivia pressed her face against the surface of the door. He was behind her towering over her. Without even looking at him she knew he was shaking. His breathing was ragged.

Olivia took in a breath that made her insides ache and she turned to face him. "Why Gabe, it might be true. Maybe it is and I've been lying to you all along. Maybe… maybe I slept with your cousin Shawn."

"Stop it Ollie," He warned.

"Or what Gabe? Shawn was overseas with us. He wasn't doing any relief work mind you. He couldn't stand the thought of the sick and hungry getting too close to him. No, all he wanted to do was run through the nurses or village girls and gamble. No? Not Shawn then maybe one of the other doctors, hell all of them,"

"I know you didn't. I would have smelled him on you," he said finally

"Which one? You know what? It doesn't even matter."

"You have this sweet smell when you're wet. Couldn't place it at first. On the drive over, it came to me. Same scent you had the first time we made love. Same scent you had that first night in here. Same scent you have now."

She was hearing him and then she wasn't. Did he believe her? He was right. God help him Gabe was spot on and as much as she was throbbing and the wetness between her legs began to seep down her thighs, she refused to believe what he was saying. He was angry. He was trying to get her back. It was any of those things; all of those things but what her heart longed to hear. The words cut a path through her mind tossing her resolve back and forth to such an extent that had he not been standing there she probably would have fallen to her knees. Instead, she tried to walk past him, and he blocked her path.

"I don't want to fight with you Gabe.

"Evidently you do," he taunted.

She looked down and away from him.

"Don't look at the floor Ollie look at me."

She heard his quick intake of breath and cringed knowing every word she spoke was a lie to make him hate her. Hate was easier. If he was angry then maybe she could do it again. Leaving saved their lives before and after arguing with Shawn the choice was so clear.

"It was a mistake to come back here," Olivia kept her head down as she struggled to keep her composure.

"Answer me. Why'd you come back here?" he asked.

Olivia shrugged and he closed the distance.

"Do not. Shrug your shoulders at me. Talk." He said hoarsely as his green gaze burned down on her.

"In all honesty Gabe, I figured you left this place long ago. I came back here because it was the last place, I was every happy. What a beautiful mistake." Olivia inched around her desk and shoveled her paperwork into a folder. "We can't be friends, okay? We—" the shock of the words lodge in her throat.

"Same reason I came home." Gabe let his hands fall to his sides.

The astonishment on his face was obviously genuine making her regret every word she spoke.

"Oh, I travelled the world trying to get you out of my system," he said backing away from her. "Then I realized why should I? The happiest times of my life were here with you. So, I came home and because maybe if I did—"

Olivia tried to back away and he stepped forward closing the distance between them. He ran his thumb down the back of her neck and she arched her back as a moan escaped from her.

"You could be anywhere in this world," He whispered in her ear before he dragged his open mouth across the area just below her ear. "Answer me, why did you come home?"

She could feel the tear as it spilled from the corner of her right eye. Gabe kissed it away then he stood back far enough to look at her full on. She slipped a hand around his neck and pulled him down against her hungry mouth. He crushed her to his chest as he drank her in. Her breasts mashed against the hard wall of him as her arms slipped around his neck. He grabbed the lapels of her lab coat and snatched it from her shoulders before he hoisted her up against the wall behind her door.

Olivia pushed his jacket from his shoulders before she smoothed her hands over his neck and up under the black skull cap, he was wearing and removed it. He smoothed a hand up her thighs pushing the fabric of her skirt and slip higher. He hooked a finger into her panties and bathed his knuckle in her juices. She gasped as he snatched the scrap of lace aside.

Her fingers worked feverishly at his belt buckle and clawed at the front of his briefs. He took a step forward positioning her over his hips and he drove himself deeply into her heat. She gasped against his mouth as he groaned.

Over and over, he drove himself into her as he covered her mouth with kisses that he smeared across her cheek and down over her throat. Over and over his hips ground into her in a circular upward thrusting motion that pushed her thighs high on his hips. With each hard thrust, she answered him with a sharp push of her own.

Gabe hooked his arms around her thighs as he backed away from the wall. He fell against the door briefly before he lifted her higher and walked into the middle of her office and lowered her down against his thrusts. The friction, the pressure of her sweet body meeting his thrust pushed him deeper and deeper inside making her sob against his mouth. The sound of her sopping wet sex punctuated the whimpers and moans of pleasure that rippled through them.

Olivia gripped his biceps as he drew his arms up higher making her spread her legs even wider. Gabe dragged his open mouth across her face and down to her throat as he licked and sucked at the soft hollow space between her collar bones. Olivia slipped a hand behind his neck as she pulled his face to hers.

Gabe turned his face up to hers and she swept her tongue against his lips and pushed his teeth apart as she pushed her way inside. He answered the thrust of her tongue with one of his own as their mouths mimicked the rest of their hot sticky union.

Olivia leaned back from Gabe taking his face in her hands. "I came home to find you."

The last of her words were lost in his mouth as he lifted her higher and began to slam her harder against his thrusts. He picked up the pace moving faster, harder as he erased all distance between them. She ground her hips down against him and then she cried out against his mouth as every nerve in her body converged in a thunderclap of passion that made her cry out against his open mouth. He dragged his mouth across her cheek as he moaned in her ear. Olivia the sweet walls of her sex contracted against him pushing and pulling until at last he erupted within her. Gabe held her back from his chest.

"Look at me Ollie. Look at me."

She looked deep into his eyes as her breaths came in short hot gusts. His eyes searched her the bewitching green she'd grown to love glittered and became darker. His eyes widened as the wave of her orgasm drew and even harder one from him. She moved to lower her legs and Gabe wrapped them around his waist. He took her face in his hands and lined her jaw with kisses before he gave her mouth one long slow languid kiss.

Rather than crush her between his chest and the wall, Gabe gently cradled her against his chest as he walked over to the sofa. The further he walked the more his pants slipped down to his knees. He gripped her hip to maintain his connection deep within her as he sat down. He cradled her head against his shoulder, pressing his ear to her mouth as he listened to her trying to quiet her breathing. She tried to sit up and he wrapped his arms around her.

"Stay with me."

She nodded and breathed a sea of kisses down the side of his neck. After a while, he smoothed her hair back from her face then leaned back far enough to see her face. Her hair fell forward shielding their faces and their reconnection from the world.

"Are you okay, Ollie? Did I hurt you?" He mouthed the words into her fevered skin.

She brushed her nose against his then she pressed her face into his neck. "I was afraid you wouldn't want me," she said in a watery whisper.

Gabe leaned her back from his shoulder. "Hey, look at me. I never stopped wanting you, Ollie. "Never." He kissed her then crushed her to his chest once more.

"Are you okay? Did I hurt you Gabe?"

"Hurt me? Only in ways I liked a lot," He chuckled

"Gabe, what if I'm too heavy…" Olivia moved to get up and he slid his hand down to her backside

Gabe groaned.   "Hardly, but if you keep moving like that—" his eyes widened. Gabe was momentarily speechless as Olivia ground her hips in a circular motion.

"Apologies in advance then," She whispered as she nipped at the warm space between his neck and his shoulder.

Gabe moaned as he eased Olivia to the sofa and stretched out on top of her. He rocked his hips forward as he pulled one of her legs higher against his ribcage. She arched her back and matched his rhythm when his phone rang. He paused long enough to look in the direction of his phone. When he faced her, she cupped his face in her hands. He ground his hips into her again. His cell phone rang again, and she looked in the direction of the phone.

"What if it's important?" she asked

"You are important." Gabe growled as he drove himself deeper.

Olivia brought his mouth to hers as he delivered a series of hard thrusts that made her body thump hard against his. His phone rang again, and Olivia stilled him with a kiss, "It's ok Gabe. Answer it."

Gabe flattened himself against her. Olivia wrapped her arms and legs around him briefly. "Go on Gabe."

Gabe muttered a curse as he got up and fixed his jeans.

Olivia sat up on the sofa and watched as he tucked the phone between his ear while he worked the buckle on his belt. The muscles on his broad shoulders rippled beneath his shirt making her long to rest her face against him. He continued to give one-word answers and then his head shot up.

"Why can't night's handle it? Fine. What's the address? No. I'll meet you there." He hung up and returned to her.

Olivia pushed herself to her feet. "Is there anything I can do?" She asked before running a hand through her hair.

Gabe sat down and kissed her. "You've done enough. We're checking the leads you gave us tomorrow morning. My night crew found something."

She nodded as she hooked two fingers in the collar of his jacket. "Put this on Gabe. I don't want you to get sick."

He took the jacket, shook it out and wrapped it around her. "Exactly why you should be wearing it. Where's your purse and briefcase?'

She looked over behind her desk.

"Okay grab it and let's go," he quipped as he tugged on her hand.

"Gabe your phone call. You said…,"

"I know what I said but it's late. This building is deserted and I'm not leaving you here by yourself."

"I can take a cab."

"What kind of man do you think I am" Gabe asked.

"A busy one," she said pushing at his arm. Gabe slipped it around her waist. Then he leaned over and looked at her arm and frowned.

"Gabe I'm fine," she insisted trying to pull away.

"That bruise is anything but fine. Get your stuff, the very least I can do is get you home safe."

"But Gabe…"

Gabe moved closer and slipped a lock of her hair behind her ear. "Hey, let me take care of you. I've been wanting to for a long time."

Olivia shook her head as she grabbed her purse and headed for the door.

CHAPTER THIRTY-TWO

Gabe sat down at his desk hard. He thought about how she looked as she leaned in her doorway.

The world had changed.

Olivia was home and back in his arms and nothing else mattered. She was a living breathing answer to a prayer and the longer he stood there looking down at her, the more he wanted to walk in and forget the case and the world for a while.

"You racking up overtime, G?" Calvin asked.

Gabe locked yes with his friend.

"You're not wearing the clothes you had on yesterday, but that don't mean shit. You keep a change of clothes here."

"Got a call from night shift about a lead. Turned out to be a dead end. Apparently, my cousin moonlights over at one of the Transplantation Centers. He tripped the alarm while screwing one of the secretaries," Gabe said as he swiveled in his chair to finish a report.

"You talk to Olivia?" Calvin inquired.

Gabe cleared his throat and started shuffling papers on his desk. Calvin pulled out his chair and sat down.

"Subject change?" Calvin offered as he tapped the button to turn on one of his computer monitors.

Gabe licked his lips and instantly regretted it. There was a hint of her cherry flavored lip balm still clinging to his bottom lip. The memory her legs wrapped around his waist and her sweet cream drying on his thighs made him smile. He almost regretted taking a shower that morning, because it felt like he was washing away their night together.

Gabe glanced over at Calvin who grinned and wriggled his eyebrows.

"We finally got the 911 tapes. From the first night," Gabe said returning to the safety of his monitor.

Calvin grabbed the sandwich bag containing the last of his peanut butter cookie. "Well, at least your coloring is better, and you don't look like you're going to kill the next person that says Good morning to you."

"I wasn't that bad," Gabe countered.

Calvin took a bite then chased it with some coffee; all while staring at Gabe. "From the look of you, she must have given your raggedy ass a come to Jesus moment."

Gabe put his head down and smiled. Calvin raised an eyebrow in defiance as he popped another piece of the cookie in his mouth. "Alright. Now what I want to know is what Christine's favorite flower is. You're an inside man now. Get me some deets. You know, phone number, favorite flower, or snacks. On second thought forget the food. She is a pound cake and a growing boy like me loves to eat."

"What about Marcy?" Gabe reminded as he moved his mouse to the print icon and glanced at the printer sitting in the space between both of their desks.

Calvin put his hand on his chest in mock indignation, "Are you trying to keep me from my Amazonia?"

"Says the man that wants my mom to screen his girlfriends," Gabe said with a grin.

Calvin flipped Gabe the bird and Gabe laughed out loud. "Subject change for real. Where's this 911 tape?" Calvin said as he shook the empty plastic bag and frowned.

Gabe grinned as he cued up the tape on his desktop computer.

"911 what's your emergency?" a nasally female dispatcher.

"Yeah, I'm out here near the picnic area near The Barrens? There's this white male in his mid-thirties, bleeding from the posterior right lower quadrant."

Gabe rocked back in his chair as Calvin walked over to the coffeemaker and poured two cups. He came back and handed Gabe one. "Play that part again, G."

Gabe clicked the rewind arrow on his screen.

"Well, shit. That's about the most helpful 911 call I've ever heard. I mean this guy was nice enough to tell us who to look for and what the nature of the injury is." Calvin took a swig from his green travel mug.

Gabe nodded as he took a sip of the coffee and winced. He sat his cup aside and replayed the call again. "Almost sounds military or medical."

"Well, the dead guy was a doctor. He don't sound like anybody over at the hospital. Cheap voice box disguise or not. Think Olivia might know this guy?" Calvin rocked back in his chair clutching the travel mug in both hands.

Gabe listened to the call again. "She doesn't know every doctor in Shadow Bay Maryland Calvin." His voice was loaded with ridicule.

"Judging from the way they gave her the red-carpet treatment at that shindig, she knows enough of them." He quipped before taking a long sip from his mug. "She looked like royalty walking through there. Never seen two people more suited to each other."

"I'll ask her, but you're asking about Christine yourself. Want to head over there now?" Gabe asked as he locked his computer and reached for his coat.

"Nah, let's bang on a few doors from the good doctor's list and you can buy me breakfast or lunch or both for the next day or so."

"For what, pray tell?" Gabe patted his pockets then reached in the drawer for the black key fob. His keys jangled as he tossed them in the air and caught them.

"Getting you back together with your soulmate." Calvin grinned, "And I fully expect all the rights and privileges of a best man, godparent and all around Funcle."

Gabe chuckled as he looked over at his wall calendar. "I got lunch, but all of that is put on hold. We got Gun Safety Classes this morning, and what is a Funcle?"

"The Fun Uncle." Calvin rolled his eyes and looked at the ceiling. "Ah shit. They couldn't have planned this a little better. Amazonia needs my special sauce."

"Not sure that's what the word means," Gabe thumped Calvin on the shoulder as he walked by. "Gun Safety Class is every third Wednesday and it's been that way for the last five years. Your hot and heavy with Amazonia will have to wait."

Calvin groaned as he fell in step behind him "Easy for you to say. You found your Angel of Mercy. All I want is her side kick paying attention to my never minds."

Gabe thundered down the steps then looked back at Calvin sulking as he made his way down to the second landing.

"Special Sauce Calvin? Really?" Gabe chuckled.

"Shut up man!" Calvin laughed.

CHAPTER THIRTY-THREE

Gabe sat back against the wall watching Calvin pace the short distance from the door to the gurney. It hurt to breathe deep but watching his partner of nearly ten years agonizing over the whole incident bothered him.

Calvin came from a large family teeming with cousins, but no siblings. Everyone at the academy had partnered up. Plenty of their classmate's male and female raised an eyebrow and silently asked to couple up with Gabe. Rather than answer, he sat on the bleachers in the gymnasium above them all watching the whole things transpire like some weird matchmaker session.

Everyone passed over the heavy-set class clown with an easy smile and fondness for vending pork rinds and coffee. When Calvin was the last on the floor Gabe wordlessly made his way down the bleachers and thumped him on the shoulder.

"Come on, Calvin. We have work to do." He called over his shoulder before walking out of the gymnasium.

Gabe smiled at the memory and settled back against the wall as the heavy stinging sensation in his chest gained weight making it hard to sit up straight and even harder to lie down.

He followed Calvin's line of vision to the bulletproof vest thrown in the corner with the chest sunken in. The powder burns and the jagged tears through the fabric and the blood marring the chewed-up fabric were enough to turn his stomach.

After the EMTs helped him out of the vest Gabe realized that pieces of shrapnel had sliced the side of his neck enough to make it bleed like a knife wound. He glanced at the curtains in the emergency room cubicle they stashed him in. "Cal I'm fine. Stop looking like my vest failed."

"Where are they? They said they'd be back." Calvin shot him a look before he continued to pace on the other side of the room.

Gabe slouched down against the wall as he pulled a knee to his chest.

"And they'll come back. Right now, they're dealing with the people that really need help,"

"And you don't?" Calvin spat as his gaze drifted to Gabe's chest. He started pacing once more. "You got shot for fuck's sake!"

"Calvin, they just told you I got a good thump to the chest. It will make for an ugly bruise in the morning. Betadine or a styptic pencil can take care of anything else so just calm down,"

"Calm down?! Calm down!? You almost clocked on me mother fucker! I would have had to go see Ms. Alana and tell her I failed to keep you safe. Your Moms man!" Calvin continued to pace. "She'd kill me on the spot, and I wouldn't blame her."

Gabe inched forward on the gurney with a grunt and let his long legs dangle over the side as he attempted to stand, "Mom would never blame you. I'm just glad I don't have to deliver that news to your mom or Marcy."

Calvin turned and looked at him as if he were insane. "Where the fuck are you going?" He walked over and put his meaty palm on Gabe's shoulder. "Get your ass back on that stretcher and wait for the nurse."

Gabe eased back down on the gurney and chuckled and instantly regretted it as the pain spread in his chest making it hard to sit up straight.

Calvin walked over to the curtain and looked out into the hallway. He muttered a curse before turning around "And why are you talking about Marcy at a time like this? She doesn't want no parts of me good job or not. She thinks I'm some adrenaline freak hanging out with your crazy ass."

"I wasn't the one threatening the EMTs into a hat dance because you felt they weren't moving fast enough." Gabe clutched at his chest as he tried to stifle a giggle.

He looked up at Calvin to see him roll his eyes then put his head down and laugh. "I was emotional."

"Yes... very," Gabe teased.

Christine pushed her way into the room holding an armful of supplies. Gabe smiled and tried to sit up straight.

"Hey Christine. How's my Lady? What did she eat today?" he asked.

Christine came in and threw the supplies on the gurney muttering a curse under her breath. She looked over at Calvin then back at Gabe before she folded her arms.

"You're guess is as good as mine," Christine laughed to cover the annoyance in her voice, "She may be on Administrative again and out the door if she can't keep her hands to herself. She almost broke Shawn's nose; I mean Dr. Prescott's nose."

"What punch?" Gabe asked shooting a look at Calvin.

Christine chuckled bitterly as she ripped open some packages of gauze, "Are they cousins or something?" She asked, directing the question at Calvin.

Gabe sat forward, and Calvin started crossing the room.

"He's, my cousin. What did he do?" Gabe squinted at the woman as he dropped one long leg off the gurney.

"He never said. After I cleaned him up, he just left. Sold wolf tickets saying she had no idea who she was messing with. He was no worse for the wear this morning during rounds. Olivia was late and she's never late. Beacham even noticed. She's never late."

Gabe squirmed on the at the prosect of causing Olivia any problems on her job. Calvin gave him a knowing look that he ignored.

"Don't say anything to her about this. Is there another doctor around to take a quick look so that I can go?" Gabe moved to the edge of the gurney. Both Calvin and Christine reached for him.

"She's trauma so Olivia got the alerts before any of us did. She's probably on her way across campus as we speak. It was a dumb move." Christine threw one of the bandages back on the tray and put a hand on a hip. "She could have broken her hand or really hurt him."

Gabe let his gaze slip to Calvin then he looked back at Christine. "Knowing my cousin, he deserved it."

"That man and his team have the best organ transplant stats in the area. Other than Olivia, Shawn— Dr. Prescott is the only surgeon that can perform the surgery that could save my son's life. It was selfish. They both were," Christine rubbed her eyes.

Calvin shifted against the wall and Christine glanced over her shoulder.

"Excuse me gentlemen that was out of line," Christine mumbled as she picked through the gauze.

"I'm sorry to hear about Cory. His illness is bound to be taking a toll. I'm sorry to be a bother. We'll be on our way," Gabe said with a grunt as he attempted to stand once more.

Calvin reached for him as Christine stepped into his path. "And Olivia would never forgive me if I let you leave before you could be checked out."

Calvin cleared his throat. "She's right, man."

Gabe shifted his gaze to Calvin and smiled. "Christine, this is my partner, Calvin Ford. Maybe he should be checked out too. I landed on him. I think he cut his hand on some debris."

Calvin's eyes widened as he shook his head no. Christine turned and walked over to Calvin who smoothed a hand over his beard then tried to pose against the wall as if he were bored.

"This fall, did it knock any sense into either one of you?" Christine asked.

Calvin opened his mouth to speak when the curtain fluttered, and Olivia came through the door with a nurse trying desperately to fasten the yellow gown ties at her back.

Gabe stood up and Olivia flew into his arms. He grunted as he lifted her from the floor and sat down on the edge of the bed. He frowned at the tremors the racked her body. He pressed a kiss into her shoulder and pushed his face down against her ear

"Hey Ollie…. Babe don't. Shhh. It's okay. I'm fine. Ollie, I'm fine."

He heard her gasp and snatch back from him. He winced at his blood smeared across her cheek. She zeroed in on a cut in his neck before leaning back to further assess his injuries.

"Doesn't look serious though. You won't need stitches," She tried to turn from the gurney to the table.

Gabe tightened his arm around her forcing her to face him. "Ollie, look at me. Babe, look at me, please?"

But she wasn't looking at him. The doctor in her was forcing the woman he made love to further away. She turned her head in the direction of the nurse that tied her gown.

"Lisa call Marty in Radiology. I want X-Rays. If he was hit hard enough, Gabe could have some deep contusions to his heart or fractured ribs. Christine help me." She called over her shoulder.

Christine moved closer and Gabe pointed at the door. Calvin nodded as he hustled Christine and the other nurse back through the curtain. Gabe crushed Olivia to his bare chest trapping her arms down at her sides. She struggled against him briefly before she went limp and started to cry.

"Ollie stop. Babe stop, please? I'm okay. Let me hold you. Just let me sit here and hold you alright?" he asked while breathing in the fragrance of her shampoo.

"Stop saying that, Gabe. This is not okay." She tried to shake her head no and he cradled her head to his shoulder.

Gabe leaned back far enough to press his forehead to hers. "Can I hold you?" he asked.

She wriggled in his arms until he loosened his grip enough for her to look up at him. "How is holding me making you feel better?" She asked as a tear leaked from the corner of her right eye.

His throat started closing over his own unshed tears. He chased one of her tears down her cheek with a kiss. "I don't know it just does. You're going to have to stop all this crying or you're going to make me cry and it won't be all pretty like you. It'll be ugly snot and all," he said with a sly smile as he looked down into her face. "I might even wipe my nose on your lab coat. Ultra-sexy I know."

She burst into a mixture of tears and laughter as she buried her face in his neck. Gabe chuckled as he felt her dig her head in under his chin. He leaned back a little more on the gurney and she slid further between his thighs. He bit on his bottom lip and groaned as an unholy stab of pleasure heated his groin.

"Unless you think I need a physical exam?" He brushed his nose against her before giving her bottom a pinch.

She laughed again, but it quickly turned into a storm of silent tears. "I just found you Gabe…. Please…. I can't. I can't lose you."

"I'm right here, Baby. I'm not going anywhere," He whispered. "You're home and I'm right here."

She pulled away and he plucked the pen from her hair and watched it spill around her shoulders. He looked down into her upturned face and frowned. He reached past her and snagged a piece of gauze from the table and started wiping at the blood on her cheek.

"Uh oh made a clean spot," he murmured as he kissed her cheek.

Olivia dropped her head and stepped further back looking at the bruise on his chest, but Her eyes widened as she ran her fingers over one of the passages close to the bruise, "Langston Hughes was always one of my favorites."

Rather than answer right away he pulled her closer and hid his face in her hair as he murmured one of the verses in her ear. She leaned back far enough to look at him. The remnant of a tear track shimmered under the lights overhead. He erased it with his thumb as he traced her bottom lip. He blinked slowly as if drugged before he leaned in and nipped at her bottom lip making her kiss him back.

"Yeah, well at the moment, we're both on the injured list so I guess we'll hold each other together for a while." She murmured into the warm space between his neck and shoulder.

"Sounds like a plan, my Lady," Gabe smiled as his gaze locked on the hellfire eyes watching from across the room. Alana moved the curtain aside just enough so that she could lean on the door frame. She nodded as if answering a question. Her gaze drifted to Olivia and a strange smile tipped his mother's lips. She gave him one last pointed look and then she was gone.

Olivia pulled back from him and searched her pockets for her phone. "We have to call Ms. Alana. She'd want to know."

Gabe took her phone and sat it on the tray and hugged her tighter. "She already knows I'm in good hands."

CHAPTER THIRTY-FOUR

"Well for a man that almost bought it yesterday you're positively glowing," Mark said as he dragged Gabe into a bear hug.

Gabe winced as his chest bumped his uncle's shoulder.

"I'm fine Uncle Mark."

Mark held onto him for a moment longer before he sat on the edge of his desk. Gabe tried not to notice the relief on the older man's face as he flopped down in one of the chairs. From where he sat, Gabe could see Calvin in the middle of an animated phone call.

"Still can't figure out how Alana knew. Your Dad was the same way about her like some kind of symphonic pain."

Gabe squirmed a little in his chair and looked back out the window at Calvin writing in his usual awkward overhand way as if he were trying to hug the desk and write at the same time.

"How is my mom this morning?" Gabe said as a pang of fear stole into his gut.

Mark moved to his chair and sat down. "Holding her own. You wanna tell me what really went on out there before you ruined your shirt?"

Gabe draped a leg over the arm of the chair and tugged his blue long-sleeved tee shirt sleeve up around his elbows. "Same story I told the brass. It was just another place to check out on that list Ollie gave us."

Mark scribbled a signature on a document and tossed it on a growing pile. "Anything new?"

"The manager said they had a patient in mumbling about a harvest. She got him out of there before the people in the lobby got too suspicious."

"Incisions sites?" Mark asked before meeting Gabe's gaze.

"Lower right side. I was writing down some names and next thing you know, all hell broke loose, and my shirt got ruined," Gabe glanced out at Calvin on the telephone.

"So, what's your plan? Are you heading back over there to finish?" Mark asked still shuffling papers around on his desk.

"Fisher and Graham already divided up the list. I was going to stop by and check on my mom then hit a few more blood banks why?" Gabe asked as he thought about what to bring Olivia for lunch if he got the chance.

Mark glanced up at him then back down at the table. He signed off on one set of paperwork before tossing it on the pile that was growing on the edge of his desk.

"You know Uncle Mark; I know you like hanging around here, but it might be easier to handle running the city from Olympus." Gabe offered. "If it will make you feel better, I'll move a box in."

Mark threw his pen on the desk and sat back in his chair, "Gabe, she went back inside."

Gabe removed his leg from the arm of the chair and sat up. "What?"

"She thinks she missed something during the first visit. Kept rambling on about Maji and September. Have you seen Maji?"

Gabe pushed himself to his feet with a grunt. "No, her receptionist keeps giving me the runaround. What could my mother have possibly missed? Hell, what did she find Mark?"

"Maji Speaks and September Dade were business partners for years. Dade went in on a RICO charge and was effectively flushed away for life. She was also an organ transplant recipient. Records were sealed but, you know how your mother and Nicolas Levine roll. It was easy enough to verify, plus a list of others that included Egan St Clair. Some of the inmates have been selling their organs to take care of their family on the outside."

"Who's performing the surgeries?" Gabe scrubbed his face with his hands then looked through the window at Calvin.

"That's what she went back in there to find out. She thinks Dade lied to her," Mark leaned forward and gripped Gabe's shoulder. "She's not there to stay."

Gabe brushed his uncle's hand away. "You could have tried talking her out of it or calling the warden to make him refuse her."

"You don't think I tried?" Mark hands placed belligerently on his hips.

"So, she takes one look at me at the hospital and just decided to go take part in Family Day at CIBEX Detention Center?" Gabe muttered a curse and sat back. "She give you a timetable on when she was coming back?"

Mark looked down at the desk. "True north Gabe. In the middle of a shitstorm, her compass is true north."

Gabe resisted the urge to laugh. "None of this is legal. Even if she finds something this could easily be misconstrued as fruit from the poisonous tree."

"The Dade woman refused council and went on record corroborating everything your mother ran down a few hours ago. Deathbed declarations are still admissible, G," Mark said returning to his pile of paperwork.

"If the Dade woman is dead then why is my mother still in there?" He barked.

"Gabe she's perfectly safe." Mark said slowly before facing Gabe once more.

"She give you a timetable on when you can go back to pick her up or did, she close that door on you too?" he snapped.

Mark pivoted in the chair and looked out the window facing the Fire Department Business Building across the street. "She would have done it with or without me G. Just as she did things without your father's blessing. Saved your life…. mine… the life of my family. She did it all without anyone's permission."

Gabe left his place at the door "I brought her to this," Gabe said as he put his head down. "If she gets hurt or dies in there. It's on me."

"You can't go to the prison and try to extract her, Gabe." Mark warned.

"Of course not. Even if I did get her to come to the phone room, she'd just tell me to leave," Gabe rubbed his mouth with the back of his hand.

"G, son, I know it feels like…" Mark started.

"No Uncle Mark it is exactly like that. I mean what are the odds. The two most important women in my life and neither one of them listens to me."

Gabe looked over to see Mark grinning at him.

"What?" he asked trying to sound annoyed.

"Alana pulled back the curtain enough for me to see you two. Looks like you two made up. You always did back then, even when you were an ass which was most of the time. Olivia could handle you."

"Hey, she can be pretty annoying too." He stifled a laugh as he looked away.

Calvin knocked on the door before walking in. He was mumbling to himself as he approached the two chairs in front of the desk. "While you two in here bonding I got a call from Max. Found DNA on one of the organ coolers belonging to Shawn Prescott. They also typed the blood on that stuffed giraffe."

Gabe turned to face his partner. "And?"

"It's Olivia's. No anti-coagulant." Calvin looked up from his notes.

CHAPTER THIRTY-FIVE

Painting the world black was for amateurs. Smearing the globe in body glitter or sex candy red, made the galaxy bump. The long line of patrons snaking around Maji's club twisted and writhed in time with the wicked bass emanating from the two-story black brick building. Situated at the end of the cul de sac known as Hump City to the locals and Baltimore Street to the tourists Maji's had more visitors than all the museums in Washington combined. Signature drinks like the Curse Nasty and Candy Licker were blamed for affairs and babies in equal measure.

The bar ran along both sides of the wall with patrons crowding in placing their orders. Scantily clad wait staff waded through men whooping and hollering at one of the many dancers strategically placed on small stages and the poles located on the second level.

"Calvin keep up!" Gabe yelled as he eased passed one man deep in conversation with one of the dancers.

Calvin smiled and nodded as he stuck his middle finger in the air. Gabe returned the gesture as he was swept into a crowd and carried to the safety of a smaller bar kiosks in the middle of the dancefloor. Gabe recognized the bartender as an undercover cop from Vice. The leggy blonde turned around and smiled and stuck out her hand. Gabe kissed the back of her hand as she swayed with the music. He joined in and spun her around once before leaning in.

"Hey Gabe, what are you doing down here?" the woman yelled as she swayed to the music.

"Living my best life Trudy-Girl is Maji around?" he asked scanning the crowd.

She gestured with her head toward the back office and Gabe squeezed her hand again. Calvin was still a few feet behind him with a twenty-dollar bill stuck to his forehead. As he shimmied under a stripper hanging upside down on a pole.

"Calvin!" Gabe shouted. Calvin jumped and peeled the twenty from his face and stuffed it back in his pocket.

He waded through the group. "I was on my job. Just helping Chante out, a little something to put away for college," Calvin replied as he moved his shoulders in time with the music.

"Her name is Rochelle and she's finishing up her doctorate in Astrophysics in a week or two. Stay focused man we're not here to stay," Gabe said as a waitress covered in body glitter and a rhinestone G string sashayed by.

"A nerd with a booty like that?" Calvin nodded at the woman appreciatively "Like you don't notice all this free love floating around. Half the girls in here probably stuffed their numbers down your drawers before you got back here."

"Not likely. Most of them are married, in a relationship or all about business." Gabe pushed his way through the patrons and stopped near the dark curtains in the corner. One of the performers rolling around against the mirror threw herself at him. Gabe barely caught her before he sat her on the floor in front of him.

"Hey G!" she squealed before throwing her arms around his neck.

Gabe squinted then gave the girl a hug before she pulled him back behind the stage. Gabe reached back through the curtains and grabbed Calvin by the arm and pulled him back there with him.

"Hey Sabrina." He hugged her and stepped back. "How are you and the kids?"

"I'm good. Ms. Alana stopped past to check on me and the girls. Stayed for dinner and gave the Misha and Nena those hand knitted winter princess hats she promised them."

Calvin stood there staring at the girl's backside covered in sweat, glitter and very little else. Gabe looked over at Calvin and grinned.

"Like I said. Free love just falling or in her case jumping on you."

"Calvin Ford, this is Sabrina Jones," Gabe grinned with a flourish and a bow.

"It's Sable to the customers Gabe." She pinched his arm making him jump.

"My bad, Sable. My partner is having a very hard time wrapping his mind around his current predicament," he said directing his conversation to Calvin. "My mother got her out of a pretty dangerous situation."

"Is this any better?" Calvin replied facing Gabe.

Sable turned on Calvin so fast he backed up. "What are you trying to say about Ms. Alana? She got me out, but I chose to come back. Where'd you find him Gabe can you send his ass back?" Sabrina was about four foot nine and barely cleared five feet in heels. She still managed to back Calvin into the corner.

Gabe touched her shoulder and she turned around. "He meant no harm Sable. All respect anybody with me. You know that. I called earlier. I'm supposed to be meeting Maji tonight."

Sable flipped her hair back before giving Calvin a once over. She ran a tongue over her top lip and walked around him running a finger up his arm. "He looks kinda scared G. Bring him back tomorrow night. Luna Love will pop his cherry for him."

"Sable," Gabe warned "Respect goes both ways."

She rolled her eyes and smiled. "You right. My bad, Detective Ford. Maji back there in the office. I don't know if she alone though. Night's young and she ain't one to pass up no appetizers."

Sable gave Calvin another look then she bumped him with her hip and disappeared behind the curtain.

Calvin threw his hands in the air. "Will I ever get used to the company you keep? I mean damn, man!"

"Calm down Calvin," Gabe said as he glanced over his shoulder at the office door sitting ajar.

"And your moms? Man, she is scaring the hell out of me right now," Calvin inclined his head.

"As well she should gentleman. Alana don't suffer no company lightly and neither do I." The southern drawl seemed to crawl from the office with a creepy grace.

They both turned to the door that was sitting ajar. Gabe walked over and pushed it open. A red-haired woman hopped down from the desk in front of the dark-skinned older woman with platinum grey dreadlocks. The woman smoothed the fine strands of fiery red corn silk hair back up into her ponytail before smoothing down her black leather skirt. She draped a linen napkin over the woman shoulder pushing the dreadlocks back over her shoulder. The red head went to put the bottle of whiskey back on her tray as a fine trickle of blood seeped from a neck wound.

"Leave the bottle, Fancy. Little Hades came to visit his Godmother in the Underground. Grab an extra shot glass. His friend looks like he needs something to take the edge off," Maji said with a cackle that reminded Gabe of something guttural and a lot less than human. "What's the matter boys? You not into blood play? Don't knock it till you try it."

"Uh no thanks Ma'am, I'm fine," Calvin offered as he backed away from the woman switching through the door. Gabe bowed his head and waited for the woman to disappear beyond the curtain.

"Evening Maji. Thanks for agreeing to see me." He took a chair in front to the desk. Gabe glanced over his shoulder as Calvin looked around the room in awe before he sat down in the other chair.

Looking at Maji Speaks full on was to see a perfect concert of confusion. On the one hand, she very much looked like an older almost wizened grandmother complete with the platinum grey locks that snaked from her dark chocolate scalp like twisted vines.

On the other, the silver full length beard adorning her high cheek bones made the rugged masculine side. Her pale grey eyes looked more menacing as they slid back and forth between the two men. She hooked a red lacquered coke nail under one of the arms on her steel rimmed spectacles before arranging it behind an ear. "Appetizer gentlemen?" she offered as she dabbed at her mouth with the napkin. "Or would you prefer the main course? Male female, something else on the menu, hell I don't discriminate. Got plenty to share." She leaned in as her smile made of dagger fine pointed teeth glistened under pit lights in her ceiling. She ran her tongue over one of the points drawing a thin line of red on her tongue.

"No thanks. We already ate," Gabe said glancing at Calvin. The mixture of fascination and disgust on his partner's face made him chuckle. "As I said thanks for meeting with me."

"You were a baby the last time I saw you. Most babies see me and scream and cry. Showed you my fangs and you just smiled back."

"No Ma'am. Last time I was in here I was seventeen."

Maji's eyes lit up as she settled back in her leather admirals chair and steepled her long slender fingers that were manicured into fine sharp claws.

"I'd almost forgotten about that. You and your cousin came in here with fake IDs a five-year-old could have made. Alana walked in and picked a coaster up off the floor right near your sneaker." She cackled before clapping her hands.

"My cousin Shawn and the others scattered like rats leaving me behind per usual."

Maji's cold grey eyes crawled over them with a predatory slowness. "Paid for your drink and the others before you left. Fifty dollars total. Much respect for any man that pays his debts." She plucked her shot glass from the tray and downed the brown liquor and lapped at the lip of the glass. "Now here you are looking every bit like a male version of her. You need a job? You'd be one hell of an enforcer. I'd bust a nut to see that shit." Maji giggled as she settled back in her leather admiral's chair.

"Took a while to catch up with you," Gabe continued.

"You know I have that allergy to pork. Keeps me busy staying under the radar." She said letting the chair sway beneath her. Her face closed as if guarding a secret "Would have kept you waiting til I died, but if Alana is at CIBEX then the harvest must be ready, or we got some sloppy sharecroppers out there. All we need now is a reaper's scythe and here you are."

"Yes, Maji about that harvest." Gabe started as he fished his notebook from a pocket.

Maji scooted up to the desk and poured a finger full of whisky in the shot glass shaped like a small skull. She ran a finger under her moustache before belting back the whiskey and pouring another.

"Why she wanna go wading through that pile of shit is beyond me. Guess you and your people are responsible for that. The newsman says ya'll got yourselves an eager beaver playing in the Barrens." She snapped her head back and gargled with the whiskey before she swallowed.

"There's a mass grave out there, Ma'am— Sir-- uh," Calvin trailed off while shooting a look at Gabe.

Under the lights, Maji's pale gray eyes were magnified in her bifocal lenses making red rimmed twin pools of scrutiny appear even more frightening. "Profound and profane is good enough for me. Take your pick son I ain't particular." She regarded Calvin with the kind of disgust one would hold for an insect. "On the outside I resembled the other little girls all decked out in barrettes and bows. Under my skirts? Well, that was another story entirely. Never thought anything was right or wrong with me til the games started with Daddy."

"We found the remains of three missing children out there all in the same area. Their names were—" Gabe flipped through the pages of this notebook and clicked the button on his ink pen and frowned. Olivia's pen was missing and the prospect of losing it irked his entire soul.

Maji raised her hand. "I know who I buried out there alongside my Daddy. Wasn't no sense in trying to find families. They flushed them away a years ago."

Gabe sat up in the chair. "What are you saying?" he asked leaning forward.

"September disappeared for months, but then she came back better.

She got that kidney transplant. I don't know if it was Toby or Garcelle or Felicia, but one of them saved my Seppi and we got back to work building this place," Maji pointed to the walls around her.

Calvin looked over at Gabe then leaned in. "So, what you're saying is some doctors, harvested human organs and what…sold them here in Shadow Bay?"

"Charity begins at home, Pork," Maji said with a grin "Excuse me detective that was rude. Here Barbados, Uganda what's the difference? One of them saved my best friend's life. She came back here and helped me build this place for people like us with nowhere to go."

Gabe ran a shaky hand over his mouth. "Three children, countless others are dead and—"

Maji moved the whiskey bottle over and folded her hands neatly on the ink blotter, "Alana wanted all of us to get clear. Her life's mission was to spare us from the horrors she endured. Some of us even landed well. A lot more didn't. She got us to the extraction points but some of us weren't built for life beyond it."

"We have a current case we are trying to solve Maji," Calvin said barely containing the exasperation in his voice "What does any of this have to do with--" Calvin stopped talking as Gabe waved a hand to silence him.

"Careful Pork. We can always put your ass in the back yard while we grow folk finish talking," Maji said leaning forward.

"You can try to pretty this up as much as you want like it's some noble cause, but the fact remains. Your friend betrayed another. They benefitted from another child's death, "Gabe said cutting Calvin off.

"I did worse. Alana did her best to do right by us. Got beat to shit more than once for one of us stepping out of line. They kept saving her a space to get on the fucking van, but she kept going back getting one more always one more. Most of us didn't even deserve it."

Gabe sat back. "You told."

"Alana had become the biggest human trafficker on the eastern seaboard, getting people out to safety. Like some kind of red Moses. It was the only way I knew to get her clear." Maji tossed back the shot and poured another. "Had to be done. Some of us belong right where we are. Hell can be home too." She raised the glass to her lips, though better of it and sat the skull shaped glass on the desk. "Her first husband beat her within an inch of her life for it when he found out. She was bleeding his profits right under his nose. Phaedra Khalid was the first to betray her. I was the last, the worst one, and she forgave me anyway. I'd kill of die for her even now. It ain't noble. It's just right."

"The doctors are they alive?" Gabe snapped trying hard not to envision is mother in a bloody broken mess.

"Even if you cut the head off that particular snake, the world has changed. Mediocre organs are just as valuable as the pristine ones. You find a readymade crop and you can live like a God. Ask your cousin. Poor as a church mouse. He's nothing like you. Plenty of markers, half of them unpaid. He does extractions over at that Transplantation Center." Maji settled back in the chair and let it sway gently beneath her. "That boy don't care nothing about getting his hands dirty to settle his debts. Let a few of Regulus Chastain's acquaintances use him like a public toilet to settle a Super Bowl marker."

Gabe tucked his notebook away and moved to stand.

"What about Dr. Olivia Calderone? She ever get her hands dirty like that?" Calvin blurted out.

"Calvin!" Gabe yelled.

Maji stopped rocking and turned to face his partner. Her nails dug into the arms of the chair leaving deep grooves in the leather. "Now that was rude." Maji hissed as she rose from her chair. "Cutting out a vile tongue ain't polite Pork. Say her name again and I'll make an exception," Maji hissed then she turned on Gabe. "Get him out of here while you still can."

"Was that a threat?" Calvin said rising from his chair.

"Threats are for pussies. Prison or death don't scare me, boy both are a vacation for evil bitches like me." Magi's forked tongue darted from her mouth as she rose to her full height, only a foot shorter than Calvin, but her girth made her an equal.

"Enough!" Gabe roared and Calvin and Magi both backed down.

"Answer his question, Maji."

Maji swung her head in Gabe's direction. "You'd do her dirty like that? She's better than blood and you'd do that to her? Get out of here, both of you."

"I'm trying to solve a murder investigation here, Maji. Just. Answer him." Gabe said moving between them. "We have to ask questions about anybody that surrounds the case."

"Bullshit. Should have got her away from both of you sooner. Fighting over her soul like dogs." Maji said as she swept everything from her desk. "Get out of here!" she roared lacerating her tongue on one of her teeth. The blood dripping from her mouth made her look even more fearsome. "You are your mother's child and your father's son. Whatever grace you had died here tonight. Now get gone."

Gabe heard the unmistakable click snap of the clasps on Calvin's holstered gun open with a malevolent snick. Without looking, he put his hand on Calvin's chest and shoved. "No."

"Olivia's only crime was loving you and doing her job. You don't get to pin another man's sins on her jacket!" She growled turning on Calvin as she gnashed her teeth.

"What man? Shawn? Does this have anything to do with Shawn? Answer me Maji please."

"Him. You. Her boss. The military? What's the difference?" She swung her fist knocking her lamp off the desk. Maji hissed. "None of you will be satisfied until she's dead and buried! Uganda wasn't enough. How long she gotta pay a debt she doesn't owe? You leave her be."

A loud thump drew their attention to the office door as the music beyond was joined by people screaming and glass shattering.

"Never mind the nightly barroom brawl gentlemen. Maji is in a killing mood. Get out while you can." She hissed.

***

"So, we're not going to talk about what just happened back there, G?" Calvin's voice hardened ruthlessly as he reached the truck.

Gabe thumbed the lock on his key fob and got inside. Bloodlust thumped in his head harder than the base shaking music making his tinted windows vibrate.

Calvin got in and slammed the door. "I asked you a question LT Garrett."

Rather than answer Gabe put the key in the ignition and sat back, "It's my fault. I should have come alone. I knew better." Gabe struggled to quiet his breathing. Each breath soured under the fragrance of salt and blood.

"Seriously?" Calvin ground the word between his teeth. "She could have killed us."

"You need to catch a ride with the patrolmen back to the station." Gabe's voice was stern with no vestige of sympathy in its hardness. He started blankly through the windshield.

"What the actual…" Calvin asked spacing the words out evenly.

"She started by killing her father. No one knows what she did with the rest of her family. All we have is her word and Maji doesn't lie. The crack heads Ollie was sold to… they're still looking for the heads." Gabe felt the chords in his neck tighten as he faced his friend. "Had you done anything but what I said. You would have been delivering that death notice tonight or I would be delivering one to your mother. Please Calvin. Get out of my truck."

"I don't believe this." Calvin stroked his beard with a shaky hand, "We just gonna let that freak of nature go? G, is that what you're saying?"

Gabe's cellphone buzzed in his pocket, but the ringtone blared through the speakers in the cab. Calvin flinched, but Gabe continued to study him. He slid his thumb over the answer button.

"Hi Gabe, it's Olivia, just touching base. I'm home and, oh okay your outside. Hang on."

Both men turned and looked at the dashboard to see Olivia's name crawling in marquee fashion across the screen in his dashboard.

"Ollie, don't open that door!" Gabe roared.

Over an explosion, shattering glass, and gunfire, Olivia screamed.

CHAPTER THIRTY-SEVEN

The large bay window shattered as the first percussion bomb exploded. Then one smoke bomb and then another bounced across the carpet near the front door. The noxious fumes filled the air both blinding and choking her instantly. Olivia turned to run for her bedroom when a pair of hands bit into her upper arms and slammed her against the gallery wall. The same arms pulled her back to repeat the assault and Olivia bought her knees to her chest. Then, using an old bouldering technique called smearing she planted her feet on the jagged remains of a frame. She took several steps across the wall and just as she was nearly vertical to her attacker, he caught her and slammed her against her front door knocking the wind out of her.

Registrar la casa. Rapidemente

Evi Aramark

The two distinct male voices gave the same command in Spanish and Turkish were the same.

Search the house.

The owner of the arms imprisoning her, spoke in English with a thick European accent,

"The American promised not to hurt you. We did not. Where is my shipment?"

***

Gabe put all his weight behind the boot he put on her front door. The ornate French door splintered near the handle before crashing against the wall inside. Gabe choked on the thin haze that cloaked the room. Calvin brought up the rear with uniforms spreading out to check the perimeter.

"Olivia!" Gabe roared as he moved through her place with his side arm in one hand and a flashlight held tightly in the other. "Ollie? Olivia Calderone!"

He moved thorough each room leading back to her bedroom with Calvin right behind him. Reaching her room, Gabe used an elbow to flip the light switch. Feathers from her down pillows floated to the floor as two officers cleared the bathroom and her bedroom closet.

Walking back out to the living room, Calvin tapped the dimmer switch on the wall. Olivia's gallery wall was destroyed. Large shards of glass still hung in the frames, but the floor was littered with photographs. Gabe stooped down and fished a few of them out of the sea of glass on the floor.

"Jesus," Calvin breathed as he stepped back and looked at the wall, "Did she run up the wall?"

Gabe glanced up at the wall and stood. Taking in the several small footprints marred the mounting paper in the frames.

"It's an evasive maneuver. My mother taught her how to get away from someone twice her size by either dropping to the floor or running up the wall so that she could—" Moving closer to one of the jagged remains of a frame, Gabe drew his weapon and aimed at the wall.

He waved a hand to silence everyone in the room. He pointed at his ear and then the wall as a soft thud emanated from somewhere behind the frame. Gabe stuffed his gun down the back of his pants. Taking both hands, he pressed on the wall. A soft click opened a false wall. No sooner had the door slid open, Olivia, bound and gagged spilled into his arms.

CHAPTER THIRTY-EIGHT

Olivia turned her face into the spray as bits of glass tinkled against the sides of the tub. The scratches on her back and arms stung under the unrelenting spray from the shower. She squeezed some cherry blossom bath wash into her hands and lathered her body twice before rinsing and turning off the water.

Taking the edge of the rich, chocolate colored towel, she wrapped herself in. Olivia made a clean space in the right corner of the guest bathroom and looked at herself in the mirror. The old black and blue marks on her arm were nothing compared to the newer ones that slowly materialized on her bare shoulders in the shape of large male fingers.

Olivia cleaned more of the fogged glass to see the familiar crochet shower curtain and liner in the bathroom Gabe shared with his older sister Monet. Tears beveled her view as she traced the soft blue and white flower accent wall in the bathroom next to the sink.

I'm taking her to the safest place I know.

Walking into a dream paled in comparison with the landscape that stretched out before her. The sidewalks were clear, but remnants of the last snowstorm still clung to the small slopping hill. The large oak tree cradling Gabe's tree house sat silently with the tire swing patiently waiting for either of them. The vast lawn beyond, ended near a small staircase that led to a closed in porch with white Adirondack chairs stationed in twos across the deck. Olivia leaned against the passenger window as memories of Gabe and Olivia racing up the steps afterschool filled her mind.

Once Gabe put the truck in park, He was around to the passenger side gathering her to his chest. He carried her up the small hill leading to his parent's front door and only sat her down long enough to unlock the door as she limped inside. When the door closed, his arm became a band around her waist as he hauled her back against his chest. His ragged breaths against the back of her neck made her tear up.

"Are you okay? Answer me." The edge in his voice hurt more than the scratches and the bruises.

She turned and he pressed his face against the side of her face. "I'm fine Gabe. It's not that bad. I'm okay, really."

"Should have been there. Never should have left you," he said in an anguished whisper.

"Gabe, stop it. I'm not fragile. Olivia grabbed his face and shook him into a gasping silence. She whispered. "I'm not fragile. I won't break." She kissed him hard and deep as if to prove her words.

He snatched away. "I just found you hog tied in with your bloody footprints on the wall. Don't tell me you can't break."

Olivia stepped up on his boots and put her arms around his neck. Gabe lifted her high and pressed his forehead to hers. "I'm here Gabe. Right here." She buried her face in the side of his neck and sighed.

Olivia covered his mouth with hers and he groaned and dragged his open mouth across her cheek to her ear. "Not letting you go this time. I—"

Olivia gasped as his fingers graced a cut on her shoulder. Gabe eased her hair out of the way to see the wound.

Olivia twisted in his grip. "Gabe it's not bad."

Rather than answer, Gabe swept his arm under her legs and carried her upstairs.

***

After a hot shower, Olivia turned out the light and padded down the hallway back to Monet, Gabe's older sister's old room. A crack in Gabe's bedroom door drew her closer. Pushing the door open she felt for the light switch. She palmed the switch and the room she spent much of her childhood, came into view.

The rich caramel carpet whispered beneath her feet as she neared the window. His treehouse sat dark and silent. Clutching the towel in one hand she attempted to open the window and failed as Gabe's old paperback copy of Treasure Island fell on the floor. As she stooped to picked it up, the floorboard just outside his door creaked.

"Sorry Gabe. I didn't mean to intrude," she said as waves of anxiety washed through her. Olivia secured the towel around her before standing to face him.

The mixture of relief and the last traces of fear made the moisture on his eyelashes stand out. "You spent about as much time here as I did. I started referring to it and the treehouse as our home." Gabe gave her a sad smile. "Let me get you something to put on," he offered before making a beeline for his dresser just below the window.

"I'll head back to Monet's room," She murmured as she retreated to the door.

"Ollie" his voice was barely above a whisper as he closed the drawer hard enough to make her flinch. "Please don't."

"It's okay, Gabe," she said praying her voice sounded steadier than she felt.

He moved through her blood like a measure of music. One minute he was clear across the room and the next he was right behind her, tracing one of the scratches on her shoulder and followed it with a kiss. Pushing her hair out of the way as his mouth found another scratch and then another. Warm tears spilled across one of the scrapes making it burn. He kissed it before pressing his face against the back of her shoulder.

"At least let me get the first aid kit." He whispered. "Ollie I am so sorry."

Swallowing the sob swelling in her throat, she looked up at him. The mixture of lust and regret on his face made her slip an arm around his neck and to pull his mouth down to hers. Gabe pulled the towel from around her and dropped it in the hallway. Slipping to his knees, he parted the folds of the sweet cleft between her thighs with his tongue. Every long languid sweep delved deeper and deeper until her pearl rested on the tip. He latched on her throbbing pearl and twisted his head to the left sealing his mouth over the aching bud.

The hard sucking kiss to her gem delivered a shockwave that made her knees buckle. Olivia bit down on her bottom lip as each wicked flick of his tongue was punctuated with a stroke that teased her slick velvet folds. He tore his mouth away and gripped her thigh and draped it over his shoulder. His eyes glittered with a black fire expecting complete surrender while demanding even more.

"Stop biting your lip. I want to hear you," He growled, the silky rough texture of his beard set the sensitive skin on her inner thigh on fire. "I want to hear you," he growled nibbling at the muscle near her knee.

Olivia cried out as he pulled one orgasm and then another from her. Gabe stood and guided her back into his bedroom as she traced his lips with her tongue.

"I need you inside me." Her voice broke into a husky whisper

Something intense flared through his entrancement as he put her hand on his belt buckle. And then he went still. He glanced over his shoulder then back at her.

Olivia cupped his face in her hands, "Gabe what is it?"

Gabe snatched her up to his chest and bolted for the door stopping long enough to slap the light switch on the wall plunging them into darkness. He moved further away from his door before loosening his grip enough for her to slide down his body.

"Someone's outside," he said before kissing her hard and deep," he released her long enough to take his shirt off and push it into her hands. "Put this on. Stay here."

Olivia tugged the shirt on and grabbed his arm. "No, I'm going with you."

Gabe pressed his forehead to hers before he stooped down dragging her with him. The snaps on his ankle holster popped open as he extracted the gun, checked the clip, and pushed it into her hands. As he stood, Gabe moved in front of her pulling the gun from the waistband at the back of his jeans.

She caught a glimpse of her name in the brilliant Cyrillic script across the back of his broad shoulders. For every step he took down the steps, Olivia's disappeared into his. As they reached the landing a thunderous knock landed on the door repeatedly. Gabe released her hand long enough to sweep her behind him as he peered through the gap in the curtain.

"What is she doing here?" He asked before disengaging the lock and pulling the door open, "How did you get this address, Christine?"

"Christine, what—" Olivia attempted to move out from behind him and Gabe swept his arm around her, "Gabe don't." She gripped his hand before moving to his side.

Christine face was little more than a glowering mask of tearful rage. Gabe Moved to sweep her behind him once more and she stepped out from behind him.

"Wow, Olivia. This is rich. My son is dying in a hospital and you're too busy getting laid to answer your goddamned phone?" She spat.

Olivia looked down at her bare thighs and moved closer to the door ignoring Gabe's gaze. "Christine, you know my phone was stolen."

Christine held out Olivia's phone "You mean this one? You left it on the sink in the locker room like you always do before surgery. I know you got a new one. I saw it."

"I don't have it with me. Christine, I got attacked in my own home tonight. The new phone is still sitting on my charger where I left it. So, you see I couldn't answer either one."

"They found a donor Olivia," Christine moved closer. "If you answered your phone, you'd know that and come to help."

"But I just told you I don't have my phone. Besides, Shawn Prescott does organ transplants. Not me." Olivia handed Gabe the gun and reached for Christine.

Christine threw the phone and Gabe batted the phone out of the way as he shielded Olivia's face. The phone bounced off his hand and fell to the floor.

"And that somehow justifies throwing a phone? How did you get this address?" he repeated as he put his body between the two women.

Olivia put a hand on his side as she ducked under his arm. "Shawn does transplants Christine. Not me. You know that."

"He told me what you did in Uganda. He said your hands were small enough to help my Cory. Besides, he can't come. He's across town scrubbing in."

Christine grabbed Olivia's wrist and yanked her forward. Pain shot up her arm as Olivia pried at her friend's fingers, "Burt in Urology or Stan. He's on call. Christine. Christine let go."

Gabe clapped a hand over Christine's and pulled Olivia free. "Christine I'm sorry about Cory. If you want to come in and talk that's fine. What you won't do is—"

Christine looked at Olivia "You can make them reconsider. It's not a precise match but with the anti-rejection drugs it could work. You have clout you can talk to them. You see how sick Cory is. He needs a kidney now."

"Pristine or not if he's not a match, Christine you already know." Olivia tried to step out in front of him and Gabe put an arm out to sweep her behind him once more. "It's okay Gabe. Christine if they are performing the surgery on someone else then Cory wasn't a viable candidate. Organ rejection could kill him."

Christine spilled to her knees and sobbed. "You have clout! You gotta try. Please? Please Olivia you have to help. He's sicker. His doctors are saying he can't wait any longer. she sobbed and sank to her knees. "Please help us. Please?"

Olivia slid down next to her friend and rubbed her back. "Christine. There is nothing I can do. If he's not a match the surgery could kill him. You know how aggressive the anti-rejection drugs can be. I'm sorry Christine,"

Christine snatched away so hard that Olivia fell back against the door jam. She pulled Gabe's sweater down over her thighs as Christine rose.

"You, bitch! You won't even try? You failed Bimbi so now every other kid must suffer? You selfish bitch."

Gabe moved between them again. "I think you better leave,"

"Selfish bitch. I thought you cared about Cory," Christine snarled. "I thought you were my friend!" She screeched as Gabe gently ushered her to the steps.

"You're done here Christine. You're upset I get that, but you need to leave. Now." He commanded. "I won't say it again."

She snatched away and thundered down the steps and bolted back to her car. Olivia could just make out someone in the driver's seat before she crawled back in the house and settled beside the door. She spotted the phone on the floor and ran her thumb over the shattered screen.

***

Gabe came in and kneeled beside her closing the door. "Babe," He whispered as he smoothed her hair away from her face.

Olivia was staring straight ahead with tears shimmering on her cheeks.

"I loved how they were together, your parents. Sometimes I'd see them in the kitchen, sharing the same cup of coffee near the sink. When they danced, your dad would just hold her so close, and I thought whatever she'd done, however she was broken that your dad knew how to put the pieces back together. There was so much love in this house. There was even some left for me."

Olivia blinked sending more tears down her cheeks as she focused on something painful beyond the kitchen. "Tiana and her wife were on a milk run."

"Ollie a milk run is for drug dealers. People that invest in a large drug shipment like seed money. What are you saying?"

"Erin, Tiana's wife wanted to open some high-end club so that they could become influencers on social media." Olivia raked at her cheek with the back of her hand. "They were only gathering girls that wanted a better life for themselves and their families. They lied and sold them as sex slaves." Olivia sighed and sank into his embrace.

"Bimbi's village was their reup. It's where I met them. Erin refused to tell where they stashed them. They executed her." Olivia winced at some private pain before she looked at him. "I don't remember getting shot; just Bimbi under me… not moving. There was another child hit too. My hands were small enough. Trying is lying, but I did try Gabe. He died in my arms. It's why I refuse to perform surgeries of any kind on children, I can't risk failing again."

Olivia climbed from his lap and stood. Gabe followed.

"Shouldn't have come here," she said finally

Looking up as she approached, he studied her openly, "Olivia you are in no condition to go anywhere. You don't have to do this."

"People are dead because of me." Turning blindly, she stumbled, and his arm became a vise holding her back against his chest. "Thought if I could save one or two them, maybe Bimbi would forgive me for not keeping her safe."

"That is *not* true." Gabe pressed his face against the nape of her neck, and she stiffened.

Olivia tucked the phone in his hand and pulled away and walked to the staircase. "Yes, it is."

CHAPTER THIRTY-NINE

The air was thick is pain. Fear clung to the very walls around them. As they stepped off the elevator, Calvin stood and came to them. Olivia walked over to the nurse's station and Tiana threw her arms around her neck.

"The boy. Did he—"

Calvin pulled Gabe further down the hallway.

"What happened?" Gabe asked as Tiana pulled Olivia behind the Unit Clerk's Desk and made her sit down.

"G, we gotta bring Olivia in." Calvin's mouth took on an unpleasant twist as he glanced at the Nurse's Station.

Gabe focused on his partner and tilted his head as if he hadn't heard him correctly. "Come again?" he asked with a deceptive calm.

Calvin pointed down the hallway and started walking. When they were a safe distance Gabe gripped his partner's shoulder. "So, talk."

"Her blood was found in the Cargo area. Place was refrigerated so the blood was preserved. It was all over a stuffed giraffe toy; her blood and someone else's."

"She got shot Calvin. Somebody must have carried Bimbi's stuffed animal in there." Gabe tried to move past him, and Calvin put a hand in his chest.

"Are you listening to yourself right now? You're grasping at straws. The paper that was taped to her mouth matched the medical paperwork she used while working at the MASH unit. It was a physician's order form for an organ extraction. Carbon testing discovered her signature is at the bottom."

A wave of nausea washed over him. "No. She didn't do this any of this. I don't care what you found."

"G, listen to me. I think you need to ask yourself if you really know her. It's been a while. People change."

"Not Olivia. She is a surgeon. She signs off on orders all the time. I'm sure she signed plenty overseas," Gabe said the words with the certainty of a man unwilling to relinquish a dream. "She got hurt Calvin, obviously somebody is after her."

Calvin stepped back momentarily rebuffed before he leaned closer "Not that bad though. All of her injuries were mild in comparison."

"Somebody tried to pull her arm out of the socket. That's not serious enough?" Gabe said as he walked briskly down the hallway. Calvin jogged behind him, and Gabe spun around. "You didn't see the scratches on her back… the bruises. Some asshole ripped her shirt down the back and damn near off her body. Did she zip tie herself and stuff herself in that hole in the wall too?" he roared.

"She could have had help, man." Calvin offered. "How many times have we seen victims fake being sick or hurt?"

"I'm not hearing this. You *showed* me the blood on the walls. We both saw her feet," Gabe said as he walked further down the hall away from Olivia. "You know what? Here. "Gabe extracted Olivia's phone from his back pocket and held it out. "She said it was stolen. Christine brought it to my house tonight. It may have been cloned. Get it to forensics. Check it. Did you tell Christine where to find me?"

"Now what do you think? For all I know you're the safest place was your crib." Calvin took the phone and put it in his coat pocket. Christine also said the night she was attacked in the emergency room it looked like they knew Olivia. Looked like they were having a conversation."

Gabe pulled out his badge and service weapon.

"What are you doing?" Calvin stilled his hand.

Gabe pulled away and collected his gear "What I promised. I'm not objective. Take the phone. Check it. My cousin was overseas with Olivia. He has a raging gambling debt and connections to God knows who over there. He had a string of ex-girlfriends back here that followed him around like a God. Shawn knows where my parents live. It's not out of the realm Calvin."

Calvin put his head down. "They found another body G. Her stethoscope and badge were found not too far from the body. The liver was missing. Kidneys too."

A scuffle up the hall drew their attention as a female officer started walking Olivia to the elevator. While another pinned Tiana to the Nurse's station. Gabe rushed back down the hallway.

"You can't do this. She didn't do anything!" Tiana screamed as she tried to get away from the female officer currently restraining her.

Gabe walked down the hallway as Tiana craned her neck to look at him. "You can't let them take her! Do something!" She shrieked.

Gabe glanced at Olivia. Her hair spilled into her face as the uniformed officer finished mirandizing her. Instead of answering the officer's question about understanding the charges, Olivia called over her shoulder. "Tiana it's okay. I'm fine."

Tiana struggled in their arms. "Tell them Olivia. Just tell them! It was me and my wife. We were the human traffickers! We sold people into the sex trade! We moved them!"

And just as the officers started moving toward the elevator, Cory walked out of the hospital room holding Christine's hand.

"Ms. Olivia?" he called as he rubbed his eyes.

Olivia sank to her knees and the boy walked over and threw his arms around her neck. "Hello my sweet boy. What are you doing up so late huh?" She asked before resting her cheek on his shoulder.

The elevator doors opened and Beacham, Mark and the state's attorney stepped out into the hall. Beacham moved forward.

"And you can take your hands off my doctor and her scrub nurse. Uncuff them. Now," Beacham barked. "Do I need to repeat myself. You people do speak English, right? Uncuff my surgeon."

"Now wait a minute," Calvin said moving forward. "She's not being charged; we're just bring her in for questioning."

The state's attorney in her smart navy-blue silk suit and matching purse directed her comments to Gabe "A federal judge signed off on it, Detective Ford. This is highly irregular, but you can and will release her under special circumstances. An organ just became available for that little boy. Car crash out in Bethesda. Organ procurement is on the way here by helicopter. Considering the boy's age and the gravity of the situation, Dr. Beacham feels like Dr. Calderone is the best one to perform the surgery if she agrees. After that you can bring her in."

Gabe moved forward "Hillary, Uncle Mark, Ollie didn't do anything but get attacked in her own home and here at the hospital. Where is all of this coming from?"

"It's just like she said Gabe. Release Olivia Calderone and her Scrub nurse. Once the surgery is over, we will bring her downtown." Mark walked over and stooped down near Olivia.

As the uniformed officers removed the handcuffs, Tiana shrugged them off and went to Olivia. "Like Olivia can perform a surgery after what you bastards just pulled. Besides, there's no organ available. We would have got the call."

Beacham held up a form. "Parents gave consent. Can you do this Dr. Calderon?"

Olivia cradled the boy in her arms for a moment longer before she put a loud smacking kiss on the side of his head. He giggled as Christine pulled him back against her legs. Tiana pulled Olivia to her feet and put an arm are around her. Olivia cupped her friend's cheek and nodded once.

"Tell them what we did, Olivia, what *I* did. Please. It doesn't matter anymore. Erin's dead. I can't lose you too."

Olivia pressed a kiss on the side of Tiana's head. She whispered something that made Tiana's shoulders sag as she clutched Olivia to her chest.

She took her time scanning the crowd before her eyes locked on Gabe. A sad strange smile whispered across her features. "Give me a few minutes to scrub in."

CHAPTER FORTY

"We've known each other since third grade Ollie. You can tell me—" His voice cracked as he looked up at the ceiling and swallowed hard.

"When I woke up at Walter Reed a couple of years ago, I could have sworn I saw your dad sitting in a chair by my bed," Olivia cradled her head in trembling hands, "He gave me that big old smile and he said, Come on Ollie- Girl. It's time to go home."

Gabe thumped the back of his head against the wall. "Ollie, just tell me. They're going to lock you up. Whatever you've done—whatever it is, baby please let me help you."

Olivia waited for him to look at her. Gone was the little boy that shared his granola bars with her. Only the man she longed to grow old with remained. Her hand moved on its own volition to his jawline.

"I made a promise Gabe. It's not my story to tell," She moved to the door and Gabe whipped her around so fast that she bumped into his chest before he pinned her back against the wall.

"Did you hear what I just said? They are going to lock you up for the rest of your life. Is that what you want?" he asked so viciously that she wondered how she could have ever though him kind.

Oliva said cupping his face in her hands. "What kind of woman do you think I am?" She asked.

He pressed his forehead to hers before kissing Olivia hard and deep. "A good one. The only one I want to grow old and die with."

"Do you trust me?" She leaned into him lightly tilting her face toward his.

Gabe leaned back. "With my life Olivia," His gaze was dark and unfathomable.

Olivia bit down on her lips nodded once. "So, did they, before I killed them," and walked out.

***

Gabe stared after her for a long time. Leaving wasn't an option. Even if he wanted to the thought of Olivia being handcuffed and trooped through the lobby and out through a sea of reporters raked at his insides.

The door swung open, and Brenda stepped in. "They are prepping Cory for surgery. Come with me,"

Gabe pulled his arm away. "Where?"

"Observation unless your squeamish," Brenda grabbed his coat sleeve again. "Cops say somebody needs to be near."

"She's not a flight risk, Brenda." Gabe pulled away and Brenda turned around. "I'm not a cop anymore. I'm a distraction she doesn't need right now." he said as a sensation of intense sickness and desolation swept over him.

Realizing he was no longer beside her; she bustled back down the hallway and grabbed his arm. "You love that girl?" What should have been a question sounded more like a statement or a demand. The only thing Brenda didn't ask was what were his intentions toward Olivia. She poked him in the shoulder. "Do you?"

"What does that have to—" the words caught in his throat. His thoughts tasted like gall. "More than my next breath, Ms. Brenda."

"Then help her. See her through this. That girl never asks for anything. Ever. Always pouring into everybody around her. She needs us. All of us, and that means you too."

Calvin came up the hall to join them. He moved to speak, and she turned on him. "Not you. Only Gabe. You are not welcome in there."

***

Brenda let go of his arm as they entered the gathering area just outside of the double doors leading to the operating theaters. Men and women dressed in surgical scrubs and gowns and colorful skullcaps and hoods lined both sides of the hall.

Gabe made his way through the gauntlet. At the very end stood a small group. A nurse stepped aside and immediately; Gabe saw Olivia's glasses tucked down the back of her collar. Tiana stood beside her hugging a surgical gown sealed in plastic with tears standing on her cheeks. Brenda brushed past him on her way to the group.

"Alright everyone simmer down. Every patient that comes to us is special, but this one is close. We need to do our jobs, but we also need to make room for God to scrub in and have His say," Brenda waved everyone closer then, she grabbed Gabe's hand and placed it on Olivia's neck just above her glasses.

He ran his thumb down the back of her neck praying she would turn and look at him. Instead, she took in a shaky breath. Shawn pushed through the crowd and put a hand on Olivia's shoulder. When Brenda completed her prayer Gabe looked up to see Shawn staring at him.

As the others released Olivia and went in to complete the final procedures, Shawn walked back over to a space by the wall as the low grind of a battery powered car slowly made its way up the hall. Cory sat in the driver's seat with Christine walking beside him pushing an IV pole The little boy parked the car and Christine helped him stand.

Gabe moved to remove his hand and Olivia grabbed it. "Let me get him to recovery and then get me out of here. Do this for me."

Gabe squeezed her hand and put his forehead against the back of her neck and nodded. Olivia took in a trembling breath then released his hand and gathered Cory into her arms and proceeded to carry the boy into the operating room.

CHAPTER FORTY-ONE

Olivia's team disbanded and walked toward the showers. Most were in tears while others slammed their fists against the lockers. Gabe stood just inside the recovery room door as Olivia helped the nurses get Cory tucked in. One of the nurses pulled up a chair then rested a hand on her shoulder before returning to their work with the patients in other recovery beds around them.

At one point Olivia rested her head on her arm. Her shoulders bowed inward as her body shook with silent sobs. One of the nurses came over and smoothed down Olivia's hair before she handed her some tissues. Gabe was about to walk over when Brenda stepped into the room and tapped him on the arm.

"You really going to go through with this," she scrubbed at her eyes with the heal of her hand. "You saw what she did in there,"

"Brenda, I handed in my service weapon and my badge. She—"

She tapped the glass with a finger. Gabe peered through the glass. The tubing in the butterfly IV stuck to the back of Cory's hand shined under the lights as he pulled the surgical cap, she wore from her head. Olivia raised her head and kissed the palm of Cory's hand and smiled.

"Does that look like a killer to you?" Brenda asked as she folded her arms.

***

Gabe pushed through the double doors and scanned the room for his partner and the other detectives. Shawn sat on the edge of the sofa next to Christine scrolling through his phone. The moment he saw Gabe, he put the phone away and rubbed the back of Christine's hand.

"How's the kid?" Calvin walked over to Gabe.

"Alive." Gabe pulled his surgical cap off and gestured in Shawn's direction. "Has he been here the whole time?"

"No. Rhonda and Tony said he made a few calls. He sounded like an extension on a marker," Calvin reported as Tiana burst through the operating room door almost hitting a nurse on the way. "He's been in surgery every time there was a murder. Security cams and witnesses corroborated. No fingerprints. Only hers and her blood."

She stormed past the group and went straight for the waiting room Christine jumped up and went to her. "How's my baby?" Christine asked clutching Cory's robe to her chest.

"Olivia handled her business. He's alive," Tiana rolled her shoulders backward as she stared at the woman in disgust.

Christine threw her arms around Tiana's neck. She stood there with her arms down at her sides .

Christine released her and wiped at her eyes. "Well can I see him?" She asked with a grateful smile.

"Sure, he's back through there," Tiana said shoving Christine away. "Olivia saved his life and you sold her out."

One of Christine's family members tried to grab Tiana's arm and she drew back a fist. "Stay the fuck away from me. What did you have to do Christine? Funny how one minute your boy is at death's door and then miraculously there's a kidney just waiting for him." Tiana squared on Christine again "You're living paycheck to paycheck and your insurance is crap. So, what did you do? Who do you know? Back or knees, who did you blow?"

"Nothing I'm ashamed of that's for sure. Sniffing and groveling around Olivia like some dog. She's strictly dickly, ask Gabe." Christine shot back as she searched the faces of her family members before zeroing in on Gabe. She wiped her eyes on the robe and shrugged. "I don't know what you're talking about. God provided. He always does. Olivia understands. She'll forgive me for what I said earlier," She insisted.

Tiana went after Christine. Gabe blocked her while Calvin dragged her to the far corner.

"You sold her out, you bitch!" Tiana screamed.

Christine stood there looking around at her family. "Olivia understands. You performed the surgery. You do understand right?" Christine asked looking over at the double doors.

"Lower your voices. This is still a hospital," Olivia said in a harsh whisper as she moved into the room.

"You don't have to do this, Olivia." Tiana sobbed as she clung to her. "Tell them. Just tell them! The club was my idea. It's my fault Erin died. You didn't kill anybody."

Olivia hugged her friend and waited for her storm of tears to quiet. She murmured something in Tiana's ear and the woman backed away.

"But you didn't do anything wrong! I did." Tiana whined before wiping her nose with the back of her hand. Olivia whispered something else to her and Tiana nodded once before she shoved her way through the crowd and took off down the hall.

She turned and walked toward Gabe, but Christine stepped into her path. "You do, right? You understand right, Olivia? Christine questioned as she reached for her.

Gabe stripped out of his coat, wrapped Olivia in it and walked out.

CHAPTER FORTY-TWO

Minutes bled by. Distance was all she needed. Transferring to another wing or hospital wouldn't be hard. Christine had family in the south and the medical centers there were bound to have openings for Surgical Technicians or Scrub Nurses.

In a few weeks, Cory would be heading home. In a year, he would return to school. And maybe even little league. And then there was church. The mothers at the church were already packaging frozen meals following the new dietary restrictions she had to follow. The choir was already planning to sing all of his favorite songs when he came back to church the first time. Cory was alive and Christine would live up to the bargains she made with God if Cory lived.

They'd move on. He would grow up and finish school and he'd give back to the community. She'd see to it and every year they would leave flowers at the gravesite of the person that saved her son and Olivia would forgive her. Maybe not at first, but Olivia rarely held a grudge. Olivia was good and kind. She was funny and intelligent just like Cory said. Her doing her job and saving Cory's life stood for something. They'd let her go eventually. Wouldn't they?

Christine brushed her lips over Cory's forehead as his shea butter hair product filled her nose.

"How's our favorite guy doing?" Shawn asked.

A wave of revulsion washed over her as his aftershave entered the room before he did. He paused long enough to tuck in Cory's blanket on the opposite side of the bed.

"Recovering. Is Olivia, okay?" she asked. "Cory will be worried about his Aunt Olivia. He loves her. He calls her that."

"He never called her that." Shawn sank into the burnt orange colored chair parked by the bed and crossed his legs. "You're worse than a pimp. All you saw was an opportunity like most freeloaders do when they ask somebody to be a Godparent. It's rarely about teaching somebody the ways of God, but all about that mighty dollar."

"That is not—"

"What? True? Between me you and the wiretappers, maybe it's just a little true."

Christine glanced at the guitar case in the corner.

"Case in point that guitar over there. My cousin makes that brand. Sells them for a pretty piece of change. Made the body in Olivia's image. Loved a mindless slab of wood into perfection right down to his initials where Olivia's birthmark is. Saw it once when I walked in on her changing out of a bathing suit when she was nine. All I wanted to do since then was kiss her there. I bet it strums true just like her."

"My son *does* love Olivia" she sniffled as smoothed a hand over the pillow beneath Cory's head.

"Everybody does. You remember the annual senior boat trip around the harbor?" He asked she checked the IV tubing attached to the sleeping boy's arm.

"Olivia's phone. Did you take her phone and put something on it? They have it now Shawn. G gave it to them," she said closing her eyes, her heart aching in her throat.

"Olivia was pregnant. It was his. Never got close enough after I caught her in his tree house. Gabe was bound to do the right thing unlike me I spread my seed to anyone simply willing to spread their legs like you." Shawn gazed at the western playing at a low level on the flat screen television. "Like the one I knocked up in the village. Rumina was her name. She went missing with my precious cargo. Bitch was ready to pop."

"Shawn did you set Olivia up? Please tell me you didn't do that." she begged.

"She wouldn't come to me. I loved her—tried to show her every time I got her alone. She didn't even try." He sulked folding his arms. "She even went so far as to throw in with the Militia leader instead," he said as tears leaked from his eyes. "I would have been good to her."

"Shawn what have you done," she asked rising from her chair.

"They were sixteen. Two more years and they wouldn't need anybody's permission" He wiped his face on his scrub top. "I just wanted Olivia to listen. She would have given up college for him. I knew it and wanted her to know she didn't have to. I'd support her. I'd take care of her. He could have the kid."

Shawn looked at his hands and made fists. "She pulled away… struck her head on the railing. It would have been so much better if she died. Never would have met Tiana. Never would have come back here. She would have been mine then. All. Mine."

Christine wound her fists in the draw sheet beneath her son and pulled him toward her.

Shawn blinked as if drugged. "He went in after her. Pulled her out more dead than alive. He knew. Gabe always seemed to know. Tried to tell him it was an accident. Told him I was sorry, but he didn't hear me." Shawn reached for the back of his head. "Only stopped smashing my head into the floor when she came out of the room and called his name. Not mine. Just his. Always him." Shawn scrubbed his face with the scrub top once more and stood.

Shawn reached over and straightened the blanket, "After all the brilliant work she did, Cory shouldn't be moved. Olivia really is gifted you know."

Christine shook her head no, as she grabbed the draw sheet and proceeded to pull Cory closer. Shawn rounded the bed and eased her aside while he tucked the boy in.

"What was on that phone, Shawn?"

"Shh. It's alright Christine. No one would blame you. It is the truth after all." He kissed the side of her head as his phone went off in his pocket. Shawn peered into his breast pocket then put a finger to his lips. "Just keep telling yourself. You did what any good mother would do. No one would blame you. Right?" The bemused smile he gave made her turn and be violently ill.

CHAPTER FORTY-THREE

"Whenever you got put in time out at recess, I'd do anything to be put there beside you," Gabe settled on the interrogation room floor in front of her.

Olivia couldn't bare the sight of him without breaking down. He put his hands on the backs of her calves and drew her closer.

"You can't spend the entire night looking at the floor. Talk to me," his voice was little more than a whisper. "Please tell me what's going on. Maji was ready to put a switchblade into my eye over you."

Olivia stole a quick glance at the wall clock as she was being booked. Tiana still had time to get word to Maji. She thought of her old guardian that took pains to make herself look like a gargoyle. Maji's circle was a living breathing at will entity.

She remembered her old friend's warning in her head. Tiana's loyalty was rock solid until it wasn't. Everything boiled down to saving herself and if one option wasn't available, she had no qualms about betraying anyone's trust to get herself to high ground. On the strength of that fact alone, Olivia knew they were living on borrowed time. With Olivia in prison or close to it, all bets were off and that was where her old demon of a friend came in.

Maji didn't trust anyone there was bound to be a Plan B and the rest of the alphabet in place as necessary. After all, how else did they know when to descend on her home. Regulus and a few of his men swept in and shoved her into the panic room Maji had commissioned especially for Olivia.

The soft scrape of metal on metal made her raise her hands and look at the carbon steel cuffs. "This isn't recess Gabe. You shouldn't be here."

"Where else should I be? Where could I possibly go that wouldn't have me worried sick about you?" he sighed bathing her in concern. "Why wouldn't you let Tiana speak? So, she was on a milk run that went south. Her wife died in the process. If she knew more about all of this, something that could set you free. She should be here instead of you."

"The club was Tiana's idea, and her wife is dead. Isn't that punishment enough?"

"Ollie." He breathed.

Her throat was raw with unuttered shouts and protests. She exhaled sharply then gave a resigned shrug. Gabe trapped her forehead against his and swallowed hard.

"Don't shrug at me. Talk," he said in a harsh whisper.

Olivia pressed her lips between his eyebrows. "Too much is at stake."

He snatched away from her. His expression was like someone who had been struck in the face. His broad shoulders were heaving as he breathed. *"We* are at stake Ollie. *Us."*

Olivia was suddenly overwhelmed by the torment of the past few weeks. The hiding. The delays. The failed launches and the close calls. Bringing Rumina into the hospital to deliver the baby was a risk. Getting her back out of the hospital without notice was even harder when she found out that Shawn was on the roster for that month. Four shipments in all and the final one was on the last mile, known as the danger water.

The hearings were still a few weeks away If the group stayed beneath the radar, the closer they were to exposing the truth. And as much as she trusted the man before her, the risk was too great. The last man she told was the coyote, the guide she paid to get them through the tall grass. As they pulled Olivia and Bimbi from the mass grave, she saw the man's body on a stretcher a few feet away with a woman screaming and crying over him.

It was one thing not to see him all those years. Gabe walked naked through her mind and followed her down into her dreams. Even as the nurses helped clean her up after the miscarriage, part of her still carried the memory of their unborn child across the miles and the continents.

Her spirits sank even lower when she looked up to see tears turn his green gaze into a glittering pool of despair. Olivia licked her lips as a new anguish seared her heart.

"You and I— we were pregnant Gabe. I miscarried the same night as the boating accident. There was no full ride scholarship anywhere," Olivia said sniffling as she raked a shaky hand through her hair. "Maji paid for all of it all. Refused to let Ms. Alana do anything but keep you away from the hospital that night. Maji was the one that found me in that crack house when I was little. Sat outside the closet they kept me in until Ms. Alana could come get me," Olivia covered her face with trembling hands as she struggled to remain in control.

Gabe tugged at one of her hands. "Finish it, Babe." The hurt and longing lay naked in his eyes.

"It was the only way I could think to keep you safe. Had I not come out of the room, you would have killed Shawn in front of his parents and yours," she said flickering her gaze at him. "It would have split you in two, destroyed you. One of us had to leave."

Gabe sat back from her. "He deserved to die. He knew you couldn't swim."

"And then I'd have to watch you die a little more each day for killing him and ruining your future. We loved you. I loved you too much to condemn you to that."

"Which was exactly what my life was like without you all these years." Gabe scrambled to his feet and walked across the room. "Little by little I've been dying inside since you left—since I drove you away."

A knock at the door invaded the tension filled room. Calvin poked his head in. He looked at Gabe and then around the door at Olivia.

"And the abnormal shit keeps coming. Do either of you speak Afrikaans." Calvin scratched the back of his head and frowned.

"What dialect," Olivia and Gabe said in unison.

Olivia tried to inch back against the wall as her leg shackles rattled.

"Keys. Now," Gabe demanded while holding out a hand.

Calvin tossed his set. Gabe caught them and unlocked the shackles Gabe cradled Olivia to his chest and stood in one swift motion before unlocking the handcuffs and throwing them in the corner and tossing Calvin the keys.

"Go on answer her. What dialect." He snapped.

Before Calvin could open his mouth, a woman's screaming and crying echoed down the hallway along with the unmistakable sounds of an infant. Above the mixture of ranting and raving in Xhosa and Afrikaans was repeated.

Malaika... Angel

"Rumina," Olivia breathed as she moved toward the door. "Is Xavier with her. Where is her baby?"

"Olivia! Let her go!" the woman continued to scream. In Xhosa

Calvin blocked her way, and she rested a hand on his chest. "Please, you have to let me go to her. The labor was hard. She shouldn't even been out of bed or out of hiding."

Calvin looked over her head in Gabe's direction. "You came in here looking for her. Let her through," Gabe said moving up behind her.

CHAPTER FORTY-FOUR

Rumina was a few inches shorter than Olivia with skin like midnight velvet. The girl couldn't have been more than fourteen years old. Her hair was swathed in the tribal print of her homeland. What little Gabe knew of the African Inlands was enough to write a decent paper, but little else. The culture and their use of dyes and ancient knitting techniques are what captured his imagination.

The moment Olivia walked into the room the woman ran to her nearly crushing the infant between them. She slid to the floor dragging Olivia with her. "They conversed in Xhosa for a while before Olivia gathered them closer.

"Several of us were pregnant. Only two of us remained. The others, my kinswomen were sold along with their babies. When Lupita returned her womb was as empty as her arms. All she had left was a hand full of corn and the blanket she made. No one asked her why the white blanket she made came back bloody."

Gabe glanced over to see his mother come up the steps followed by General Roth. They moved aside as Cassiel Garrett managed the last few steps on his own.

***

"Girls as young as five were being sold off or married to men twice their age. Rumina told me about the others before the village fell, Bimbi was next. She was four. Her brother Adama was a child soldier with the militia. He gave her to me and disappeared. Few weeks later he died on my operating table." she said clinging to the memory like a life preserver. "The only way I could get Bimbi's family out was to use the mule routes Tiana and Erin were planning to use. And then, I got shot and…"

Cassiel cleared his throat and Gabe looked up at him.

"There's a price on your mother's head. I went in her place to bring Olivia back home and then I realized what she was doing."

"I could have helped Dad."

"We needed him alive to expose the other routes which he did."

Gabe was so quiet next to Alana that she wondered if he was holding his breath. She regarded him with a somber curiosity. "Someone had to try Gabe. Took a while but we finally got them out and, in a few weeks, Rumina and the others will testify here and in front of the Hague. General Roth works with the Department of Homeland Security. He's working with them to grant asylum for them and—"

Gabe pressed his face against the side of her head. His lips trembled against her ear. "You could have trusted me with this, Ollie."

"I made it a point to not know where they were or who they were with when they were enroute. If something happened to me, they'd still be able to testify. Couldn't tell you what I didn't know."

Rumina walked over and Roth draped his trench coat over the woman's shoulders. Olivia pressed her lips to the cuff on the baby's hat before she rose and handed him over.

"Ms. Alana and Mr. Cassiel brought the last through the catacombs at CIBEX this evening. Maji got them others to the black sites so that the Levine's people could get them into protective custody. Said something about being allergic to shellfish and pork," Roth mumbled with a shrug. "You'll probably be up for another medal that you won't accept."

Olivia gripped his bicep and smiled "None of this helps with your case. I'm afraid Detective Garrett, but I retained counsel for Olivia regardless. Cairo Sharaf is on a plane heading here now. Until she arrives, I am Dr. Calderone's representative."

***

Olivia's voice filled the small room as Gabe moved closer to the one-way glass.

"Bimbi and I never made it to the port. Even if we had, they wouldn't have carried us aboard. Weighting us down and throwing us in the water would have made more sense." Olivia ran a hand through her hair and shook her head. "None of this has any bearing on the deaths here. My badge and stethoscope were found on a body. Where?"

"That's beyond the scope of this conversation. Where were you the other night?" Calvin interrogated.

"Helping Brenda clean apples for tomorrow's snack time." Her voice sounded tired as she raked a hand through her hair. "Earlier this evening? You already know. You and Detective Garrett pulled me out of a wall. Have you grilled Richard Beacham or Shawn Prescott? Both men were there in Africa with me. Sleeping with and impregnating underage girls." Olivia tilted her head to the left. "Your probable cause is coming apart detective. Did you check the whereabouts of all the other doctors you didn't bring in, or am I special?" She taunted.

"Your blood was found in that shipping container on a stuffed doll," Calvin insisted as while flipping through his notes.

"Of course, it was. I was carrying Bimbi when I got shot. I never made it to the ports. The doll could have been carried in by the people who found me," Olivia said firmly. "Was my blood anywhere else in that shipping crate?"

Calvin took his time in looking up at Olivia, a tactic Gabe knew well. Whatever he said after that was his partner's trump card that made a suspect cave." Beacham was at a function and Prescott was performing surgery," Calvin said as his phone went off. He dug in his pocket and read the text. "You're free to go Dr. Calderone."

Roth gathered some paperwork and tucked it in his briefcase. "Any further contact with Dr Calderone will occur through her counsel," he said glancing at his watch. "And I am running late to pick her up so unless there's something else?" He paused long enough to study Calvin before closing his briefcase. "Come on Olivia, let's get you home."

Olivia fell back in the chair and studied Calvin. "It happened again, didn't it? While I was here in custody. Oh my God." Roth grabbed her hand and started walking toward the door, "Wait let me go! Tell me who it is."

Calvin turned and looked at the mirrored wall. As Olivia was ushered out by her attorney. Calvin walked over to the window and put his phone against the glass. Gabe backed away.

"That's Tommy Marsden, one of her residents," Gabe answered before walking out the door.

CHAPTER FORTY-FIVE

"So, you a cop or what?" Calvin asked as he held out Gabe's service weapon and badge."

Gabe stared at the gear but made no attempt to retrieve it. "You were supposed to turn that into Uncle Mark."

"I tried and he told me hold onto it until you came to your senses."

"That's not all he said. Gabe mumbled while staring at his shield.

"Well, you're right about that. He said if you were turning it in then you needed to put it in his hand your damned self," Calvin sat the gear on Gabe's desk and headed for the door.

"So, now you believe she's innocent?" His voice was courteous but patronizing.

"Never said I didn't. You handing in your badge solidified it for me. Ve a atraparme un monstruo," Calvin paused at the stairs. "Did I get it right? It's what your moms said right?"

"Yeah, it means go catch me a monster." Gabe grabbed his weapon and shield.

"Okay then let's go hunting." Calvin started down the steps.

Gabe stared down the hallway.

"Lawyer took her out the back way with your parents," Rhonda called over her shoulder before sprinting down the stairs. "We got eyes on her just as a precaution."

***

"I don't think they used anesthesia. That sour smell in the air is adrenaline. Blood on the ceiling tells me things went south quickly," Max said as he zipped the bag. "Awful sorry to see this one. Few more years and Marsden would have been a fine surgeon."

Even with the face mask on the faint scent of rusted pennies came to Gabe on the night air. Reconstructing any crime scene was a slow process that involved measuring tape, evidence collection and preservation. While Calvin worked along the perimeter of the room, Gabe stood at the center taking in the scene.

Max came up and stood beside him. "What do you see Gabe?"

Gabe studied the door as ghost images filled his mind. He pointed at the front door sitting ajar. "This was a blitz attack. Marsden had no time to react. Most of it happened here judging from the blood volume. Whoever it was, he knew them. No signs of forced entry."

"According to the neighbors there was no noise other than some loud moaning. They figured Marsden had a date. About an hour later a car drove off. Found this though."

Calvin held out an evidence bag. Gabe turned Calvin's wrist and panned his flashlight at the barrel of the ink pen.

"I plucked this pen out of Olivia's hair that first day. Lost it during that fight with my cousin, Shawn."

Calvin cocked his head to the side not understanding. "How fresh is the body Doc?"

Max shrugged. "No more than an hour or two tops. Body is still warm."

"Blood type?"

Gabe headed for the door ripping his gloves and mask off as he went. By the time he reached the entrance, Gabe was running as he mashed the speed dial button for Olivia.

CHAPTER FORTY-SIX

Olivia studied Christine's sleeping form from the doorway. Dr Oberon peered over her shoulder.

"She's been like that since we brought him up here. Won't leave his side unless one of the nurses come in and sit with him. You did great. Cory tests results are looking good. Way to go doc," she said patting Olivia the back before continuing up the hall.

Olivia grabbed a blanket from the shelf, unfolded it and placed it around Christine's shoulders before retreating to her office.

"Did Tiana come to you, Maji?" she asked, not trusting herself to speak freely in the elevator.

"You already know. Told you that bitch would betray you. Pulled a gun on me. I'm still picking her skin from under my nails. There's a clump of her purple hair in my garbage can too if you must know."

***

The Administration wing still had a few lights on in offices. Someone from housekeeping was running a vacuum cleaner several doors down on the other side of their suite of offices perched on the top floor.

Olivia slowed her steps as the odor of cheap cologne and sweat made the hair on the back of her neck stand up. Olivia paused near her doorway and peered through. She slid behind Ms. Sittler's desk and grabbed the woman's quad cane as she neared her office. Olivia patted the pockets on the jeans she was wearing for her phone and cursed. Her new phone was still sitting on the charger on the nightstand at home.

Olivia studied the shapes in her darkened office looking for any sort of movement. Nearing the door, Olivia checked her grip on the cane once more. Reaching inside she groped for the light switch. As her office flooded with light, Olivia shoved the door open hard enough to make it hit the wall behind it dispatching anyone stupid enough to stand behind it.

Her desk phone jangled to life making icy fear twist around her heart. Olivia closed her door and thumbed the lock in place before she grabbed the phone.

"Shawn, is that you?"

"Olivia," Tiana whispered.

She spilled into the chair as the energy drained from her body. "Tiana, where are you? It was a stupid move to go after Maji. Where's Shawn?"

"I made it right, Olivia. For me, for Erin and Bimbi. For all of us. He can't hurt you anymore. It's out now." She sighed as the line went dead.

"Tiana where are you?" Olivia asked as her gaze fell to a folder sitting on her coffee table. Olivia tucked the phone between her chin and shoulder before reaching for the file. "Hang on Tiana."

"He can't hurt you anymore. It's all there... Folder. Rumina confirmed it. So did Sable. She told me about Christine."

"Tiana what are you talking about. Look stay where you are. I'll come and find you." Olivia sat the receiver on the counter as she snagged the folder and a hand full of plane tickets spilled in her lap. The C Swipe card in her door sounded, and then the world went black.

CHAPTER FORTY-SEVEN

"Lock this place down now!" Gabe shouted as he burst through the emergency room door and ran to the security desk. "Spread out and help me find her!"

Christine came out of the café with a cup of coffee and a small white bag. Gabe spotted her and stormed across the floor.

"Where is she? Did she come back here?"

Christine dropped everything and started to cry. "I don't know. I never saw her come in. She was with you!"

Gabe dropped her arms like she was hot as he scanned the lobby. Panic like he had never known welled in his throat as the soft ding from the elevator drew his attention.

"Oh my God no," he whispered as he took off toward the elevators.

Calvin, fast on his heels dived into the elevator before the doors closed. The elevator took and eternity to sink to the basement. Once the car stopped, Gabe pounded on the button to open the doors. The second they opened. Gabe wedged his fingers inside and shoved the door open.

Gabe drew his weapon and raced down one corridor and then the next. As he neared the double doors leading to the cadaver room, the air began to burn. Threw a shoulder into the door and a thicker mist made his eyes and throat burn. Gabe barreled through another door and tripped over something and slipped on the wet tiled surface. Falling to one knee, he scanned the area. All of the shower heads above the autopsy tables were on full blast purring gallons of water down the drains and out onto the floor.

Calvin came through the door coughing. He hooked an arm around Gabe's and tried to pull him back to safety. Gabe rubbed water on his face and eyes as he struggled to focus.

"Jesus Christ," Calvin exclaimed as they both looked over.

Tiana was flat on her back with a bullet hole in the center of her forehead. Gabe snatched away and stood.

"Olivia! Ollie answer me!" he yelled as he moved further into the room. He drew in a breath to call for her again when he noticed what looked like a pile of clothes lying on the floor under the hard spray of the water hose. The familiar black and yellow stripes and the letters on his waterlogged jersey was still clear enough to read.

Gabe scrambled across the floor and ripped the lid open. Olivia's head was tucked down against her chest. Gabe pulled the bin over on its side and Olivia's lifeless body spilled onto his lap.

As Calvin and three other detectives approached him Gabe crushed Olivia to his chest and began to rock back and roared.

CHAPTER FORTY-EIGHT

The world just needed to be silent, not quiet. A lack of sound meant that something could fill it or change the shape of it. Silence swallowed everything That kind of peace could be pocketed for home, scattered like salt, or rubbed into wounds that never healed.

Fumigating and cleaning the Cadaver room cleared the air of anything living except the man sitting on the spot where he found her. Gabe didn't bother to raise his head as Calvin pushed the door open and walked in and sat something on the end of an autopsy table. He pulled a metal stool from the corner and sat down.

"G, you breathed in a lot of that stuff."

"Ollie breathed in far more," Gabe said as a fine thread of rage pulsed through his resolve.

"That burn near your eye."

Gabe raised his head and stared at his friend. "Olivia's skin came off in my hands Calvin. She couldn't even scream."

"There's no reason to believe Shawn is still here in town."

"He's here. He wouldn't miss this for the world. Besides, he has to play it to the end. Same way suspect go to their victims' funerals."

"It's been an hour G. We didn't have him flagged until a few hours ago. His house is empty. All we found was some shrine to Olivia in his bedroom and this," Calvin raised a small evidence bag with an oxygen tank, condoms duct tape and zip ties and airplane tickets.

"It's why she was stuffed in a case, Cal," Gabe tilted his head in the direction of the black case up ended in the corner. "Something stopped him. Marsden stopped him. Just a few more minutes. And when he arrives——,"

"You can't kill him," Calvin said flatly.

Gabe took in a shaky breath and smiled. "It's why I chose you back at the academy. You're my conscience. Everybody says I look like my mother and people were right to fear her. My father was worse, and I am every bit of him. All the love… all the hate and rage."

"And you still can't kill him, G. You can't." Calvin drummed his fingers on the table.

"It's why Olivia left instead of coming to me. If I knew then what I know now." Gabe grabbed his gun and handed it over butt first.

The walkie talkie in Calvin's pocket squawked and he snatched it from a pocket. His eyes never left Gabe's as he took in another shaky breath. "Just like clockwork, Calvin. He wouldn't miss this for the world."

Calvin pressed the speaker button. "He's on his way downstairs sir."

"Clear his path." Calvin held Gabe's gun out to him. "You can't go into this unarmed."

"He doesn't want to kill me, Calvin. He wants to be me," Gabe said with a tired smile.

Calvin grabbed his hand and thrust the gun into it. "Humor me."

Gabe grabbed the gun and stuffed it down the back of his pants as Calvin went back into the neighboring room.

***

Gabe took in another shaky breath as an outer door opened and closed. Shawn peered through the window before pushing the door open. "G you in here?" His voice echoed in the dead air surrounding them.

"Over here Shawn," he said quietly rising from the floor.

Shawn crossed the floor and hugged him. Gabe steeled himself against his cousin's embrace. As the distinct smell of betadine filled his nose.

Shawn held him back from his chest.

"I came as soon as you called. It's not even real man, Olivia's dead? What happened?" Shawn's tone was apologetic as he gripped Gabe's shoulder.

"By the time I found her she wasn't breathing. She was broken. So broken." Gabe's voice shook as he looked down at his raw hands. The sight of her huddled under the showers with chemical burns through her clothing built horrifying images in his mind.

"Do you know how it happened?" Shawn asked while searching his pockets.

"She knew her attacker, "Gabe said slowly as he walked over and took the chair Calvin vacated. "They must have really hated her. I mean what could she have possibly done to make them hate her so much?"

"It wasn't hate." The thin sheen of sweat on Shawn's forehead and top lip glistened as he pulled up a chair and sat down. "You can't hate someone like her. She was a rarity. Maybe once in a lifetime. If she smiled in your direction, you felt blessed. Girls like her are a drug. One hit, in the form of a smile and to hear her laugh," Shawn gazed off in the direction of the area on the floor where Gabe found her. "People like her are just filled up with love. How could you not love her? Even when she looked through you, past you."

"I watched her in that operating room saving that boy's life. Why would anyone hurt someone like that? Why take her from everyone that loved her?"

"Hurts to be ignored, Gabe. I did everything right in school and for my parents. I tried hard to be the perfect kid and then you were born, and everything just came to you, even Olivia. She wouldn't even look at me until I made her."

"Olivia was entitled to a life beyond Shadow Bay and me. Maji was right to get her out of here."

Shawn said boldly meeting his cousins' eyes. "It's your fault really. She never got over you. No matter how hard I tried, she wouldn't give in to me. She even went so far as to take up with a militia man over there in Africa. Never once did she look at me."

"She didn't love you, Shawn. She never would."

"She could have tried! If she had just come to me, I would have stopped. She was perfect Gabe. In time there would be other children. Our children."

"Olivia didn't love you. She would *never* love you."

Shawn snorted. "Olivia? Who said anything about her? Bimbi was far more valuable. Rumina was a two for one. Don't you see? They were O negative, universal donors. Have you any ideas what those organs would go for on the market?"

Gabe folded his arms and leaned on the table. "Where did Olivia fit into all of this?"

Shawn glanced at Gabe. The astonishment on his cousin's face made his gut grow cold.

"She was better than a pig rooting for truffles." Shawn lifted his chin meeting Gabe's gaze head on. "Every village she helped, I harvested."

"Your children Shawn, what about them? We know about the plane tickets and what you had planned for them."

"I owed a lot of people money. One man's kid needed a transplant. He was willing to forgive my debt if I could find a heart."

"They were *your* children."

"But so many would benefit from my sacrifice."

Gabe got up and started for the door. "Gabe wait, you have to understand. They already killed your father. They were coming after my Mom next. I had to do something."

The words were like a fishhook in Gabe's back. He glanced over his shoulder. "What did you say?"

"I wanted to make it up to you. I tried. Rumina could have more children. Olivia messed everything up when she hid them. Even my son Cory could have benefitted if she had just left well enough alone. I had to harvest on the fly. It's Olivia's fault. It's why I framed her don't you see?"

Gabe crossed the floor in three strides, grabbed Shawn by the throat and body slammed him on the autopsy table. Shawn clawed at Gabe's hand as he gasped for air.

"My Mom didn't have any money, Gabe. She already lost the house, Gabe. I was trying to replace what I lost. Your father was just in the wrong place at the wrong time."

Calvin and the other officers burst into the room. Gabe released Shawn and threw him in the corner. Once Shawn was handcuffed and read his rights, two uniforms escorted him to the door.

"I wasn't afraid to face you tonight. I wanted you to know it was me that took your father and Olivia. They're mine now." He cackled. "I won."

"Bring him back here."

"Gabe," Calvin warned.

Gabe put a hand on Calvin's shoulder, "Bring him back here."

Calvin groaned. "Do what he says."

The officers looked at each other before bringing Shawn back into the room.

"Cameras."

Shawn looked around at everyone and grinned, "And what does that mean?"

"It's what Olivia said before I took her upstairs to be treated. She's there right now with *both* of my parents." Gabe let his gaze drift to Shawn's left leg, The blood stain over his left knee began to spread. "Everything you said. Everything you did was caught on camera. I like the part where she drove that switchblade into your thigh and broke the blade." Gabe said as he walked past his cousin. "My mother never taught her that, but it worked."

"Wait. Gabe wait!"

Gabe pushed his way through the double doors and went to the elevators. As the elevator door closed, Shawn continued to scream.

***

He walked the gauntlet congregating around her hospital room. Some were crying while others cast fearful looks over their shoulders. Brenda walked out of the room wiping her eyes. He slowed down as he reached her.

"What happened?" he asked. Without waiting for an answer, Gabe rushed into the room to see Alana combing Olivia's hair back over her shoulder. His father Cassiel sat in the chair beside them resting his chin on the hand that clutched the intricately carved black wooden cane.

Olivia took a step toward him, and he closed the space and slid to his knees. As he crushed her to his chest, Olivia pushed her face down against his ear.

"I love you Gabe," She whispered.

EPILOGUE

"Hey, Doc, you need a colonoscopy?" one of the inmates cackled Shawn covered his face with his pillow.

She looked so beautiful sitting next to his cousin in court. Olivia's hair looked like black cornsilk spilling across her shoulders. The trial was a blur, Olivia wasn't. He barely heard his mother wailing at the sentencing hearing. Nothing else mattered. She didn't even seem sore about what happened in the basement of the hospital. But then he knew she wouldn't be. Olivia would never hold a grudge. Even with Gabe's ring on her hand he knew she could talk him down and make him see reason.

The plea bargains fell through. No matter how many names he gave up the answer was the same. Everything he said was beyond the scope of their conversation.

Rumina even brought his son to see him, and Sable brought the girls. No one was mad because they understood it wasn't personal. He had responsibilities and men took care of their responsibilities and paid their debts.

And then the first poker chip arrived. Flushing them down the toilet did nothing to stem the tide. But then they stopped, and the uneasiness settled in. No poker chips meant his debts were settled, but by who?

Shawn thought of his aunt with the hellfire eyes and her demon of a son. Had they shown him the mercy he so craved? They weren't answering his phone calls or letters, but maybe… maybe. He rolled over on his back and unfolded the newspaper clipping with a picture of Olivia being whisked away in a black government issue SUV. Her eyes were so full of love and compassion.

He barely noticed the dull clang of something metal against each bar like a child with a stick against the slats of a wooden fence. Slowly, rhythmically the rattle and hum continued until it became the only sound in the world. The fellow inmates and their catcalling fell away as a thicker silence descended. The cherry juice mixed in with the heady scent of marijuana reached him first. Shawn scrambled into the corner of his cell and tried to hide behind the toilet bolted to the wall.

"Olivia forgave me. Ask her! Just ask her!" He shrieked as the buzz of his door being opened filled the room. I paid my debts! Alana Symone paid my debts! Just ask her!"

The door slid noiselessly open, and Shawn looked down at his urine-soaked jumpsuit. "That's not funny you cheap turnkey. I'll talk to the warden all about this! You'll hear from my lawyers!" he shrieked.

Maji slid the door open with the tip of her aluminum baseball bat. The dents in the tip were stained with something red.

It was rust, right? It had to be. If it were the other thing then it would hurt.

He looked helplessly around his cell before wedging himself in a corner.

"How's the harvest Doc?" Maji asked in her slow southern drawl as a satanic smile spread across her cheeks. The fork in her tongue darted between her lips tracing each side. "Is it white?"

Maji pulled the door shut, and Shawn began to scream.

ABOUT THE AUTHOR

Stephanie M Freeman is a Hybrid author that began her professional writing career back in 2012 when Crimson Romance, an imprint of Simon & Schuster published her novel, Necessary Evil. Since then, she has explored different writing genres including, Mysteries, Thrillers, Romantic Suspense and the Paranormal. Stephanie is also a member of Naleighna Kai's Tribe Called Success and the Cavalcade of Authors.

She often jokes that with a shot glass or a cup of coffee in one hand, she is known for writing an erotic tale or two. Stephanie has amassed a loyal group of fans who eagerly await her latest releases. Her Diamonds, Blood and Shadows Series is a fan favorite. Her other books include Unfinished Business, Nature of the Beast and A Letter from Yesay. Writing as Aracyne (Air Ruh Sin) Kelly, she also wrote: Peculiar Kindness and Heaven's Girl.

Stephanie is the host of the wildly popular Club House Event called Murder, Mayhem and Mysteries (and the people who love them). With multiple five-star reviews of her work, Stephanie M. Freeman continues to push literary boundaries.

Visit Stephanie on the Web:
Website: https://bit.ly/Stephaniemfreemanwebsite
Newsletter: https://bit.ly/stephaniemfreemannewsletter
Sociatap: http://bit.ly/StephMFreemanST

Necessary Evil: Book One in the Diamonds Blood and Shadows Series

I've spent the nights in dumpsters and the bedchambers of kings. The dumpsters were better. Telling you my name won't make any difference. There have been so many over the years. Some even made sense. Others were little more than a cautionary tale. Caveat emptor. Beware the buyer. Shed most of them like a snakeskin. Sins are my sable. Scars are the rags I wear beneath.

Shannon was my friend, and I watched her die. She called herself an Acquisitions Manager. Procurement was her sole duty. She was smaller than me, but older. She was patient. Far more than some I'd seen. Many were experts at luring frightened little things getting off of busses from Nowhere headed Elsewhere. She understood the rules of engagement and trained me well.

Duck and dodge this one and you live to see another day. Follow that one home and you'll never return. Smiles were acceptable. Conversation was optional. A misplaced laugh could be deadlier than a rejection. Be smart and charming and submissive and maybe just maybe a meal was thrown in or drugs to dull everything. There were some among us that honestly believed their boyfriend loved them even after being passed around like blunts.

Shannon forgot her place or maybe she remembered. Exhaustion hung around her like a cloud filled with hard rain. She'd gone for a drive with Julian to talk about the future. Last thing she told me was that all retirements are bittersweet.

Didn't take long to find her. Sat with her until sunrise holding her rapidly cooling hand. We both made promises neither one of us would keep.

Many will never understand why some of us stay behind, or why we endure. Save as many as you can or die trying. When we do, we win.

Shannon's gaze focused on something in the distance as the morning sun warmed the pale blue sky with a hint of peach. She kissed the back of my hand leaving behind a red smear.

As I closed the trunk and prepared for my journey home the vanity tag hanging from a lone screw caught my eye.

Alana.

Alana. Seemed as good a name as any. After a while, they all hurt. The names… the memories… the purpose. There's no moral to my story. All that remains are the shades and shards of a girl that could not be. I imagine clouds gathering in the distance with a hint of rain in the air. If I'm lucky, perhaps retirement will find me too.

Unfinished Business: Book Two in the Diamonds Blood and Shadows Series

Blood didn't move like water. Water was mindless yet persistent. Blood was deliberate, louder than an ocean, better than a scream. The panic room was the deal breaker. Monet Symone-Garrett wanted to attend college in Connecticut. To do so, she had to agree to live off campus in a place of her mother's choosing with armed guards. The gun in her lap was a birthday present from her father, Cassiel Garrett. The shooting lessons were her graduation present from her mother, Alana Symone.

Vincent was dead.

The fact that he was motionless on her bedroom floor was minutia compared to the dark patch of blood that spread beneath him in a gruesome cartoon bubble. Vincent looked as if he were craning his neck to see where she'd gone. His dark blue gaze was vacant, but even on the closed-circuit television in the panic room, it still looked like he was staring at her, blaming her.

No one knew what her mother Alanna Symone was and that was a mercy. The life expectancy of anyone that discovered her mother's peculiar kindness was drastically shortened.

Imagine a demon raising a child.

When Vincent said it, the envy overshadowed the fear. Monet couldn't hear, but she never needed to. She knew her mother wasn't like the others that took their little girls to soccer practice or baked cookies. Saturdays were for tactical training. Summers were for boot camp. Winters were for survival training and Sundays well Sundays were for reading.

Monet watched as the stain continued to spread. Splotches of red marred the duvet hanging from her unmade bed. She remembered how the other mothers straightened their backs and hurriedly fixed their clothes and hair whenever Alana walked into the PTA Meetings. The fathers were no better with their eyes crawling over her mother's frame until they got closer.

Mamma scared them. Why didn't she scare you, Vincent? You were brave or stupid. Maybe a little of both. I'm sorry Mamma. Should have listened. Should have paid better attention.

Monet smeared the tears across her face with a pajama sleeve. It didn't register at first. The cartoon bubble of blood was still there on the carpet, but something was missing. Vincent was missing. He was the only one that knew the code to open the door and how to disable it if the door ever jammed.

Center of mass for everything, Monet. Remember, Mamma said you can't afford anything else.

As a slice of yellow light poured though the crack in the Panic room door, a stillness swept over her as she palmed the butt of the 15-round magazine to the Glock 19 in her lap.

Mamma showed me what to do. With blood running down her chin, Mamma always knew what to do.

Nature of the Beast: Book Three in the Diamonds Blood and Shadows Series

Hush now; you're dying. The golden hour has come and gone. With the extent of your injuries the recovery would be a slow and painful process. But you're in luck. Mercy is my stock and trade.

Now now, we both know that licking your lips to lubricate the lie was the first mistake. And please, excuses are little more than truth turned inside out. So many apologies but they all go against the grain.

May I join you? Not in dying silly. That's your job, now. The previous one I gave you well… Can I be frank? My name is Kevin Francis Greer but, in discussions like these honesty and nicknames go hand in hand.

You think me a monster and you're right. Wasn't always like this. When I was ten, Mama held my foot to a hotplate for some real or imagined slight. Papa watched from his grey recliner in the living room inhaling the acrid smoke from the cigar he lit with a match.

Wooden ones were best as the tobacco burned evenly. Lighters are infinitely more personal. Hold one under a person's nose and it will light like the wick of a candle and burn forever burn until there's nothing left that looks human, but then you know that now, don't you? Don't you?

Yes, I think you do.

This whole dirty business was nothing like the red coil feasting on my heel at the time. The hot plate with its lone eye worked as desired if not as designed. The orgasm that leapt from me left quite the mess on the maroon shag carpet. Mama's disgust became my inspiration. Papa's pride became my muse.

Music like pain is an acquired taste, unique to each person. Your short shallow breaths remind me of a young Vivaldi or an older Beethoven. Both were poets for the dead as am I.

The assignment was simple Endicott. Follow Willow Daniels. Make yourself indispensable to her. Protect her at all costs. The MacGuffin beneath her skin is more valuable than gold or flames. Lost in the folds of her mind is an answer to a question I asked forty years ago.

Nearly killed her when I asked in person. My passion got the better of me, I'll admit, but pain makes a captive audience of us all. Nothing seemed to work on the boy with her, though. Peppering him with questions after each slice did nothing but solidify his resolve to remain silent. Sirens wailing in the distance cut my interview and their date night short.

My ex-wife was neat in her grave, nigh ten years. Such a cunning little beast she was. Hiding our son. Adopting him out was a stroke of genius. Hot plates and cigars were not part of his future. Short money filled my bolt holes and bank accounts to the brim. He would have been a God among insects. So much to tell him. So much to share. A dream deferred to be sure.

You failed so horribly. But then, thinking is a chore for mammals like you. Romance was not in the job description. It's why the scent of your aftershave was replaced by the fragrance of soot and burning flesh. Of course, I'll dab away the tear spilling from the remains of your eye. As I stated earlier, mercy is my stock and trade.

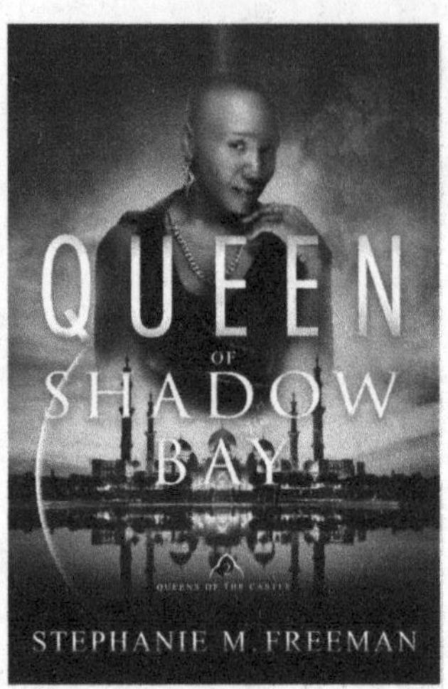

Queen of Shadow Bay: Book Two in the Queens of the Castle Series

Smothering his wife was easier than watching her sleep. The bovine, simpering way she scampered after him was cute in the beginning. Her serving him hand and foot even tickled his dick once. Just. Once. Now her 'Yes, Baby. Whatever you say Honey Man' made his skin crawl.

Gerald Newland sat his keys in the small wooden bowl his wife lovingly placed on the table near the staircase. The gorge burning the back of his throat intensified at the prospect of lying down next to his dearly beloved. He'd perfected the skill of not flinching when she touched him, but even that was beginning to fray. He glanced at their wedding portrait on the wall and admired the smug look on his face.

Carpathia "Carrie" Newland stood before a church filled with all her rotting menopausal friends wearing a cream-colored pants suit and a colorful scarf that reminded him of cheap stained glass. The bouquet she carried was little more than a Styrofoam ball with a stick shoved up its ass. The hand crocheted pink and white flowers stuck to it matched the one in her platinum grey wig with the baby hair combed into place. What old prune had baby hair? Most of that shit ran to the back of their heads by the time they hit fifty.

Why the old bitties insisted on telling her she looked like an angel was beyond him. Anyone with beer goggles could tell the woman was no prize.

"A little make up or paint makes even an ugly one what she ain't." He whispered before kicking off his shoes and heading upstairs.

But that stock portfolio mmmm hmmm, that thing alone put all the pretty little bitches to shame. The old girl was smart with her money and that was a plus. What Gerald couldn't run through the damn sure intended to spend on anything and anyone that pleased him including his stepdaughter Pamela from his first marriage or was it the third. He'd lost count over the years.

9 781736 798584